A KILLING AT RIMROCK

HELLBENDERS THREE

RICHARD PROSCH

WOLFPACK
PUBLISHING
— EST 2013 —

A Killing at Rimrock
Print Edition
© Copyright 2021 Richard Prosch

Wolfpack Publishing
5130 S. Fort Apache Rd. 215-380
Las Vegas, NV 89148

wolfpackpublishing.com

eBook ISBN 978-1-63977-033-5
Paperback ISBN 978-1-63977-034-2

A KILLING AT RIMROCK

Forever for Gina and Wyatt

JULY 1860, LAMBERT'S FERRY, THE RED RIVER

BROTHER LAMBERT'S ferry was almost half-way across the silver ribbon of the Red River when its forward guide rope snapped, tossing Lin Jarret's tall Concord coach into a skid to starboard. Lin's spooked horses reared up in terror on slippery wet oak planks as the boat yawed off its straight-line course and spun clockwise in the current.

Lin stumbled on the boards, tangled up in the lead bay roan's hooves, bit his lip, and tasted blood.

Suddenly set free of tension, the boat's madly spinning crank unleashed a torrent of frayed hemp as the swirling river threatened to suck them down to perdition.

Beneath the serenity of the Red's deceptive gently sloping banks Lin realized just how treacherous the river waters could be. With the instant clarity of a rifle blast, he understood why the teamsters preferred to cross the Red River from Texas into Indian territory and continue on to Fort Smith, freighting their goods by way of the Arkansas River. The Red was too uncertain, too fickle for even the most experienced steamboat navigators.

The angel of death flapped a route over the water like a bat, waiting for a freighter—or ferryman—to make one simple mistake.

Lin's forest-green wagon gave out a groan as the horses shifted their weight back and forth to compensate for the swirling of the ferry.

Rust-colored brine slopped over Lin's boots and trickled down to his toes.

The late afternoon sun beat down hot and indifferent on his neck.

Hooves slippery with sandy loam, the horses lost their footing and danced backwards away from the swirling water, cranking the stagecoach into a precarious jackknife position in the middle of the boat.

Lin was a tall Texas Ranger, crossing the river to Rimrock Station with his partner in the coaching concern, a gal named Reece Sinclair. Their job was to carry a man named Dale Hemlock to the Regional Cotton Growers Association meeting, but right now Lin's concern was with his bay roans.

"Let go the wagon brake!" Lin said.

He only hoped Reece heard him as the animals slammed back in their traces with a thud and a crack. He hoped the impact from the boat's violent spasm hadn't flung Reece from her place on the driver's bench into the river.

"Wagon brake's off," Reece called, and the coach's iron-rimmed wheels rolled backwards, taking a load off the four-in-hand as the ferry lurched once more.

In an instant, Reece was down on the ferry boards in her linsey-woolsy shirt and jodhpur britches, drenched to the skin—as they all were—her young slender frame moving around from one roan to another, holding fast to their leathers, issuing firm but soothing commands. Her ebony hair was long and pulled back in a severe braid. Her rolled up sleeves revealed taut, powerful muscles.

At her hip she carried a Walch Navy 12-shooter in a lambskin holster. The trick gun was a vanity, but she was a dead shot.

Almost as good with her gun as Lin was with his Colt-Walker .45.

Desperate to control the boat's erratic pitch, Brother Lambert ordered his three men to thrust long poles along the starboard side.

"Mind your horses, dammit," he told Lin, from the portside bow. "Mind them four unless you want the whole team to go over the side. I can't handle everything at once."

Lambert was a big Chickasaw with close-cropped dark hair and a dark Sunday-go-to-meeting suit befitting his status as the wealthiest man in the Indian Territory. When he cast aside his jacket, freeing his cordwood arms to heave his boat back on course, he was something else: a collection of gristle and bone who raised Rimrock plantation from the banks of the Red and cleared a hundred dollars a day in river road traffic.

"Mind yourself, Cap'n," Lin said, as he held tight to his lead gelding's rein and grabbed a fistful of the animal's wind-whipped mane. The horses strained against collars and breastplates, tripping to port across the wide planks as the teetering bow of the platform heaved toward the sky.

Together, Lin and Reece soon got the animals

under control, then Lin made his way to the ferry's edge.

"Throw me a stick," Lin said, and Lambert complied. Lin liked the heft of the long, cottonwood pole and thrust it into the water, hitting bottom sooner than expected.

"Put your shoulder to it, Ranger," Reece said. Lin grinned and put all his weight behind the lever, popping three buttons from the top of his saturated blue cotton shirt.

"Mind your horses," he said, repeating Brother Lambert's command, but this time a whisper.

The boat came around to its original perpendicular course from south to north, the inertia from the snapped line dissipating in the shallow current.

The coach slowed its back-and-forth rocking.

The Concord was similar to the coaches used by the Butterfield-Overland express—though slightly smaller at eight feet tall. Fitted with three-ply leather thoroughbraces, the carriage could accommodate heavier loads than normal, and this wagon was fitted with additional storage space front, rear, and a well-hidden compartment beneath the cabin floor. The black spoked front wheels reached chest-height on Lin, and the back wheels neared his shoulders.

Today the rear boot was packed with gear and covered with a stitched leather awning, the front boot likewise heavily loaded. Up top, the coach carried two camel back trunks wrapped in iron bands and secured by fat padlocks—traveling gear for the Jarret-Sinclair line's living cargo, Dale Hemlock.

Lambert called out, "Hold steady your side, Ranger." Lin relaxed his effort, and the ferry began to come around.

"Get the second line secure, goddammit."

They were closer now to the river's edge, and at Lambert's command, two workmen plunged into the current, holding to the barge while pulling up slack from the broken frayed end of rope, then tossing the coil toward a barrel-chested man who wallowed in the wet loam on shore.

"How's our passenger weathering the storm?" Lin said.

Reece poked her head into the coach. "You okay in there, Mister Hemlock?"

Inside the cabin, his thin face as murky green as the water, Dale Hemlock was wrapped in a cocoon of his own thick wool clothing. The sole occupant of a space which could accommodate nine passengers, he hunkered down in his seat, an expression of stunned terror stitched across his face.

Hemlock was the head man for the Regional Cotton Growers Association and one of twelve agricultural big wigs from Texas, Fort Smith, and the Nations meeting for a week at Rimrock Station.

How a pipsqueak like Hemlock got to be in charge of anything more than a nest of termites, Lin couldn't figure. But the old man sure seemed accustomed to firing off orders and having people obey.

During the trip to the border the old prune had done nothing but complain. The road was too bumpy. There were too many flies. The sun was too hot. The rain too cold. He was one of those men who had a better idea about everything, but no practical experience.

When true adversity struck, Hemlock stayed frozen in place—unwilling, unable, to help.

"Hey, Hemlock? The lady's talking to you."

Under a round derby hat pulled low over his brow, Hemlock blinked slowly at the prodding. Without speaking, he raised his arthritic hand and waved anemic foxtail fingers.

The man was pitiful.

But thank God he hadn't been knocked overboard and drowned.

Lambert let loose with a lusty, "Land, ho," and Lin shouldered his pole into the shallow bottom of the river, helping bring the ferry within spitting distance of shore.

The danger was over, and they floated in with unexpected aplomb.

Lin pulled off his wide-brimmed hat and slapped it on his knee, splashing out the water. "Wasn't planning on taking a bath until tonight," Lin said. "Guess the river had other plans."

"The Red, she's a hard mistress," Lambert said. "You got to know how to handle her." He patted each of his three burly men on their shoulders and turned to Lin Jarret. "You know what I'm talking about, yes?"

"I never learned," Lin said.

"How to handle the river? Or a woman?"

"Neither one."

Lambert's eyes carried over to Reece Sinclair, but he didn't say a word.

"Once we get up to your house, I want my crossing fee returned," Lin said, only half-joking.

"Once we get up to my house, we'll spend your crossing fee on a drink."

"We're across the river and officially in Indian Territory. I thought there was no alcohol of any kind was allowed in the Nations?"

Lambert quietly eyed Reece. Offhanded, he said, "Apple cider, of course."

Lin grinned and Lambert showed his own straight white set of teeth.

"Of course."

Reece led the Concord team off the ferry boat, her head held high, her ebony braid swaying across her back as her hips moved with confidence. Lin walked beside the coach, grateful for the journey's end. He thanked God nobody was hurt.

Within minutes, Lambert's men had the long, heavy platform tied to its moorings. A fine black Arabian horse appeared on the scene as if by magic. The horse's handler appeared from behind the stallion. The burly Chickasaw Indian wore a heavy wool uniform with shiny brass buttons. Lin was hot just looking at him.

"My foreman," Lambert said, "Daniel Martin Ray."

Stoic but not unfriendly, Ray reached for Lin's hand and said, "Good to meet you."

"Cigar," Lambert said, and Ray produced two tight rolls of tobacco from inside his dark jacket.

Just as Lin had heard, what Lambert wanted, Lambert got—immediately for the asking.

Eight hundred acres of timber, cotton, and hay were the old man's to command. A grist mill and a saw shop, a broom factory and a blacksmith. An armory, and the Chickasaw's police headquarters. All of these, and more, graced the clay loam bluffs and sweet clover meadowlands of Rimrock. Spring fed streams coursed through the local geography, and the valleys were lush with vegetation. Scores of sheep grazed, and wild fowl was abundant.

Lambert offered Lin one of the cigars, then climbed into his saddle and pointed his horse up a winding white rock trail through a grove of cedar. Above the tree line, the roof of a tall house was visible on the summit.

"Join me at my home for supper," Lambert said. "Let us say, two hours from now." He tipped his head toward Reece, then spurred his steed forward. Ray followed suit, and Lin watched the men ride away.

Lin and Reece had been given the honor of watching the big man himself pilot his ferry through a dangerous turn. Now Lambert had other matters to tend to.

He poked the cigar into his mouth and casually patted his damp shirt.

"Don't it beat all," he said. "No matches."

Safe on solid ground, Dale Hemlock roused himself inside the cabin and leaned on the side panel, hanging his head outside the window. His round hat fell back on his head and his string tie was worried and frayed.

By way of contrast, Hemlock's voice demanded to be heard.

"When I pay for safe transport, I don't expect to ride a butter churn," he told Lin through the window. "I asked your commanding officer for clear roads and safe passage. I'll have compensation for today's upset."

"Considering Reece and I are the commanding officers of this stagecoach, you're welcome to try."

Dale's brow was a gray thundercloud crashing down over the bleak tundra of his sallow face. "You know who I meant. I'm talking about the Rangers."

"And the Rangers will refer you to Brother Lambert."

"If it were me running this ferry, I'd lose the hemp lines and invest in steel cable. Shoddy material is hand-made to mischief. This man, Lambert, invites sabotage with a gold place setting."

"Who said anything about sabotage?"

"You think it's a coincidence I happened to be on board the ferry when its line broke? I am an important man, seeing to important work. With all these damned fire-eaters screaming about seceding from the union?

With the Knights of the Golden Circle about? With the Ivory Compass up in arms?"

"Accidents happen," Lin said, "even to men like Brother Lambert. You'll find they happen to folks like you and me now and then. There's no accounting for it."

"Don't try to duck your responsibility, Jarret. You and Miss Sinclair want the prestige of running a coach, then the both of you will be held accountable." The man barked like an angry puppy. "You're not just a partner in a coach service, your part of the Texas Rangers, and I'll expect an official letter of apology from them, an apology from your commanding officer at the very least, and an apology from Brother Lambert, too. Don't you try to duck out of it."

Lin sucked at his swollen lip. "I'll give you something to duck," he muttered.

"What did you say to me? What did you say, son?"

Lin pondered his recent prayers and changed his mind.

It would've been better had the old coot drowned.

9

2

On the white rock road to Brother Lambert's hacienda, Dale Hemlock railed on, and Lin Jarret chewed the tip of his expensive cigar to mush.

Carrying Hemlock was a favor to Lin's commanding officer in the Rangers. Hemlock was correct about the southern rebels stirring things up, and the Texas road between San Antonio and Lambert's crossing was increasingly hounded by mischief makers of all persuasions. Rimrock itself was rumored to be a contentious oasis fueled by black powder and alcohol—the latter being illegal on Chickasaw land this side of the Red River border.

He couldn't help but wonder how forthcoming Lambert would be about his troubles. Some men were ashamed of failure, tried to cover things up. Lin didn't get such an impression from Lambert, but things always weren't the way they seemed.

Lin ran the back of his hand across the rough stubble of his chin.

Take Dale Hemlock for example.

In spite of the skepticism Lin had shown Hemlock,

he couldn't help but give some credence to the old man's suggestion of sabotage.

And, in spite of Lin's low opinion of the man, Hemlock was an intelligent fellow, important to his own society. The Texas Rangers wanted him delivered safe and sound to the cotton growers' meeting, and Lin had delivered.

Now he held his tongue as Hemlock continued to rant.

Once the man's tirade ran out of steam, Lin tipped his hat, then hurried to catch up with Reece. When he did, he took up the right side of the lead roan, a horse called Meg, while she strolled along on the left.

Reece always named all the horses Meg.

"Sounds like you and Mister Hemlock are getting along quite well."

"I'll be glad to be rid of him," Lin said. "Thank heavens we don't have to cart him back home with us."

"Which brings up the topic you didn't want to talk about this morning..."

Lin's feet squished inside sloppy boots, and the afternoon sun beat down on his neck. "Aw, Reece, not now."

"If not now, when?"

"After supper. Tomorrow. How about we talk about it tomorrow?"

"Why can't we talk about it now?"

"Because right now I'm halfway irritable thanks to Hemlock Dale back there. Not to mention I'm wet as a newborn calf and got the skin chafing to prove it."

"And exactly where is your skin chafing?"

"Cut it out, Reece."

"Want me to rub a little talcum on your problem areas?"

Lin scowled.

"I might kiss it and make it better?"

"Darn it, I said cut it out." Lin dropped Meg's rein and stomped ahead. Reece Sinclair got under his skin faster than a deer tick in summer.

Back at the Concord, Reece refrained from any more teasing. She knew their assignment had been a favor for the Rangers. They made the run as an official duty, and it was important to Lin.

He was overly conscious of the fact his captain had been forgiving of their dalliances with the stagecoach, pretending not to know about Reece Sinclair's abolitionist ways and Lin's sympathy. More than once, Lin's commanding officer had looked the other way with regard to certain emancipatory adventures the two Hellbenders had embarked upon.

Trouble was, thought Reece, most of it was on their own dime.

During the summer months the Hellbenders had taken too many charity jobs.

While she had inherited the coach and a Rio Grande rancho from her parents, Reece knew enough about business not to back a loser. The next job needed to pay for itself.

Lin knew it too—which was partly why he sported a bug on about it.

"I'm sorry," she called ahead to Lin. "We all had a bit of a scare on the river."

Over his shoulder: "Damn right we did."

"Otherwise, the trip was without incident."

"You're saying the trip was a waste of time?"

"I'm saying we should be grateful. Which you well know."

"If you said it was a waste of time, I wouldn't blame you."

"We can talk about the return trip tomorrow. Like you said."

They walked a while more in silence.

Then Lin waited on the side of the road to let her catch up. "It's fine. We can talk about it now."

They wound around the road in a dusty cloud left behind by Lambert and Ray, leading the team and stagecoach across a wood bridge over a small creek.

The more they stayed quiet, the more sorry Lin was for his outburst. "I apologize, Contessa. Old Hemlock is a burr in my saddle."

The long sloping grade to Rimrock mansion loomed ahead.

"Our dance on the ferry boat left us with some damage to the rigging," Reece said. "We've got at least one cracked trace. A couple torn straps."

"I suspect Lambert's people can fix up the tack."

"I hope so. I don't want to take the coach back empty. We won't do ourselves any favors traveling all the way back home without passengers or freight."

Lin had to agree with her but was short on ideas. "I suppose we could wait until the cotton meeting is over. It would mean a layover of four weeks, maybe five. See if somebody is traveling in our direction?"

"A month is too long to lay idle. Besides, Hemlock said most everybody is moving on north to Fort Smith with the Dalton Company's wagon train. Assuming they arrive on schedule, Hemlock will accompany them to market after the meeting."

"I wouldn't make another trip with Hemlock even if the Daltons don't get here. Still, there might be somebody who needs a ride."

"Mr. Lambert had a suggestion."

Lin's voice was flat, and he did his best to suppress the jealousy poking at his heart. "Oh, yeah?" He couldn't help but notice the way Lambert looked at Reece.

"A squaw man called Vern Klein makes his home here in Chickasaw country. He's a drummer of some kind. Lambert suggested we talk to him."

"What kind of merchandise does Klein deal in?"

"Lambert didn't say."

"You two seem to get along well enough."

"Who?"

"You and Lambert."

"Now who's teasing?" Reece said. "The old fella's twice my age."

"Just so, he was awful nice to you when he met us on the Texas side of the river."

"He was awful nice to you, too."

"I ain't gonna argue."

They topped the crest of the hill, and the splendor of Rimrock revealed itself. "Besides, we're here."

The acreage wasn't so much a plantation as a small town, complete with a post office and sign reading Rimrock Station - Established 1853.

More than the site of a single residence, the 800-plus acres was a healthy, vibrant community of men, women, and children. Before the rope snapped, Lambert told them more than 3000 immigrants had crossed the ferry during the past few months. Families from Iowa, Arkansas and Missouri were all looking for a better life in the West. Some of them would find it in the Lone Star state, some of them would move on down the trail to Mexico and eventually, California.

A few of them stayed in Rimrock.

Lin said, "If you want to get Mister Hemlock situated in his quarters, I'll look up Vern Klein."

"Let's do it the other way around," Reece said. "I can hunt down a name as well as you can."

Lin patted the Walker-Colt .45 pistol in its holster on his hip. "The difference is, I don't trust myself another second with Hemlock."

"Now who's teasing?"

"Only part ways."

"I'm carrying a gun too."

"Point taken." Lin pulled a silver eagle from his pants pocket. "I'll flip you for it. Heads, you track down Klein, tails—I will."

The silver coin flipped over and over into the air.

But before it could land, Klein made himself known.

"Look alive, folks, it's a fire!" Hemlock cried.

———

REECE SINCLAIR HAD NEVER SEEN flames burn so hot or so long. Or crackle so loud.

At first, she thought the towering cyclone of whirling heat in front of Lambert's house was a structure fire, but the closer they got, the more it was clearly something else, a glowing white-hot heap in a circle of scorched blackened grass next to the road. A big brushfire, perhaps, but certainly not deliberate? Not so close to the hacienda's wide front portico with its grand colonnade of fluted columns. It didn't make sense.

A celebratory bonfire?

But no, at the first sign of smoke, Lambert and his men had bolted ahead, and the big Chickasaw was in the thick of it, directing the formation of a bucket brigade leading back to a brushy creek behind the house.

The event was quite evidently unplanned.

Reece parked the Concord back from the flames

15

under a blooming poplar tree in front of a building adjacent to the house. The long, open pole barn was evidently a livery stable, and Reece saw two men with Brother Lambert's Arabian horses, and a remuda of animals in the pens beyond.

As a dozen men ran from behind the barn to help quench the blaze, Reece quieted her team of roans.

Yoked by Lambert's booming voice, the men pulled together with buckets and shovels to confront the conflagration with water and topsoil.

"What the hell?" she said.

"Hell's for sure," Lin said.

"Shouldn't we move on to safety?" Hemlock said from the coach.

Tremendous gusts of searing heat threatened her eyebrows as embers floated high, twirling on the currents over the rooflines of a nearby livery barn filled with hay.

"We're safe enough here," Reece said.

"It's a wagon on fire," Lin said, springing into action.

Before Reece had time to react, Lin was already at the edge of the water brigade, grabbing a copper pail from a young black man, passing it along to an older Chickasaw, fitting himself into the line.

The flames spiraled sideways and up with a roar akin to a mountain waterfall.

While she watched, and in spite of the men's initial efforts, the fire towered high above them with an angry roar, and a fresh volley of sparks erupted from the eye of the blaze.

Reece tied the team to a hitching post, abandoning Hemlock to join a crowd of women and children at the perimeter. "What was the wagon carrying? Are the animals clear?" she said.

"Aye, and Vern Klein's only got one animal for his wagon," said a red-haired broomstick at Reece's left shoulder. "He's an old ox named Harvey and he be over yonder."

Reece turned her head toward the livery but didn't see Harvey. Instead, she saw a rawboned gent draped with overalls and a gray cotton shirt. Bare headed, his wrinkled dome gave rise to a wispy patch of silver corn silk waving in the wind, and a similar crop of whiskers poked from his chin. By his worried expression and nervous gyrations, Reece guessed the old man was the owner of the ruined wagon.

A fat lady standing next to Broomstick verified Klein's identity.

"He's a no account for certain," she said. "Vern Klein's gonna get himself killed one of these days. I pray God he doesn't take us all with him."

"How did the fire start?" Reece said.

"How didn't it start until now is the question ye ought to be askin' yourself."

"I don't understand."

"Klein's a freighter, he is. The man's on the road most of the time, runnin' his damn ox and wagon."

"Not the wagon anymore, Clair," said Broomstick.

"Not anymore, no," said Clair, crossing herself.

For several minutes the women stood at the edge of the open flame, watching the men pitch water and sod at the conflagration, watching as the billows of black smoke slowly cleared and turned to steam.

Broomstick said, "Of course Klein will find some way to leave his wife and child anyhow, you can make dollar on it. Even without a conveyance, he's not one to stay at home underfoot."

"And he ain't the only one to be starting fires these days."

"Right as rain, dearie. There's a market for what Klein's peddlin' for sure."

"You won't believe the things I've heard over at sewing circle."

"Oh? Do tell…"

There wasn't any space for Reece in the conversation, but the comment about the origins of the fire compelled her to interrupt. "Miss…Clair, is it? You said something about people starting additional fires?"

Clair looked at Reece like she'd sprouted horns and a pitchfork.

"It's Missuz Clair to you, stranger. Clair McFarlane, and I ain't got nothing to say about any additional fires."

"But you said—"

"She didn't say a thing to you, dear. You Mex gals maybe need to get your ears washed…with soap, if it ain't a dirty word to ya." Broomstick gave an audible sniff.

Reece addressed the bigotry with low tones, speaking to the woman through grinding back teeth. "I will not be addressed in such a manner. My mother was Jada Sanchez, heiress to a centuries-old Spanish porciónes where sits Rancho de Jada."

"Aye, and me mudder's the queen of Ireland, but it's clear enough what begat this pyre. Klein dabbles in the Devil's chemistry."

"Hush," said Clair.

"An' why should I hush? Ain't he got it stored up all around Rimrock? It's common knowledge."

Reluctant, Clair had to agree. "Up and down the river. All over the place, as far as anyone knows."

"The man is a public menace," said Broomstick.

"The man delights in burnin' things, so he gets what he deserves."

In front of the livery, Klein sat on the ground, his head caught between his two hands.

Reece was forced to interrupt. "He doesn't look too delighted to me. What exactly does he freight?" She did her best to keep the impatience from her voice.

"I thought I told ye, lass," said Clair. "It's matches. Phosphorescent matches. Last word was Klein had around half a ton of the evil things squirreled away in these parts."

"Half a ton of the Devil's playthings and all fixin' to explode," said Broomstick, "Between you and me, I won't have them in my house. They are unholy wicked if you ask me."

"Half a ton. And now without a wagon, Klein can't move 'em away from Rimrock?"

"Who's gonna freight the damn things out of here is what I want to know," said Clair. She turned to Reece. "Who would be fool enough to carry a wagon load of matches?"

Reece shook her head. "I can't imagine," she said.

3

Once Klein's wagon fire had been subdued and the crowd dispersed, Lin lost a second coin flip. After he and Reece unpacked the Concord, he accompanied Dale Hemlock inside Rimrock's guest house where other members of the Cotton Growers Association congregated.

Reece agreed to meet Lin at Lambert's hacienda, then led the bay roans and the coach to the livery stable. The one-eyed hostler in charge of the livery station promised to tend the animals and, for a larger than average fee, agreed to replace the broken traces.

The repairs would take every last cent Reece carried.

After the long trip, she didn't feel like arguing, and they still had a few provisions to see them through the trip back home.

She dropped half the fee into the man's gloved palm, the second half to be delivered on completion.

The experience reminded her they needed new revenue.

Leaving the horses, she found Vern Klein still

sitting by himself on a patch of rocky ground next to a livery hitching post. He raised his bare head as she approached, lifted his gnarled hand to his brow to shield the sun from his watery blue eyes.

"Mister Klein? I'm Reece Sinclair. I own the Concord coach back there." She hooked a casual thumb over her shoulder and offered the old man her most ingratiating smile. "I sure am sorry for the loss of your wagon."

Klein put his hand to his slack jaw like he was loosening the brake before letting the words roll out. When he spoke, his voice was quick and trembled like a field sparrow, his sentences clipped off at the ends. Reece was reminded of a mercantile man from her childhood who sold string by the inch. A length of thread whirled from the spool lickety-split, only to be cut off with a flash. Klein talked in just such a fashion.

"Don't know why you'd care. Ain't y'r wagon. What's y'r business with me?"

"Thought we might be able to help each other out."

Klein was old enough to ignore Reece's more obvious assets, and his attention settled on the Walch Navy pistol on her hip.

"You a gunner?"

"I've been a lot of things."

"Ain't old enough to be a lot of things."

Reece saw a way to continue the conversation, so she removed the big double-hammered sidearm from her holster and handed it over. The old man's grip was unsteady, and his arm dropped under the gun's weight.

"Hell of a thing," he said. "Two triggers."

"The cylinder holds twelve charges of powder. Twelve balls. Six percussion nipples on back fire the front load, the other six fire the rear end."

"Hammer and trigger for front and back?"

"That's right."

"What if you shoot off a back load before you empty the front?"

"You don't."

"You might. And if you do it, you might not ever shoot again." Rather than return the gun to Reece, he tossed it on the ground in front of him. "Damn foolish, if you ask me."

Reece squatted down to retrieve her gun. When she did, she looked at Klein straight on. "I don't appreciate your manners, Mister Klein. You, a man who deals in phosphorescent matches, calling me and my gun foolish. I had thought we could do business. If you'd rather act like an ass, so be it." She wiped a spot of dust from the barrel of the Walch and slotted it back home on her belt.

Standing tall, she looked down on the old man. "The way I hear it, you've got merchandise to freight."

"Maybe I do, maybe not."

"They say you've got matches stored all around Rimrock."

"Maybe if you had the eyes of a sharpshooter you'd know where my hidey holes were. Otherwise, nobody else knows."

Reece shrugged. "I've got an empty coach headed south. You change your mind about your behavior, I'll be staying at Brother Lambert's. Ask for me there."

Reece let her stride carry her down the road past Lambert's three-story brick and stucco home. Across the street, she paused behind a wrought iron rail on the hard crest of the hilltop. The rocky bedrock formed a natural patio hanging out over a thorny green bosquecillo. The long view of the river was stunning.

Lambert's men had the ferry back in operation, and

it skimmed across the glittering spackles of the Red, a white spatula on quicksilver gliding to the far shore. On the Texas roadbed, a train of six wagons stacked high with bales of cotton waited with eight horses and a score of men.

The sides of the wagons were painted to read Dalton Company.

This was the life blood of the south, pure and simple.

Market demand for cotton in the northeast and Europe was high. Recently, Reece had read a newspaper story reporting nearly half of Great Britain's exports were comprised of cotton textiles, the raw material for which came from the American South.

From her vantage point on the Rimrock bluff, Reece watched the Dalton crew of a dozen Africans wheel their oversized wagon loads onto the ferry. Under the yoke of a few white men, the slaves labored in the sun. Reece pondered the economies of scale, the philosophical and financial tradeoffs she saw, the growth of the nation she still belonged to. For how much longer?

Hard days, with hard decisions were ahead of everyone, whether they wanted to admit it or not. Harvesting and freighting cotton was a labor-intensive job and one of the main rationalizations for slavery. She didn't agree with the idea and favored a solution that didn't include captivity for hundreds of thousands of people.

Aside from being morally despicable, the current system was ripping the country apart.

It had already torn Lin's family in two. It threatened his status with the Rangers and the Southern sympathizers in his family.

The troubles gave rise to dangerous organizations.

The Order of the Ivory Compass had vowed to see a new empire arise, a nation encompassing parts of Texas, Mexico, and Central America. The New Order would be based on cotton, the African Slave trade, and a fanatical belief in mystic pre-destination.

They had also vowed more than once to see Reece dead and buried.

Conversely, her status as a Texas landowner made her a target for pro-Union militias.

Dark powers had already marshalled their force against them and would in the future. When the time came and everything came to a boil, as it surely would, she and Lin were going to be caught in the middle amidst a hail of bullets and a ring of fire.

Sick for her Rio Grande rancho, she suddenly wanted to go home.

"Sorry," came a gruff voice from behind.

She turned around and kept her back to the iron railing. Her hand hovered near the butt of her gun. The late afternoon breeze smelled of honeysuckle and mint.

"What was it you said, Mister Klein? I'm afraid I wasn't paying attention?"

"Sorry," Klein said.

Reece pursed her lips and took stock of the old man.

Klein's overalls were a size too big, and the gray shirt draped over his frame looked like the remnant of a wallpaper-hanger's drunken folly. He stroked his thin beard, unconsciously clawing apart the tangled whiskers, pulling the gray wisps into a twist.

"Wanna do business?" His voice was plain. Honest enough.

There was even a hint of desperation. "Thing is...in all the fool confusion, I forgot what day it is. Today's

Thursday. I got to get my matches into Harbor Springs on the Brazos next week."

"Harbor Springs is south of Fort Belknap," Reece said. "It's where the fort initially got its water before digging a well a few years back."

"Yeah, it's about seven miles from the fort."

Reece scratched her head. She was good with numbers and could figure time and milage to the hour. Fort Belknap, on the Butterfield Overland road, was a week away under the best of conditions. Seven days was pushing it. They would have to switch out horses at stations along the way. They would have to travel all night.

And who knows what the road was like between the fort and Harbor Springs? It might be silk ribbon smooth, or completely impassable.

Reece thought about the Concord's broken traces. "I'm not sure it's possible," she said. "Last I heard, Harbor Springs was abandoned by the Army?"

"Ain't delivering to the army," he said with a sheepish grin.

"Who, then?"

He told her.

Without a second thought, she thrust out her hand. "Fair enough, Klein. We'll make it work. But it's gonna cost you. Let's talk money."

———

ONCE HE HAD GOTTEN Dale Hemlock situated with the Cotton Growers, Lin Jarret met Reece and Brother Lambert in the spacious flower garden beside Lambert's home. The Chickasaw led them on a cobbled path around back and then inside through a pair of glass paneled French style doors.

The open dining room was home to a long walnut table, chairs, and an enormous rock hearth. Open windows and doors beckoned in the fresh air. After helping quench the fire in Klein's wagon, Lin welcomed the comparatively cool touch of evening. It was the time of year when late at night the stars seemed like flickering crystals of winter frost, even if the days were straight up scorching.

But for now, the three of them sat on cushioned chairs and sipped cool tea with mint.

Catching Reece's eye across the table, he gave her a wistful gaze.

In Lambert's polite society, they would each be sleeping alone tonight—in their own rooms at his guesthouse.

Supper was a tender beef filet, blood red and smothered in mushroom gravy with green beans, cornbread, grits with honey and rhubarb pie completed their meal. Lin drank three glass tumblers of sharp apple cider, cutting the dust from the back wall of his throat, but still he was thirsty. After the meal he accepted a mug of steaming black coffee laced with heavy whipping cream.

Lin didn't complain when Brother Lambert withdrew a steel flask from his coat pocket and added a dollop of amber to the cup. "For special guests only, and it's not the best stuff. Damned illegal runners buy up or steal it all. Even my private stock."

The prohibition against buying and selling alcohol in Indian lands went back nearly as far as Lin could remember, but it was a rule flagrantly broken.

"You ever hear the term bootlegger?" Lin said. "As in, bootleg whiskey?"

"I never have," Lambert said. "What's it refer to?"

"Just what it sounds like, sir," Reece said. "And

26

exactly what you're describing. A man conceals a flask of illegal spirits inside the leggings or at the inside of his boot."

"It's as good a name for 'em as I ever heard," Lambert said. "Maybe it'll catch on."

"These bootleggers," Lin said. "More than you can handle?"

Lambert was unsure. "Six months ago, I wouldn't have said it, but now? They're causing more trouble than I can afford here in Rimrock. This station is growing and successful because, for the most part, it's peaceful. With all the other tensions, I don't need to be breaking up drunken brawls every night."

"Every night sounds like an exaggeration?"

"Not as much as you might think. All of a sudden, I'm dealing with random mischief like the ferry mishap today or Klein's wagon fire."

"You think those acts were deliberate?"

"These varmints travel across the river by boat or on the ferry and procure liquor in Texas. Vast amounts of liquor. Then they create a distraction of some kind —like the fire—to cover their tracks smuggling back into the Nations."

"Our passenger, Mister Hemlock, believes the ferry incident was an attempt on his life."

"Or maybe an attempt to frighten him," Reece said. "The Cotton Growers have become highly politicized lately. I understand there's some sort of business agreement in the works?"

"Yes, yes—the Dalton Company is forging an alliance with one of the big South Carolina concerns." Lambert touched his napkin to his lips. "But the meeting is more than just business deals. During the month, we will entertain botanists with new varieties of plants. We'll see machinists with their new inventions, and we'll hear speakers who will point the way to the future."

"You might want to keep an eye on Hemlock," Reece said

"I don't think Rimrock's problem has anything to do with the Cotton Growers or old man Hemlock," Lambert said. "There have been odd occurrences going on for the past several weeks. If anything, it was these boot-heads as you called them."

"Bootleggers."

"Whatever the name, my foreman, Daniel Martin Ray, has declared war on them. It's a war he intends to win."

In his memory, Lin pictured the stern-faced Chickasaw in memory. "Then, I don't envy the bootleggers."

"Ray is in charge of the Indian Police here. He's sworn to kill the next man who tries to bring in illicit spirits."

Lin was quiet, brooding on the implication of Lambert's declaration.

"You don't want a powder war here," he said. "The disruption of commerce...immigrant traffic..."

Lambert agreed. "I especially don't want it this month with the Cotton Growers meeting going on. Five weeks of peace and quiet is what we need most."

"You told us you've seen three thousand immigrants pass through here," Reece said. "An astounding number."

"And just since spring," Lambert said. "We live in a restless world, and it's only going to get worse. Homesteaders from Iowa, Missouri, and Arkansas have nowhere to go. They're looking for a better land. Who knows where we will be a year from now? I pray we stay together as a nation."

Reece sipped her cider. "With half the work force enslaved?"

Lin gave her a near imperceptible shake of the head.

Lambert's expression was grim. "If I understand what you are asking, Miss Sinclair, then yes—I am a proponent of the system we now have in place. I employ nearly 300 men."

"Slaves. You subjugate nearly 300 slaves."

"I have no desire to see our union torn asunder," Lambert quaffed his drink and snapped his fingers for a refill. "Or our dinner, either. Perhaps we should change the subject?"

The black girl who filled his glass smiled at Lambert. "Will there be anything else?" she said.

He motioned her away with a wave.

"We live in a growing land," Lambert said. "Like your Governor Sam Houston, I want to see it continue to grow. I have no love for Southern disunionists or Golden Circle rabble-rousers."

"What about the Ivory Compass?" Reece said.

Lambert took a quick pull from the flask before stashing it back into his coat.

"I don't know anything about them."

Lambert's voice didn't quite ring true.

Lin said, "You're right, Sam Houston favors preserving the Union. He's the governor of Texas but, unfortunately, he doesn't speak for everybody in the state."

Lambert agreed. "As I am a member of the Chickasaw nation and not without influence in the Five Civilized Tribes. But I don't speak for them. I speak for myself. Above all else, we must maintain the Union," Lambert said. "This is where our mind should be, where our hearts are. I've seen wagon trains three miles long pull in here on their way west. And cotton trains with just as many going the opposite direction. If we hold together, the future will be glorious."

Reece was curious. "I watched the Dalton Company ride in," she said. "Why do the teamsters truck cotton to Fort Smith? Why not use the river here to market the crop?"

Lambert shook his head. "Even the best navigators find the Red River vastly unpredictable."

Lin recalled Lambert's comparison to a mistress and smiled. "Besides, the Arkansas River traffic runs day and night. With a wide variety of steamers. Prices are better up there, and the market more secure."

Lambert sipped at his coffee. "You're right, Ranger. One day we'll see better access to markets here at home."

"When the trains come," Reece said.

Lambert's expression was whimsical, but he nodded. "Inevitably." He spoke to Lin, "You have an educated woman on your hands."

"She teaches me something new every day," Lin said.

"On such a day as iron bridges span the gap between Chickasaw land and Texas, my ferry will be a thing of the past."

"We better live it up now then," Lin said.

Lambert and Reece both raised their mugs.

The outside air was split by the blast of a carbine, and men started to yell.

4

"DAMN IT ALL," Lambert said, tossing his napkin down as another volley of gunfire pealed through the street in front of his house. "I can't seem to get a moment's peace around here."

Already on his feet and halfway out the walnut carved front door, Lin Jarret drew his Colt Walker and told the big Chickasaw to stay inside. "Until we know what's going on. You'll be safe here."

"Bull roar," countered Lambert. "I run Rimrock station. I will not be cowed like a woman in my own home."

Scrambling out beside Lin with her Navy pistol in a tight grip, Reece couldn't help but laugh out loud.

"Present company accepted, I'm sure," she said.

"I'm sure," Lin said, and a third round of shooting shook the evening air.

"Over there at the overlook," Reece said.

Lin followed her gesture across the street to where a determined quartet of tall men wearing the same dark woolen garb as Daniel Martin Ray were gathered on the rocky overlook. Three of the men were

31

Chickasaw Indians, busy reloading their carbines, while the fourth man was of European descent. He wore a limp cavalry hat over his bald pate and a yellow kerchief under his trimmed beard. As Lin approached, the man tracked a moving target along the ferry road below with what appeared to be a Sharps 1850 long gun.

"Stop right there," Lin said, triggering an overhead blast with his Colt, adding his own brand of cap and ball noise to the mix.

It was like Reece and Lin weren't even there.

The Indians continued to load their rifles, and rather than heed the directive, the marksman continued his arc with a smooth glide across the river bottom. At the last possible second, before his view could be obscured by the high elm trees around the overlook, he triggered an explosion. The Sharp's heavy mahogany stock bucked into the man's shoulder and the barrel spit fire, kicking toward the sky with a trailing scarf of smoke.

Unconcerned as to whether or not he hit his target, and oblivious to Lin's advance, the man put the gun stock onto the ground and began to reload the Sharps with smooth efficiency.

By this time his companions were again ready to fire.

Now the Chickasaw carried their guns into the street, the majority of their attention on the long tree-shrouded grade coming up from the ferry. One of the men swung his rifle barrel in line with Lin's heart.

"Indian police business. Don't interfere. Get back inside."

"Like hell I will," Lin said.

"He won't be cowed like a woman either," Reece said.

For an instant, the gunman was confused. "I don't understand?"

Reece pulled back the left hammer on her gun and at arm's length leveled it point blank at the man's head. "How about now? Beginning to get the picture?"

Lin's voice took on a commanding tone. "Drop the rifles," Lin said.

The trio of uniformed Indians refused to obey. But neither did they put up a defense. Instead, they came to full attention as Lambert arrived on the scene. Cursing under his breath, a white linen napkin still crammed into his collar, Lambert demanded the men explain themselves.

"You've interrupted my supper and disturbed my guests. There'll be no end to it if the Cotton Growers are aroused."

The man with the Sharps came forward.

Lin didn't like the looks of him. Just from his tone of voice and the way he carried himself. He wore a dark beard, and his shoulders were broad. But he needed the gun to prove he was a man.

He relied on it like a one-legged man depends on a crutch.

As if sensing Lin's thoughts, the Sharpshooter offered him a mean glare, then launched a stream of spit down to the street, aiming for a spot directly in front of Lin's boots.

Lin wondered how tough the shooter would be without his rifle.

"I'm waiting for your explanation," Lambert said.

"Horseman came across the ferry with a load of booze, boss. We tracked him across the river. He's on his way up the road now."

"You know him? Recognize him?"

The Sharpshooter nodded and licked his tobacco-stained lips. "Tricky bastard. We've been after him all month. This is the fifth time he's here. Mr. Ray says we see him, we make an example of him."

"Carry on."

"Whoa, hold on," Lin said, his Walker Colt still at the ready.

"You can't just gun a man down," Reece said. "Even if he is breaking the law."

"I say what goes here, Miss," Lambert said. "More important, my foreman says it. Daniel Martin Ray is in charge of the Indian Police. I have never questioned him, and he's never let me down."

"So you sanction what amounts to an outright murder?"

More than anything else, Lambert seemed embarrassed for Reece. "Maybe your woman isn't as educated as I had previously thought," he told Lin. "Maybe she doesn't understand how things are."

"Mister Lambert, it's you who doesn't understand I'm nobody's woman except my own," Reece said.

"She's not wrong," Lin said.

A staccato of galloping hooves approached, and the three Indians raised their rifles as the Sharpshooter joined them.

"You said you know this man," Reece said.

"If he's who I think he is," Lambert said, "he's liable to come in shooting." Unarmed, he made no move to give any ground.

Instead, he turned toward the open road.

The Sharpshooter and his three riflemen lined up like a firing squad across the path.

"You aren't giving this outlaw much of a chance," Lin said.

"He hasn't earned it." Lambert's voice was cold and

34

heavy, and he nodded gravely at the four Indians. "Do what needs done."

Lin caught the look of defiance on Reece's face and marched up behind the lead gun. He and Reece wouldn't stand by and witness cold blooded murder.

"Everybody, lower your weapons," Lin said, "Or by God I'll shoot your knees out from under you."

With lightning speed, the first man in line spun around and slammed his rifle butt down on Lin's gun hand, knocking the Colt from his grasp. The gun fell to the hardpacked sod with a clatter.

"You rotten sunnuva—" Lin's fast expletive was drowned out by the crash of the Sharps and his sight clouded by thick powder smoke. He sneezed and lost track of Reece, but when he opened his eyes, she was there, beside him.

"Hold steady, Ranger," she said, crouching down. One hand stayed on his back, the other reached down to retrieve his Colt. She handed over his gun. "I think it's too late."

Less than 100 feet down the road, on the final approach to Rimrock, a buckskin clad man lay face down in the street, his hat on the ground, rocking on its crown. The body was still except for a headful of tousled hair moving in the breeze, the whorls on his spurs still spinning. A nickel-plated pistol rested on the ground under the victim's right hand.

The Sharpshooter levered his smoking weapon from his shoulder to the ground without a word.

Nobody spoke as the rider's startled gray mare continued along the iron rail of the rocky overlook. A saddle slid sideways over the mare's ribs. She carried a canvas bedroll and a pair of bulging leather bags behind the saddle. Trotting past Lin, Reece, and the gunnies, the horse continued away from them, down the street, sand and gravel crunching under its hooves.

The Sharp's big boom had set a bell ringing inside Lin's head. More than just an echo, it was an alarm. A warning bell.

Something about the man lying motionless in the road was too familiar.

Lin shoved Lambert out of the way and moved quickly to the bloody victim.

Skidding to a stop on his trousers' worn-out knees, Lin turned the body over onto its back and picked up a dust-caked hand. There was warmth, and a faint rhythm. A fading pulse.

The powerful 50-caliber Sharps had bored a hole through the rider's chest above the heart, taking out a chunk of meat bigger than Lin's fist. Blood pooled under the dying man as his sky-blue eyes moved frantically left and right.

Panic twisted the handsome features, but the jaw stayed firm, the blond sandy hair cut long and flowing. The nose was narrow, angling down over a heavy yellow mustache now stained with blood.

Lin said the man's name.

"Jim? Jim Douglas? It's me…it's Lin Jarret."

Jim's hand gripped Lin's wrist with recognition before it slipped.

Lin clasped Jim's hand. "Hang on, friend," he said, knowing there was nothing to hold to. Life was draining away into the dust, hot and red.

Reece was beside him, and Lin lifted his chin. "We need some help here, dammit. Help get him inside."

Reece shook her head. "It's too late, Lin. He's gone."

"He's not."

"J-j-jarret."

"Don't try to talk," Lin said. "Save your strength, pard."

"G-got to tell..."

Crouching down as Lambert and his men approached, Lin hissed at Reece, "Get them the hell out of here."

Reece climbed to her feet and stepped between the killer and their prey. "You all better have a good explanation for this."

"Surely you don't know this man?" Lambert said.

Lin ignored the conversation, turning his attention back to his doomed friend.

"Gotta tell you..."

"What is it, Jim?"

"C-conspiracy," he said. "Mountain...man."

"What conspiracy, Jim?"

"Mountain..."

"Mountain? I don't...I don't get what you mean."

"Conspiracy."

And then Jim Douglas slipped away, and all Lin could see was red.

FROM HIS SPOT on the ridge, Steve Gardner ignored the grinding of bones in his ankle and watched with fascination as a fast cloud of dust cut a braided scar through Snakebite Canyon. The caprock air was intoxicating, the hard blue glaze of the sky above pure and clean. His ankle was likely busted, but what the hell? He'd endured a lot worse, and bones would knit eventually.

The Ancestors agreed, rewarding Steve with a breathtaking glimpse of the herd—a thundering bunch of wild horses acting as a distant herald for a cluster of blue thunderheads towering up behind them. The roiling mantle dragged an indigo shroud across the western horizon with a rare promise of rain, and veins of lightning sliced the sky.

Damned if his heart didn't race at the view of a hundred mustangs eating up the sod.

Steve knew they ran partly from fright—the roaring clouds dogged 'em and curtains of rain pummeled the stragglers. But they ran, too, because they were free to do it. Aloof, indifferent, wherever they landed tonight they would call home.

Ever since he left home to live with the Cherokee in Tennessee, Steve felt the same calling. The lure of a greater, more personal truth. The siren call of self-reliance but always within a like-minded community. After he left the tribe, he found a society of scouts and trappers. Afterwards, the Texas Rangers.

Through his life, he carried the words of his chief, who forever dressed in memory with a tight-fitting buffalo skin crowned him with an outstretched palm. "Persevere," he had said, and it became Steve's life philosophy, and his warring cry.

———

AROUND THE WIND-CARVED isolated buttes and through shallow side canyons at the eastern edge of the Llano Estacado, the herd of wild horses circled, a wonder to behold. Hundreds of pounding hooves slashing through the scanty grass, free to run, to gallop with the dark streaks of rain at their back, the sun ablaze in their face. What Steve wouldn't give to run with them, beside them, to be caught up in the middle. Instinctively, he pulled back his shoulder-length hair and flexed the rippling muscles of his bare, sun-bronzed torso.

Breaking around a spring-fed gully, the feral horses split into bands led by blacks and browns and grays before coming back together only to disappear behind a series of blood-colored mounds. The string of scarlet dust was three miles long and led into the storm's black roiling clouds in the distance.

"Persevere," whispered Steve, lurching to his feet and holding his ten-bore coach gun in hand, jamming the butt under one arm so the 32-inch barrel could crash through the tangle of boulders and mesquite roots in his path. In his other hand, he swung his heavy frontier tomahawk, a gift from Comanche chief Tibbalo to signify the peace after he and Lin Jarret had skirmished with the tribe.

Steve forged ahead dressed only in a fringed loincloth and tough, square-toed boots.

He clamored along the 1000-foot-high face of the canyon wall, following the trail he initially blazed in his hunt for Gamble's quail. Before he'd fallen like a bumbling child. Now he smelled the sweet scent of distant rain, each stab from his ankle reminding him to be happy and count his blessings.

After all, it might've been his neck.

Step down, and his ankle complained like an old woman. Rest too long and his joints rusted tight like wooden teeth. Think about it too much and worry ducked around the edges of his grumbling stomach like nattering songbirds.

He was a good many miles from civilization. A day's ride to Gruber's Station and medical attention.

Steve shrugged off his worries. Snatching at the creeping fear, he threatened to wring its neck until dead. Clean rivulets of sweat ran down his profile, collecting at his smooth, shaved jaw. He rubbed his chin on his bare shoulder, brushing the drops aside.

The wind braced him, a blast of winter chill as the approaching storm replaced the heat from earlier in the day.

Life was to be lived in the moment, not some spotty future of shadows.

Above him, the clouds became a solid mass higher than any mountain ledge, rolling, fluffy cauliflower heads raising dark curtains over the dry ocean of land.

At the base of the ridge path, Steve's horse nickered his welcome at his rider's approach. Hanging from the saddle horn on a leather strap, a canteen of water waited patiently.

Underfoot, a mouse dodged into a narrow stone cut, avoiding Steve's boot, and a hawk circled on the gusty currents above, scolding them both for ruining its hunt. The long, piercing cry of the bird touched something deep in Steve's heart and echoed the grumbling of his own stomach.

"You and me, both, brother."

He'd been out all morning without seeing any quail.

A flash followed by a wave of thunder came across the of sky. Surprise!

Steve's horse jumped. A spit of rain plopped onto Steve's nose. The wind punched him with gusts of cold fury.

Steve was less than 100 feet away from his mount when another salvo issued forth from the clouds. The roan pulled back its ears and trembled.

"Easy, Romeo," called Steve. "Hold on, fella." But the next crash of noise came with a searing flash of white lightning. Startled, the horse twitched his ears back and forth before trotting away sideways. Steve arrived on the floor of the vast Texas plane only to watch his ride home turn tail around a stack of fat boulders.

The burrhead wasn't usually so touchy. "Damn your eyes, horse." But even as he said it, he picked up a fast-whirring alarm from behind the assemblage of rocks.

The oncoming squall hadn't been the only thing shivering Romeo's hide.

Rattlesnake!

Also known as Steve's supper.

41

There was a reason the desiccated gash along the Caprock Escarpment cleaving east Texas from west was called Snakebite Canyon. The rattling fat coil of spring-loaded meat Steve found in the rock clearing was one of them. Rattlers were as plentiful here as sheep on the Rio, and Steve preferred the tender white meat's flavor to just about anything else. Especially with a beer.

It's what he'd gotten used to.

Using his gun to keep himself propped up on the bad ankle, he fingered the tomahawk loop of his pants.

The war-axe Steve carried was fifteen inches long with a six-inch long square flint head. The wood handle was carved and stained at the end to resemble a duck's head while farther up, the grip was wrapped in soft leather. The chipped flint head was held fast to the handle by tough rawhide Steve maintained on a regular basis.

Years of carry had worn a smooth notch under the head, and the weapon fit snug in his hand. Years of practice made the war blade as deadly in Steve's hand as a six-shooter might be in another.

A rumble of thunder hastened Steve's moves. After he secured the snake, he still needed to track down his horse.

Wound tight in the wedge of space under a waist-high roughly hewn round rock, the rattler weaved its exposed head up and back, pulling in as close to its stone shelter as possible. A clean kill would be tough. Better, Steve thought, if he could lure the old snake out of hiding.

And it was an old snake. Long and fat with scales flaking around its mouth, it moved a tad slower than it should've, seemed more complacent in its danger. Oh, the rattles purred away, and the creature swayed back and forth with proper trepidation, but it didn't have the edge of a young warrior. It didn't have the spirit of a killer.

Steve had the advantage there.

Momentarily, Steve wondered about using the scattergun, but decided not to. In such close quarters, surrounded by granite and limestone, a load of shot would ricochet in a million directions, ripping into his own hide even as he cut his supper to fresh ribbons.

No, the tomahawk would have to do.

With one bold move he lunged down onto his knees, swinging the axe into a fast horizontal arc only a few inches above the sandy red clay, swiping into the space under the rock, missing the rattler by less than an inch.

Unable to stop, the snake shot out at the tomahawk's head, slapping its broadside before recoiling back to reconsider its options.

Steve encouraged the old rattler to move. "Hup to, damn your slinkin' guts."

If the blasted thing would only slip outside the periphery of the boulder, one swift motion would cleave the head from the body.

Steve got set to try again, and now the thunder came in a continuous wave.

No! Not thunder.

Hoofbeats.

"Oh, holy hell," he said, turning his head as the shadow of the first wild horse leapt over his prostrate form. If he hadn't been sprawled out, hunting the snake, he would've lost his head. A second animal careened past, a blur of elbow and knee, hoof, fetlock, and tail.

Then the pounding was deafening, and the air

became thick with the smell of sweaty horseflesh and flying dirt.

It was the herd of wild horses he'd seen before. The storm must've driven them off course, circling the bands of frothy, screaming beasts into a frenzied tear. They angled over Steve's head one after another, hooves like hard wood mallets bludgeoning away.

Steve yanked himself into a ball, pulling his legs up to his chest and embracing his knees with his arms. Pressing his right side into the rock he crouched behind, he willed himself to stay still, to become the rock as the string of crazed horses tore through the rim of the canyon.

Almost immediately a heavy club came down on his shoulder sending shards of agony through his arm and down his rib cage. A spray of gravel pelted his forehead and a limestone chip skimmed across his back leaving a stinging gash.

All Steve could do was wait out the stampede and pray he wasn't chopped to pemican.

He counted the seconds to himself.

By the time he reached thirty, Steve was nicked, kicked, bruised, and battered.

"Persevere," he said. The neighing, awful roar went on forever.

Gradually the stampede lessened, and he realized the rain of horses had been replaced by a torrent of water from the clouds. Trembling, he dared relax his arms and lift his head.

The world had been remade.

On all sides, Steve was surrounded by a plowed field of sod, thick with torn pockets of earth already filling with rain. The smallest boulders were still present but rolled here and there where they made new clusters with the bigger foundation rocks. In the far distance, Lin still heard the animals running, wondering if his Romeo was one of them now. Wondering if what he really heard was the continued ringing of his ear drums.

Then his hand fell to the ground and brushed the tomahawk even as the rattler emerged from under its safe spot. Curious as to the nature of its latest experience, and having forgotten about Steve, it wandered into the open, its forked tongue taking the temperature of the fresh new world.

With one smooth, quick flourish, Steve grasped the wood handle and flipped the tomahawk end over end with enough force to split a bison skull. The sharp flint stone hit home, buried itself in three inches of clay. On one side of the axe, the head of the rattlesnake, newly freed from the rest of its body, worked its jaws over and over, biting reflexively, its glazed skin gleaming with each flash of sheet lightning.

On the other side of the axe head, the writhing meat curled around itself and uncurled in increasingly slower spasms of death.

Steve exhaled long and hard, pressed his back against the warmth of his wet rock furniture and reveled in smug self-reliance.

They would eat like kings tonight after all.

He and his guest at the cabin.

He snapped open his eyes, realizing he might well have to walk all the way back.

Then he heard Romeo's familiar rough nicker, his breathy snort.

Pushing himself up, Steve saw a familiar figure coming through the dying rain. As the clouds began to part and sunlight broke through to the palo, he reclaimed his war axe and did his best not to give away his hurt ankle.

The old man led Romeo in past a gnarled mesquite to the tilled ground where Steve stood with his snake. "You happen to lose a horse?"

"I did, but I secured our supper."

The old man nodded knowingly and, reaching into a canvas sack tied to his waist, pulled out an identical reptile, equally decapitated. "Me too," he said. "Let's light up a fire and get to cookin'."

6

LIN DIDN'T KNOW the one-eyed jasper with the pair of leather saddle bags slung over his shoulder, but it was clear Reece recognized him. Stooped, with a grizzled white beard and a kerchief tied low around his head, One-Eye cleared his throat at the threshold to Martin Daniel Ray's office.

Stoic as ever, Ray sat behind his desk in a padded leather chair, but not as padded as the one Lambert occupied beside him. The foreman's hat hung on the wall, and the top button of his heavy dark coat was unbuttoned. His big hands, like blocks of carved wood rested on heavy oak surface in front of him.

It was hard to read his expression. Hard to read his age, thought Lin. The fanned array of crow's feet around his eyes put him over forty, but his smooth forehead and sturdy build pegged him as a man still in his prime.

"Gotcha the load here from the rum-runner," said Freddie. "We're keeping his horse in a back pen. Good looking animal. Good you didn't have to kill it. Be a shame to lose a good animal on account of some no-good, dad-blasted no account."

Lin felt his guts climb up into his throat.

Freddie bounced up and down, clinking the contents of the saddle bags together. "Guess you know what's in here."

"Fine, Freddie. Thank you for bringing it over," Lambert said. Then, for Lin's benefit. "Freddie's our local hostler."

"Got your team set up for the night, Miss Reece. Fine team of roans you got. Ain't caused me any trouble."

Reece offered her thanks.

"Just leave the bags, Freddie," Lambert said.

Freddie nodded with satisfaction, the kerchief covering the hollow socket over his left cheekbone. With a grunt, he heaved the load from his back, dumping the satchels to the hardwood floor. The sound of smashed crockery was immediate, the air filled with the pungent tang of strong corn liquor.

"Idiot," spat Ray, followed by a string of oaths, but Lambert couldn't stifle the expulsion of laughter spilling from his lips.

"Get on with you, Freddie. Get on home now. You did a good day's work." Lambert waved the chagrined oldster back out the door before Ray could get his hooks into him.

Freddie showed Lambert a nervous smile, then darted out the door.

Lambert continued to chuckle and wipe at the sweat on his forehead with a white handkerchief. "You just never know what to expect with Freddie," he said.

From his spot near the corner of Ray's desk, Lin watched the hostler scurry across the boardwalk, leaving a trail of dust in his wake.

Then he turned his attention back to the shadowy interior of the cramped square room.

After Jim Douglas had been carried to the home of Rimrock's resident doctor and declared officially dead —as if there could be any doubt—Lin and Reece followed Lambert and the Sharpshooter across Rimrock's wide open brick square to the foreman's office.

The room was half of a single-story frame structure with a tall false front. A sign across the front entrance read Indian Police and Boot Store. Ray had the door open for them when they arrived. The boot store side of things was closed, but through the glass window facing the street, Lin saw a row of shoes and a cobbler's bench. Not much else.

But for the most part, his attention was elsewhere.

Filled with clouds of rage, he was a steam engine without a pressure release valve. Every step on the way to the office had added kindling to the fire. Twice Reece reached out to comfort him, twice he shied away from her hand.

He needed to stay contained, keep his head on straight and his temper under control until the right time.

Boiling at the edges, he'd played the whole dirty scene of Jim's killing over and over in his mind more than once, coming at it from different angles, imagining opposing points of view.

No matter how things stacked up, Jim Douglas had been murdered—with premeditation and without remorse. Lin was sure of it.

The only thing he wasn't sure about was how he would avenge his friend's wrongful death.

But one thing was for sure—Lin would see justice done.

Once inside the office, Lambert immediately fell into one of two comfortable chairs, while Ray claimed the seat behind the desk. Reece sat on a three-legged stool near the wall under a pair of hat pegs, leaving Lin in the middle of the room to worry the leather soles of his boots.

He paced back and forth, too anxious to rest.

Could be why they needed a shoe repair next door.

The door opened, and the Sharpshooter quietly joined them. It was all Lin could do not to reach out and strangle him with the scruffy yellow kerchief tied around his neck. He took a step forward, but once more restrained himself.

The dour faced white man walked to a place near a side table where a coal oil lamp rested on a hand-crocheted doily.

"Go ahead and light the lamp," Ray said, and immediately the Sharpshooter used a match to ignite the wick,

Lin was struggling to find the right words to address the entire affair.

Now Ray and his Sharpshooter were on their haunches beside Jim Douglas's dumped saddle bags, carefully removing whole crocks from the sharp remnants of broken jugs. "Stupid old fool," Ray said. "He's getting too old to piss straight. I don't know why we keep him around."

"The same reason I keep you on, Daniel," boomed Lambert. "Loyalty. We share a common goal. We have common enemies."

Ray shot his boss an expression filled with venom.

Interesting. There was no love lost between the two, and the glowering look caught Lin off guard. He tucked it away in memory for a later conversation.

One thing was sure. Lin had been present when Jim

Douglas rode onto the scene, had watched his horse gallop away after the shooting.

The bags filled with broke booze crocks had not been carried into town by Jim.

The lamp cast flickering shadows over the stucco walls of the office, and the men had the smashed crockery cleaned up when Lin managed to get the words straight in his head. Ray returned to his place behind the desk, and the Sharpshooter went back to the lamp.

Lambert was the first to speak, and his tone was sincere. "Let me be the first to say I'm sorry about your friend, Jarret. If there had been any other way…"

"There was no other way," said the Sharpshooter.

"What happened today has been a long time coming," Ray said.

Lin glanced at Reece, took strength from the quirk of her eyebrows, the silent parting of her lips in affirmation. He didn't need to hear the words to know what she was thinking.

I've got your back, Ranger.

Lin ignored Daniel Martin Ray's smug demeanor behind the desk and focused on Lambert.

"Don't you dare tell me what happened out there was an accident," he said.

Lambert pursed his lips. "Nooo," he agreed. "I wouldn't call it an accident at all." He hauled himself forward and put his elbows on his knees. Face aglow with curiosity, he said, "What would you call it?"

"I call it cold-blooded murder."

Lambert let his heavy carcass fall back into the chair with a sigh. Behind the desk, Ray curled his lips into a sneer.

"You're not in Texas, Jarret. Here, across the river,

the Five Civilized Tribes are in charge. We follow Chickasaw law."

Lin confronted the Indian head on. "Who said anything about law? I'm talking about what I saw out there. I'm talking about your soldiers lying in wait for a defenseless man who—"

"Jim Douglas carried a gun," Lambert said, quietly.

Ray opened the top drawer beside his hip and dropped Jim's nickel-plated five-shooter onto the desk.

"The gun was carried high for everyone to see."

"Who shot first?"

"A question our Sharpshooter can answer," Lambert said.

Lin turned on the assassin. "You got a name, mister?"

"I don't answer to you."

"You do answer to me and Brother Lambert," Ray said from behind the desk. "Who pulled trigger first?"

The Sharpshooter's gaze never left Lin's face. With a smirk he said, "The Texan took the first shot. Don't they always?"

Lin didn't flinch under the insult, holding his hard look with a clenched jaw, but keeping his fists in check. He wanted nothing more than to pound the man into corn mush.

Not here. Not now.

You'll get your chance, he told himself.

"What you two Hellbenders need to understand," Lambert said, addressing Lin and Reece, "is Jim Douglas has been terrorizing Rimrock for more than a month."

"Hellbenders?" Reece said.

"It's what they call you, isn't it? I know damn well

who you are," Lambert said. "Nobody eats at my table I don't know who they are."

"Abolitionist scum," said the Sharpshooter under his breath. "Word's out about you two."

The man was begging for a broken mouth.

Lambert continued to dress Reece down. "Do you understand me, Miss? I know everybody walks, jogs, gallops, rides, stomps or is carried through my town. And if—by some act of God Almighty—I don't, my constable does."

"You don't know Jim Douglas."

"You're wrong, Jarret," Ray said. "We know Douglas quite well—apparently better than you do. We aren't talking about some innocent stranger here. We've watched him for weeks. He's carried more contraband across the ferry from Texas than just about anybody else."

"He wasn't carrying those bags when he arrived today," Lin said. "I was there. I saw."

Ray continued. "We have issued warnings, rebukes, punishment. I've had more than one run-in with this man, Douglas. If this is the kind of rascal you call friend, I can't imagine how vile your enemies must be."

Lin chewed on the words.

Not because of Ray's haughty attitude, or because he demeaned the name of a dead friend, though those things were true.

Lin chewed the words because there was a chance Ray was right.

Douglas had always been more than a handful.

During Jim and Lin's younger days together, taming the saloons on both sides of the Rio Grande, the line between right and wrong sometimes grayed. Moral guidelines got a little blurry for both of them.

There was the time Jim was caught, literally, with

his pants down in a conniving Tejano's bedroom with the man's supposed wife. Lin used up two six-guns' worth of powder and lead getting his friend out of that particular honey trap.

The favor was returned when Lin couldn't keep his mouth shut at a Mexican sheep ranch. All he'd done was suggest the foreman had carnal knowledge of a fat ewe named Daisy. Lucky to be alive after the knock down-drag out, Lin agreed such rowdy goings-on were the stuff from which legends were stitched.

Together, the two of them wove a tapestry some folks in Texas still talked about.

Jim's loyalty to Lin had never wavered, and the reverse was also true.

And that was the crux of the matter: loyalty.

Could Jim Douglas have been running liquor into the Nations?

It wasn't beyond Jim's abilities. Nor would it conflict with Jim's view of right and wrong.

But, even so, Lin didn't believe it.

"It's not the kind of nickel and dime scheme he'd be involved with."

"I'm surprised to hear you say so. He was a favorite of the nickel and dime ladies."

"You'll choke on those words," Lin said, launching himself across the room.

Lambert hauled himself up from the chair and intervened.

Bringing himself to his full height, standing toe to toe with Lin, he towered above the Ranger and talked down to him in no uncertain terms. "This is my home, and I will have order. Must I remind you who paid for your dinner tonight?"

"It was mighty generous of you, but—"

Lambert poked at Lin with his index finger. "I will have order."

"You will take your paw out of my face, Lambert, or I'll tear it off your arm."

"You pissant Rangers talk so damn tough," said the Sharpshooter. "Pantaloon-wearing bunch of ignorant—"

Lin couldn't take it anymore.

Between Lambert's pompous speechifying and Ray's non-stop goading.

Lin spun around and punched the Sharpshooter in the mouth.

7

WITH A SHOULDER BURIED in Lin's guts and both hands
clamped behind the Ranger's back, the Sharpshooter
drove them both out the door and into the street
where they lost their hats.

Lin's heel caught the edge of the boardwalk, and
the last thing he saw before stars was the shoe repair
window and its lineup of girl's high-top patent leather
button-up boots. His head bounced hit the tough sod
of the street like a cantaloupe, as the Sharpshooter
drove his knee into his spleen. The world was foggy
and full of pain.

The dark shadow of a fist coming down, swinging
in from the sky like a sledgehammer, warned him at
the last instant to roll. He managed to escape the drubbing only to catch a swift kick to the ribs. Lin tried for
his Colt, but another kick paralyzed his shoulder.

Rolling like a rat clipped by a wagon wheel, he
gained some ground and found his knees in time to
see his nemesis pounding toward him.

Lambert called out from Ray's office, "Let him

alone, Clay," but it was too late for either one of them to yield. Lin had too much of a mad on, and Clay had his pride.

Only one way to settle things now.

Lin wrapped his arms around his chest, whimpering and playing possum until the last possible instant when he jerked up, slamming a hard set of knuckles into the soft flesh under Clay's jaw. He followed with a staggering punch to the throat.

Now Clay was on the defense, clawing at his neck, choking and gasping for breath. By rights, the blow could've killed the man, but Lin had held back. He wanted to humiliate Clay with a good drubbing, not hang for manslaughter.

He didn't think Clay would give him the chance.

The Sharpshooter was tougher than Lin imagined, already shaking off the jab, stalking around in a half-circle, looking for a line of attack. Lin held back, measuring his opponent's mass, figuring he was outweighed but not by much.

"A bag tricks won't do it today, Jarret," Clay said. "Today you'll prove yourself with your fists. So far, all I've seen is horse-apples and granny punches. Your sweet little girl friend teach you how to fight?"

Lin cupped his hands, wagged his fingers to provoke the man. "C'mon you son-of-a-bitch."

When Clay stepped forward with a fast right, Lin deflected it with a round sweep of his left hand and slammed his fist into his opponent's nose. The satisfying pop of cartilage and whoosh from Clay's mouth gave Lin the added fuel he needed to keep going. He stepped partially to the left, then levered a hard right boot sideways into Clay's sternum.

From the momentum of the kick, Clay staggered to

the far side of the street where two ladies stood gawking. The more robust of the two women caught Clay by the shoulders, stopping his fall, and pushed him up with a knee to his backside while her red-headed companion cheered him on, "Go on and give 'im a beatin' boy-o!"

The fight was drawing a crowd. Behind the ladies, Lin caught a glimpse of the three riflemen in their policeman's uniforms.

He had a sinking feeling. Even if he won, he might lose.

The Sharpshooter was back now, red-faced, raging, eyes bulging from their sockets. Blood poured freely from the wrecked nostrils of his flattened nose, and he swiped at it with trembling fists. "You didn't think I'd stop, did you?"

"I had hoped."

"God, I wish it would've been you at the end of my sights today. You pompous jack ass. I'd enjoy putting a hole in you almost as much as your Union-loving friend."

"Say it again, Clay. Say it once more, so's I can shove the words down your throat."

"You heard me."

"You murdering piece of—"

Clay still had one good punch in him, and it caught Lin flat on the side of his head, bringing back the fog. He stumbled, trying to stay upright even as the evening daylight dimmed.

Sun's going down.

Maybe for the last time.

He blinked as the sparks flitting around his face. Fireflies?

"Yah, yah, yah," was the noise from the crowd.

"Fight, fight, fight," but Lin couldn't tell who the crowd was cheering for.

When Clay landed a half-assed slap to the opposite side of Lin's head, the applause was wild.

No doubt who Rimrock pulled for.

For a few seconds, Lin lost track of Clay as the crowd reeled past. He was fighting a two-front war now—one battle with a man, a more urgent struggle with gravity. A wall of hands and arms caught him, shoved him back toward the street.

Clay waited for him, breathing hard, bent at the waist, his hands on his knees.

Blood from his face trickled like a fresh-water spring, but he wasn't yet spent.

Lin swallowed hard and tried to clear his perception. His ribs ached and the agony inside his head was like a thousand steel-spiked balls whirling against his skull. There was no doubt Clay meant to kill him.

With renewed determination, Lin reached for his Colt.

This time he drew it from the holster.

Clay's reaction to the gun was a mocking tirade. "Knew it…all the time. Knew…you'd…give up. Knew… you wouldn't fight like a man…knew you couldn't beat me fair and square."

Gurgling with blood and phlegm, there were two Clays in the street, but Lin worked hard, pressing his left hand to his temple, willing the images to come together as one. Twin Clays fuzzing in and out of focus suddenly struck Lin as laughable.

The loudmouth had killed Jim with a coward's ambush and now he was maligning Lin's honor, accusing him of not fighting fair.

"Two…against…one," Lin said.

Everything north of Lin's collarbones felt like it was wrapped in cotton, and when he gazed down at his own torn clothing, he imagined himself as a broken rag doll.

Fighting a croaking fat frog who kept splitting in two.

The whole damn scene was ridiculous.

Lin staggered forward, holding his gun at his side. When he stood within arm's reach of Clay, he dropped the shooting iron to the ground and took a deep breath, willing his opponent to come into focus.

As soon as he had a solid target, Lin cranked his right elbow back making contact with the Clay's nose and snapping his skull back. Lin followed up with a hard left hammer to the Clay's right ear, the sharp-shooter crumpled like a sack of potatoes.

Nearly drowned by a sea of angry complaints from the crowd, Lin floated backwards, paddling toward the sound of his name.

"Well done, Jarret, well done."

He felt himself pitching forward into a pair of welcome, strong arms.

"I wouldn't have put my money on you, but you came out on top," Lambert said, setting him up straight.

Lin appreciated the praise, saw the big man reach out to pat his shoulder. "Yes, indeed. Clay's about the toughest man in these parts."

The crowd around them continued to boo and hiss.

"Only one man I can think of who's tougher than Clay," Lambert said.

Lin rubbed the back of his neck, looked up at Lambert, and smiled weakly. "Oh, yeah," he said, catching his breath, "who would be more tough than Clay?"

Lambert slammed a granite fist into his face and the sun dropped behind the horizon.

"That would be me," he said.

Then, turning to Daniel Ray, he said, "Put both of these men behind bars."

8

LIN WOKE up the next morning with the sun
threading its way through cracks in a rough built sod
wall. The musty smell of dust and black mold had a
clamp on his nose and a knife-like pain through the
base of his spine made him aware he'd slept on a hard
rock floor.

These were the least of his discomforts.

Closing his eyes to stop the thrumming inside his
forehead did nothing. Pressing the meat of both palms
into his eye sockets was a slight, but temporary respite.

He wanted to beat his skull against the floor, crack
it open, and drain out the misery.

But his shoulders hurt too, and his knuckles were
swollen and raw. Not to mention the fact the floor
smelled like more than one person had missed the
bucket in the corner.

The cell he occupied was built of earthen walls
with a single door, a barred steel frame entrance set
into solid oak beams. The overhead rafters were a
sloppy job of pine construction and patches of sod
roofing bowed down between them.

Rimrock's jail was hardly escape proof, but it was impressive. Lin's first challenge was simply to sit up.

Poking around with his tongue, an inventory of his teeth gave him some comfort. They were all there.

He pinched the bridge of his nose to confirm it was whole. It was, but touching it triggered a dull throbbing.

Recalling the previous day's fight, Lin decided Clay absolutely came out on the worse end of the stick.

The lucky bastard was probably still asleep.

An attempt to rise sent his guts into an uproar, and the churning continued even as he sank back down. He lurched onto his side and was sick but found some relief once the spasms died away. Guess he missed the bucket, too.

Lin must've slept for a while then, because when next he opened his eyes, Reece sat on a stool beside him, and the cell had been cleaned. The needle-thin shafts of light permeating the earthen walls were at a more acute angle, and this time Lin made out the detail of fine dust motes.

He decided he wasn't going to die, no matter how much he wanted to.

"Drink this," Reece said, lowering a cup of heat into his awareness.

He didn't know what it was and didn't care. The warmth soothed his sore fingers, and he carried the hot cup to his aching throat, his bruised cheek. When he sipped at the rim, he discovered pungent coffee thick with sugar.

"What time is it?" he said, surprised by the strength of his voice. He took another slow sip, letting the elixir slip down his throat.

"Just after noon," Reece said. "You were out more than fifteen hours."

"Clay?"

"Rode out of town first thing this morning."

"Damn. I thought I whipped him hard enough to keep him sleeping for a week."

"Lambert roused him before breakfast and put him on a horse personally." Reece put her hand on Lin's shoulder. "Told him not to come back."

Lin drank some more coffee.

"There's some comfort there anyway," Reece said. "Just so you know, Lambert's not at all happy with Jim's killing. No matter how he may have acted yesterday."

"I wish I could believe it," Lin said. He directed Reece's hand to the back of his neck where she massaged the hard knots there. "At least he hasn't put me on a horse yet. Or is he running us out of Rimrock by sundown?"

Reece's gentle fingers helped melt away the pain in Lin's neck and shoulders, but her words were rough.

"Sundown or as soon as you're awake, whichever comes first," Reece said.

Lin groaned and tipped the cup on end. "I guess I'm awake," he said.

"Lambert promised us safe passage back across the ferry as soon as you're up."

"Awfully big of him. Or is he planning to have us shot in cold blood, too?"

"Like I said, I don't think he's as convinced his men were in the right as he let on. This morning at break-fast he—"

"Wait—you had breakfast with him?"

"Of course."

"Maybe this restaurant you ate at will pack us a lunch?"

"Wasn't a restaurant."

"Then...where? Not in his house?"

"Naturally, yes?"

Lin straightened his back and turned to Reece, a halo of sunlight drawing an outline around her face. "Then where did you stay last night?"

"At Lambert's house. Where did you think?"

"You spent the night with him, while I was stuck in here?"

"I hope you didn't mean it the way it sounded?"

"Oh, hell, I'm not accusing you of anything. I guess I'd just expect a little more...respect."

Lin felt a wave of fiery heat rise into his face, then just as quickly dissipate in the soft innocence of Reece Sinclair's emerald-green eyes. He put his hand to her cheek, and she kissed it. "On the other hand, I guess I'd expect you to stay safe and find out all you could from Lambert."

"He's a good man in a hard situation," Reece said. "I can tell you more once we're out of here and on the road to Fort Belknap."

Lin nodded, poking at his ribs, prodding his jaw. "Give me a few minutes." He looked around the barren room. "Got any more coffee?"

Reece brought a tin pot up from under her chair and poured the remnants into his cup.

Lin's stomach grumbled.

"I've got some food packed. We'll get you some when you think you're ready."

"Later," he said. "Coffee's good for now." Then he stopped drinking and said, "Fort Belknap? What's this about the old fort?"

"The coach is outside, and the team is ready. We're all loaded up and ready to go."

"Slow down, slow down. Why are we going to Fort Belknap?"

"We have to be there within a week. Not the Fort, exactly. Harbor Springs. It's south of the Fort."

Mental calculations made Lin's head hurt, but he muddled through quickly enough. "It's not possible," he said. "We'd need to travel without stopping. Besides the gear and supplies we'll need to lay in, the extra water."

"All taken care of. Add to it, Mister Klein supplied a well-documented route with plenty of spring-fed creeks and ponds. I spent all morning securing food and supplies for the horses. The last thing I need to collect is you."

"Who's this Klein you mentioned?"

"He's the teamster whose wagon burned up, remember?"

Lin certainly remembered the fire, recalled hearing the name in passing. "But why is he drawing us a map?"

"We're taking over his freighting business for a few days."

"But he deals in matches. Phosphorescent matches."

"Yes, exactly. We have a full load waiting in the Concord."

Lin almost prayed he was still asleep and dreaming, but the coffee was still warm on his throat. For the first time since waking up, he wasn't focused on the aches and pains of his body. All he could imagine was the Concord going up in a blast of flame.

Taking the two of them with it.

"My God, Reece, do you know what you've done?"

"It's a fast trip. A bit risky."

"A bit?"

"We've made more dangerous trips. And the best part? This job actually pays. Half up front and half when we deliver."

Lin shook his head. "But, Reece, this Jim Douglas business isn't finished yet."

"It isn't?"

"Just like you haven't had the chance to tell me about the matches and Dallas, I haven't had the chance to tell you what Jim told me."

Lin was careful to bring back the words just as Jim whispered them to him with his dying breath. When he told Reece, the effect was powerful, and she was momentarily silent.

"Conspiracy. Mountain," she repeated the words. "Not much to go on. In fact, nothing to follow there at all."

"I think there is. Last night in Ray's office, before the fight, I think I figured it out."

"You think it's got something to do with the illegal whiskey?"

"I don't know. I don't think so. I think there's more to it. Jim and I go back a long way. Back to before our time in the Rangers."

"Our time? Jim was a Ranger?"

"Once, a long time ago, yeah. Back then, there was a third Ranger named Steve. A wild man. Fearless. Crazy. Mountain Man Steve, we called him. I think it's what Jim was trying to tell me. He said Mountain...man."

"You think he's had contact with Steve?"

"They were real close, Reece. Like brothers."

"Have you considered Mountain Man Steve might be the leader of this alleged conspiracy?"

"If he is, it's a conspiracy I'll get behind. Steve is true blue."

"There's one more thing," Reece said.

"Yeah?"

"You aren't gonna like it."

"Tell me."

"About Harbor Springs. The men we're delivering the matches to. You're not gonna like it."

The pain was returning to the base of Lin's spine, and he kneaded it with the knuckles of his right hand. "Well, it's okay," he said, "It keeps us even."

"Even?"

"Trust me—you ain't gonna like where we're going to find Steve."

"Where are we going to find Steve?"

"Snakebite Canyon."

Reece sat back on her heels. "You're right. I don't like it."

"What about Harbor Springs? What about these men?" Lin said.

"Comancheros," Reece said.

Lin felt the pain creep up his backbone. Reece was right.

He didn't like it at all.

9

AT SNAKEBITE CANYON, the old man was asleep inside the cabin while Steve Gardner leaned back in his wooden rocking chair to readjust his persnickety damn ankle on the porch rail. Relaxed, but careful, Steve kept his scatter gun propped across his outstretched leg and pointed at the horse and rider less than twenty feet from his front door.

For his part, the rider with the round kepi cap hadn't made a single move toward the rifle he carried in a long leather boot on his saddle, and his horse seemed content with her eyes half-closed. Behind him, three haughty columns of black smoke visibly marred the red-orange western horizon.

"Tell me more about the fires?" Steve said.

"It's like this, sir. The smoke to the left looks to be Burwell. Over there, that's Arrowrock."

Steve measured the height of the columns with his eyes, gauged the distance across the open plain. "S'pect you're right about Burwell," he said, not sure about the other town. "Seems to me Arrowrock is more off to the south a ways."

"I come through there this morning. It's Arrowrock."

"Oh, so?"

The damned pup. Steve didn't like being corrected, but he admired the kid's guts. "So they havin' a brush burnin' or what? What's the story?"

"The story is the towns are damned neared burned to the ground. Seems like a coordinated effort at arson. Three towns to start with. Two more got torched yesterday."

"Them settlements ain't much more than wagon camps anyway."

"Now they're nothing but ashes on the wind. And I ain't told you all of it. Dallas is half burned down, too."

Steve nodded. The kid was right. Dallas was another kind of hitch in the loop. He said, "Nearly 1,000 people in Dallas."

"Looks like somebody's trying to burn down all Texas."

"Not the first time, I guess."

The rider was slow to answer. "No, sir, you'd be right to say it. But this time's different."

"Different...how?"

The rider shrugged. "I'm just riding through to New Mexico territory. Thought you might like to hear the news. Maybe swap me for a drink of water and bite of food for my horse."

The young man in front of him was an expert poker player.

He was holding something back. Something he'd swap for water or grub.

Swinging his leg down from the railing, Steve slammed the barrel of the shotgun into the porch wood and used it as a crutch to stand.

A week had passed since his ankle betrayed him in

Snakebite Canyon, and he was getting damned tired of favoring the thing. He waved the kid toward the split-rail horse pen where three gnarled mesquite bushes wrestled on the bank of a jagged creek adjacent to the house. "Water your horse. Fill your canteen. Good spring water there."

"I'd oblige you for something to eat."

Steve shook his head. He and the old man had downed a few quail, but otherwise the cupboard was bare. There was enough hay and cracked grain for Romeo, but nothing to share.

The way it turned out, Steve was down to his last plug of apple-jack tobacco.

He hadn't planned to stay in the cabin so long.

If he and the old man had to wait any longer...

He laid the shotgun flat on the rail within reach, then leaned on the porch pillar. Using his heavy sharp bone handled knife, he carved a hefty slice and lipped it into his mouth straight from the polished steel.

"All's I can offer you a 'backy chew," Steve said. "Anything beyond...well, I hope y'r good with your carbine." He nodded toward the uneven western landscape. "Plenty of game if you know where to look."

The kid didn't hesitate to answer. "I get by," he said.

After a while, Steve said, "It's all I got for you, son. You gonna tell me what you know?"

"They say it's abolitionists burning stuff down."

Steve savored the tobacco juice and thought about the news. After a moment, he said, "They're sayin' it's slaves too, I reckon?"

"Slaves too. You maybe heard about John Brown and Harper's Ferry. Back east?"

Most everybody in the American south had heard about the winter uprising in Virginia. Some folks found the idea of an abolitionist revolt terrifying.

Steve nodded. "I heard about it. I found the news…inspirational."

The rider didn't flinch.

"To each his own, mister."

Abolitionists burning entire towns? A slave revolt in the heart of cotton country?

Steve didn't think so, but he'd learned not to judge things too quick.

"If I might ask," he said, "who'd you hear all this news from?"

The kid bent over and flipped open one of his leather saddlebags. After rummaging around for a few seconds, he removed a crumpled newspaper. Spurring his horse forward, he got close enough to hand it over.

"You can keep it if you want. Swapping for the water and tobacky."

Steve accepted the paper with a nod, then took in the front page with its ornate masthead. "Arrowrock Advertiser," he read. Skimming the story about multiple fires breaking out across north Texas, gleaning what information he could, he said, "There's a lot of speculation here. Not much fact. The truth is, it seems like it's nothin' more than a couple of letters written by a man in Dallas."

"All I know is what I read."

Steve pulled the paper close, peering at the story, looking for a signature to the letters. "Who's this Adam Sperling fellow?"

"Sperling is editor of the Dallas Enterprise. Dallas burned as well. The entire story's there on the front page."

"And you figure it's gospel truth?"

"Reckon they wouldn't print it if it weren't true."

"Well, son, accordin' to Sperling—if I'm takin' this right—it seems like emancipation is to blame for the fires in Dallas, the fires in Burwell and Arrowrock. Not to mention, man's fall from paradise, Noah's flood, and Jesus Christ on the cross."

"I got no stomach for abolitionists," the kid said.

Steve turned his attention back to the paper, where he read Sperling's breathless prose:

"Such a diabolical plan to devastate the entirety of Northern Texas has never been conceived in the minds of civilized Americans. White men and women, friends of abolitionist preachers and run-away slaves, do-gooders who ironically do only evil by our sacred way of life, are instigating the plot. The whole ingenious plan makes the blood run cold. These diabolical conspirators, these Hellbenders, desire nothing more than to destroy our cities, assassinate our leaders, and lay waste to our great nation."

Steve tossed the paper into his rocking chair, then cut another notch from his tobacco plug.

Addressing the rider around the wad of chew, he said, "You don't think Mr. Sperling is somewhat...biased?"

"Ain't no paper doesn't have its bias here and there, sir."

"You seem to know an awful lot about it."

The kid didn't answer, sat silent for too long, not moving, waiting. When he spoke, his mature self-esteem cracked just a little. Steve could hear the frightened boy inside the young man, "You think there's gonna be a slave revolt, Mister?"

Steve cleaned his knife blade on his loincloth and tossed the remainder of the plug to the rider. "Nope, I don't."

Another long pause.

"That's it?"

"'That's it," Steve said, examining the blade of his knife once more.

The kid tipped his kepi cap. "I'm obliged for the water."

"I'm obliged for the news."

The rider steered his horse off into a casual walk for the creek.

Steve gazed across the horizon at the twin towers of black smoke.

"More killin'," he said to himself. "More destruction."

With sudden fury, he buried the first third of blade into the porch pillar.

Damn the rabble rousers like Adam Sperling of Dallas.

Damn the complacency of men like the young rider.

They were kids at the candy counter, hell bent on war. Didn't anybody see there would be no winners in such a fight? No matter which side triumphed, the entire country would lose?

In the half-light of sunset, he caught a glimpse of himself reflected in the polished steel blade.

Was he any different? Hadn't he already picked sides? Wasn't he willing to kill or die for what he believed in?

For too long, he continued to gaze at his slender face in the reflective surface of the knife. His teeth were straight, his forehead high. His eyes were like blue chips of turquoise and his brows slightly arched. Steve put a finger to his lower eyelid and pulled it down. He poked out his tongue.

He needed a shave.

Yeah, he thought, I'm different. After sitting around too much, I'm way different.

Too much thinking, not enough doing.

The sedentary life was killing him.

Chewing hard, savoring the bittersweet syrup of the pressed tobacco leaves, he returned his attention to the smoke.

Way out there, somewhere, a nation was burning.

Better get used to it. Gonna burn for a long time before it goes out.

Steve couldn't help but voice his next thought aloud.

"Where the hell are you, Jim?"

FAR AWAY FROM the Red River and Lambert's ferry, Lin steered the team of roans across the wide-open face of northern Texas, picking his way with care. As far as cargo went, a coach full of phosphorescent matches was even more volatile than Dale Hemlock, but the slow pace made for a longer trip. The uneventful days were beginning to blur, and the cool nights in camp with Reece were spoiling him.

Every fifteen miles or so, roughly once a day, they'd come across a Butterfield Overland way station. There they could swap out their horses, stretch their muscles, and enjoy some easy socializing. The station caretakers were a friendly, talkative bunch.

The road was full of patient easy swales, and restful fields were bordered with quick runs of cypress and persimmon trees. Lin made sure to avoid gopher mounds, badger holes, or anything else which might cause the matches to strike one another and ignite inside their packaging. Each new team of horses Lin swapped for were better than the last, and they crept through a landscape spackled with sparse bunchgrass and tall indigo blue bonnets, and along streams leading to the Brazos.

Reece had the larder stocked well with bacon wrapped in paper, his favorite canned peaches, and a canvas sack of beans. The oak barrel of sweet water strapped to the rear boot was for drinking, but considering their freight, it served double duty as a comfort to Lin's nerves. The days were hot, but not overly burdensome, the nights, cool.

Buzzards and chicken hawks rode the warm air currents above in ever-widening gyres, and the sky was clear as sweet candy.

Lin was losing his edge, and more than once caught himself falling asleep on the bench seat.

At long last, Quincy was less than a day off. Harbor Springs the day after, if luck held.

Then they could rid themselves of their load and get on with finding justice for Jim Douglas.

Lin hoped the Comancheros who Klein lined up to take the matches wouldn't pose a problem.

The pleasant drive could almost make Lin believe he'd imagined the mess at Lambert's Ferry, make him believe Jim was still alive and Bill Clay wasn't back there somewhere, tailing them, spurring on the prickly warning in the back of Lin's neck which always meant trouble.

The ache of his ribs complained otherwise. The bruises on his face remembered Clay's fists only too well.

But even his wounds began to fade with the hours on the road.

If only Lin would fade from Clay's mind as fast.

Lin knew it would never happen. Clay would never let go of the drubbing Lin gave him outside Ray's office. A public whipping, especially when the village idiot knew he was in the wrong to start with, was something which stayed with a man like foot rot, stinking and festering and flaming to life when he least expected it.

Reece sat beside Lin on the bench as she always did, her carbine in hand. If she looked worried about Clay or the Comancheros she didn't let on. The late afternoon sun lit the edges of her hair like a halo, and her skin seemed to glow with a light of its own.

Lin tried to remember a time Reece ever looked worried.

Only one time, he told himself—the week before when she sat with him in Lambert's sod jail. When he first opened his eyes, she let her proper, brave façade slip.

Hadn't there been a flicker of fear?

Maybe, but not now. At the outset of their non-stop cargo run to Harbor Springs, Reece kept her fear tucked neatly away. Not even the Concord's creaking cabin filled with wooden shoebox crates, each of them packed tight with sweaty paper cartons of matches, concerned her.

"You realize Bill Clay's on our trail," Lin said.

Reece shrugged. Unflappable. "I know it's possible. But it's also possible he hightailed it before you were even awake."

"A man like Clay—there won't ever be a day's peace for him until one of us is planted underground, never a night he goes to sleep without his dreams tinted with shame."

"You're always such a glorious ray of sunshine. You spread joy everywhere you go. But I suppose you might be right."

"I can feel him out there. He'll make a run for us.

Somewhere along the road up ahead. Might be today, might be tomorrow after we turn south."

"You seem to know him pretty well. What makes you so sure he'll come after us?"

"I would. I'm the same way as him."

Reece cocked her head. After a sizable pause, she countered, "Except for one sizable difference, Ranger. I haven't known you to carry a grudge."

Lin shook his head. "I got one or two I lug along with me. I just don't yak about it like most folks."

"Grudges aren't good to carry. They wear you down. You ever think so?"

"I guess it's however you choose to look at it."

"I guess it is. The best way to go about life is to travel light—"

"Says the lady sitting on top of ten-thousand chemical explosives."

"You know what I mean. You don't allow a splinter to stay in your hand, and you don't store a burdock in your saddle. Worrisome things need to be let go."

"Forgive and forget? Doesn't sound like you."

"Who said anything about forgive and forget? The best place for a grudge is underground," Reece said, a touch of iron coming into her voice. "You never heard of the three S's?"

"I guess not?"

"Shoot, shovel, and shut-up. Any grudge I ever carried is covered by six feet of soil—every last one."

"Sometimes it's not so easy."

Lin couldn't help but think about Daniel Martin Ray, the man who had commissioned Jim's killing, but was under Brother Lambert's protection. Or Lin's Uncle Oscar, who worked for the Order of the Ivory Compass but was still blood kin. Both of these men deserved a taste of lead from Lin's Colt, but each of them found exoneration because of Lin's loyalty.

In Lambert's case it was the Ranger's loyalty to the law and the folks sworn to uphold it.

In Oscar's case it was loyalty to family—no matter how distasteful the uncle.

No, it was never as easy as Reece wanted to make it seem.

He took a moment to collect his thoughts, then he said, "The bottom line is Clay will make a run at us sooner or later. Or those three riflemen will."

"When they do, it will be whatever it is," Reece said.

"I figured you'd say something more along the lines of when they do, we'll be ready."

"If I've learned one thing this past year, it's when violence comes a callin', ain't nobody ready."

They continued to follow Klein's map, riding along the Butterfield-Overland stage road until it intersected with a trail called Rambeau Pass.

As if waking up after a long night's dreaming, Lin realized the going from here on wouldn't be so easy. Looking at the map in conjunction with the winding hump of barely recognizable roadway, he told Reece the road would be a lot more treacherous.

"Mind we don't shake up them matches," he said. "One heavy bump or upset, one wrong shift of the wagon, and the phosphorous match heads will strike each other. One unforeseen scrape, one simple spark..."

The Concord was a tinderbox, and the heaving bitch of a road could prime the fuse.

"Maybe we should avoid the pass. It'll take more time, but if we follow the Overland Road direct to the Fort, we're guaranteed better ground."

"Rambeau Pass will shave a day—maybe two—off

the drive," Lin said, "and I'm awful eager to ditch the cargo and get on to Snakebite Canyon."

Reece agreed with him. "If Klein's old horse and buggy could stand the road, I suspect we can do better."

"I figure Quincy is only a day out. We ought to make Harbor Springs by the next day."

They turned down the pass and slowed to a crawl.

A hawk screeched overhead, and Lin coaxed the wagon team over a never-ending series of deep-water ruts and prairie dog towns.

The road was nothing but a series of mounds and chuckholes.

"Tell me about these Comancheros," Lin said. "It'll get my mind off this road." The knot he'd been favoring at the base of his neck throbbed in time with his heartbeat.

One wrong turn…one heavy bump…

Lin figured he knew as much about the Comancheros as Reece did, probably more. For at least half a century, the unorganized nomad traders had covered a wide range in New Mexico and Texas, deriving their name from trade with the Comanche. Amoral and self-serving, they bartered with the Indians, swapped tools, dry goods, and slaves for buffalo skins, weapons, and favors. Comancheros were the scourge of the Rio Grande valley, and Reece's home, Rancho De Jada, had been raided more than once.

There were few bands of people she detested more.

In some ways, he was surprised she agreed to do business with them.

"Klein says the Harbor Springs men will be small in number," Reece said, "maybe only three or four. The leader goes by the name of Juarez, and we'll know them by the Circle-B brand on their horses."

"Animals no doubt stolen from the Comanche or Kiowa."

"More than likely."

Suddenly the road plunged down into a short, rocky ravine, its sandy walls closing in like pincers. Lin was instantly brought to his feet, holding back on the reins, calling on the team to brake as the wagon pointed straight downhill and threatened to come around sideways.

One of the rear wheels crashed into the sidewall, then rebounded back onto the road with a loud clattering.

Lin held his breath.

And then they were through it, and the way opened wide before them.

He sniffed loudly. "Don't smell any smoke. Do you?"

Reece inhaled deeply, then said, "Nope."

"We were lucky."

"I think the driver's skill had a lot to do with it."

"You keep talking to yourself until after we deliver the load," Lin said. "And along those lines, once we deliver the matches to Juarez, what do we get for all the wear and tear on our nerves?"

"Enough money to get us home."

"How do we know the Comancheros won't just kill us? You know these treacherous bastards—what's to stop them from killing me and adding you to their slave trade? Pretty girl like you would bring in a lot more than a load of matches."

"And be a lot more explosive," Reece said.

She had a point.

"I have no intention of walking into a trap."

"I have no intention of letting you. The bad news is, I've never been to Harbor Springs before."

"Would you be surprised to know I have? Once, when I was a little girl, I traveled to Fort Belknap with my father. We stopped at the Springs to water our horses. I remember the creek, the old outbuilding. I think I have a fairly good idea how to approach the place."

Lin should've known. "You do continue to surprise me," he said.

"Just make sure your Colt is charged and full of lead, Ranger. We'll get in and out okay."

"I can't say the same about the Juarez clan."

There was nothing more to say for the time being, so Lin watched the road ahead. As they approached Brushy Creek, the evening sun cast long shadows through a growing accumulation of trees. In the distance ahead, an ugly black gash tore through the prairie.

"Brushy Creek flows all along here, emptying into the Brazos farther south. We'll cross up ahead, make camp for the night, then more or less follow the creek into Quincy."

"A good plan, but we have a problem," Reece said, holding tight to Klein's map. "See this bridge, here?"

Lin looked at the spot she indicated, then toward the creek ahead, then back to the map.

"There ain't no bridge," Lin said. "At least, not anymore."

"It must've washed out."

Lin pulled on the reins, holding the horses back.

The Concord was stopped dead in its tracks.

"WE SPILL THIS THING, there won't be any saving the horses," Lin said. "It doesn't take much for the matches to rub together. And if that happens the whole entire wagon is gonna go up in smoke like a January Christmas tree."

Standing on the rugged bank of Boggy Creek, peering down into the wide, shallow chasm, Reece agreed. "There won't be any crossing here."

They stood beside two rough cut posts half buried in the sod and leaned into the gap, weighing their options.

The span from shore to shore was roughly fifty feet with the broken remains of the bridge scattered on the cracked mud of the creek bed.

"The bridge was nothing more than a series of thin horizontal planks nailed to a scaffold," Lin said. "No piers, no abutments."

"No guardrails."

Judging the remains of the shoddy structure, it was easy to imagine what had happened. After one of the recent long dry spells, with the loam baked granite hard, an afternoon gully-washer had roiled up out of nowhere, the kind of rainstorm the old timers called a frog-strangler. Two or three inches of rain in the space of a half-hour wouldn't have time to soak into the oven-crusted sod and the creek would fill immediately, washing away anything in its path.

Including somebody's lousy build of a bridge.

"Likely as not, we wouldn't have gone halfway before the damn thing fell in, taking us with it."

"At any rate, we can't cross here."

Reece was right. They faced a ten-foot vertical drop on each side. "Klein's map doesn't show any other way to cross," she said.

There was nothing to be done but find an access way and forge ahead through the relatively dry bed and hope they didn't tip the wagon over.

"We'll parallel the crick for a while, maybe we'll get lucky and find a more gentle slope in and out," Lin said.

"Which direction?"

The creek ran at a rough north-south angle, so Lin reasoned in the direction of Quincy.

"South it is," he said.

They set out at a leisurely pace with the setting sun on their right.

The team seemed to enjoy the dusky tramp along the dry tributary, sauntering along amiably as Lin and Reece steered from the wagon seat. Up ahead, a series of cottonwood groves cast long shadows on the ground.

"Cottonwoods like to keep their feet wet," Lin said, pointing to a group of trees. "The banks won't be as steep there. Might be a chance we can cross."

By the time they arrived at the grove, the black cottonwood shadows were crowned with the first stars of evening, and an owl hooted at them from the dark, thick foliage. When they stopped, a genial breeze picked up the smells of grama grass and moist earth, and Lin turned the reins over to Reece while he fixed a cigarette.

The acrid smoke relaxed the tight knot in Lin's back, and when he flicked away the spent butt, he felt refreshed and ready to tackle the crossing. Under the lead tree, a long slope led to the floor of the creek where a tangle of thistle grew among a twist of cotton-wood roots.

Lin decided he'd need a second smoke.

"Gonna be hell getting the horses through the thistle patch," he said, rolling his paper together and licking the seam. Striking a match on his boot, he fired the cigarette with a deep inhalation.

Then he held the lit match in front of his nose, watching it as it slowly sputtered out.

"What is it?" Reece said. Around the edge of the red ember, he said, "You see how easy matches spark to life? I'm imaging all those Lucifer's sticks back there, piled one on top of the other, rubbing together, scratching each other."

He took a long pull from his cigarette. "We were spoiled on the Overland Road."

"Are you sure there's not a better place to cross?" Reece said.

"Getting too dark. If we don't cross now, we wait until morning."

"It would be good to put it behind us."

"Agreed."

They sat for another few minutes while Lin finished smoking. Then he said, "Might as well get started."

"You stay here, hold tight to the four-in-hand. I'll

scout a path and lead them by the nose."

Lin waited until Reece was on the ground in front of the team. Then he said, "Don't get tripped up. Let's try to avoid the thistles."

"Will do," Reece said.

But there was no way to avoid the thistles.

———

TEN MINUTES LATER, hip deep in a stickery mass of thorny green leaves and perfumed purple flowers, making a snail's progress through the aptly named Brushy Creek, the flora wasn't to blame for the first wave of disaster.

It was the fauna.

With the front leads firmly in hand, Reece had led the first two horses into a long turn through the weeds, pointing them upstream toward a slow incline on the opposite shore. As they moved, step by painstaking step, a silver bright moon came around the edge of the cottonwoods and a young coyote, not more than a year old and distracted by the remains of a rabbit in his mouth, froze in the light.

Locking eyes with Reece, the coyote offered a surprised snarl, jumped up to skitter away, and was foiled by the immediately imposing bank of the creek.

Spinning in a quick circle, he pointed himself in the direction of the wagon and shot straight toward the rig, diving between the horses' legs, under the carriage, and out of the riverbed up the grade behind them.

The horse nearest Reece instantly reared up in surprise, stepping sideways, pulling the wagon off course. When the second horse followed suit, the right side of the Concord came a few inches off the ground, then slammed back down hard enough to make Lin grunt with the impact.

"Whoa, fellas," teased Reece. "Hush, now, it's okay."

The horses weren't having it.

Fed up with the barbs and brambles of the thistle patch and now scared out of their skins, they revolted, hurdling ahead, yanking along the other two horses, jerking the wagon forwards with a violent lurch.

Ducking away fast, Reece jammed her toes against a twisted cottonwood root and fell to one knee, smashing her kneecap on the exposed wood.

"Dammit to hell."

"Hang on," shouted Lin, and the wagon bucked up over the cluster of roots and crashed down hard, twisting the cabin with a wood-rending screech. A cracking noise came from the region of the thorough-brace on Reece's side and the back wheels almost rolled over her leg.

Scrambling back to her feet, she saw a flash of light from inside the cabin and even as the horses cleared the thistle patch, flames erupted from the side window of the coach.

"Stop," she called. "Lin, stop!"

But the horses were committed to action. Having been forced to plod along all day like a company of swaybacks, the young geldings were ready to go. Tearing along the creek bed, they hit one, two, three more cottonwood roots, sending the coach through a series of hard jolts.

One of the flaming packages fell from the cabin's open window and Reece kicked at it as she limped to catch up. Another tumbled free as the Concord made the opposite creek bank.

Damn poor timing to hurt her knee, she thought as she watched the coach spur up onto solid ground. As the final jolt knocked open the carriage door, a bundle of flaming packages careened to the sod, sparking hot, glowing embers into the night sky.

Then Reece saw Lin beside the wagon, scattering the blazing containers, leaning into the belly of the Concord pitching out each of the fiery hazards.

When she arrived beside him, a series of charred boxes remained along the trail, and a small blaze crackled in the dry brush. The immediate fury of the matches was spent.

Smoke tendrils came up from the prairie beside the wagon like whirling stalagmites, and Lin knelt on his knees in the flickering orange light.

Behind him, the Concord tilted at a precarious angle, the anxious horses rocking it forward and back.

"I got the brake set," Lin said.

"How bad are we hurt?" Reece said.

"Bad enough." Lin hugged both fists to his chest and trembled. "My hands are blistered up. Something's broke under the carriage."

"But you saved the coach. You saved the horses."

He turned to the south and Reece followed his gaze.

"Small comfort, I reckon."

Something was wrong with the horizon.

Streaks of red and orange flickered in contrast with a shelf of black clouds, and a heavy, sour odor filled the air. "Since when does the sun set in the south?"

"It's Quincy," Lin said. "Burning."

Before Reece could respond, four men on horseback rode up in a rustle of dust and grass and surrounded the wagon.

"Damn dirty Hellbenders," said one of the men. "Looks like we got you dead to rights."

12

ON THE SMOKEY banks of Brushy Creek, Lin knelt between the Concord's spoked wheels and Reece stood her ground beside him. Four horsemen, armed and wearing long coats, circled the coach in the grass fire light.

"You firebugs didn't think we'd catch up with you, didja?"

"We got 'em, sure enough."

"Gonna make these skunks pay for what they done."

The leader was a knobby man on an Indian paint horse. When he drew his six-shooter, Lin's arm was lightning fast. Reaching for his Colt, he beat Knobby to the draw, but immediately let loose of the gun with a grimace.

"Son-of-a—" He muttered, cradling his blistered fingers in hand.

Lin was one of the fastest gun hawks Reece had ever seen. Only her rancho foreman, Stick Carvell, came close. But the fiery packages of matches he had pulled from the carriage had taken their toll.

Knobby chuckled, then ordered Lin to stand up.

Reece stepped between them with the Walch Navy 12-shooter. She held it with both hands, pointing the barrel straight at the intruder's chest. "Drop your gun," Reece said.

"Lookee here," said Knobby. "We got us a little sissy bug."

"Don't nobody tell us what to do, sissy-bug."

"What do you want with us? Who are you?"

"What do we want? Guess we don't need to tell you. As to who we are, I'm Mal Billingsley. These here are the Brushy Creek Boys."

"We're...ah...what you might call a vigilance committee."

Reece took one step forward and her injured knee buckled under the weight. She slammed to the ground as smoke and a thunderclap of rifle fire went off in front of her. The bones of her shoulder rolled like jelly and agony enveloped her arm and rib cage. She sucked in a breath. Unable to hold the Walch, she let the gun fall from her hand.

Lin screamed out a curse, then yelled her name, but it was all too garbled to follow.

Above her, Knobby on his paint horse looked down. Standing beside him was a man with a rifle, the barrel still smoking.

"You...you shot...me," she said.

"Yeah," said Knobby like he was addressing a petulant child, "he shot you alright." Then his voice reached down low. With a bass rumble, he said, "He's gonna shoot you again, sissy. And he's going to keep on shooting you, too."

As if in a dream, she saw Lin leap to his feet and charge at the rifleman. Between them was Knobby on his horse. Spinning around quick, the horseman slammed the heel of his boot smack into Lin's chin with a sickening crunch.

Lin fell beside him like a sack of hammers.

Reece did her best to form the words, but it felt like she was speaking through a bundle of cotton wadding. "We...didn't."

"They're feisty ones, ain't they, Mal?" said the rifleman. "Caught dead to rights and still wants to argue about it."

"Half our town's nothing but ash, thanks to you," said the knobby leader, who the rifleman called Mal.

Lin's voice was distant, weak. "...you mean Quincy...we've never been there."

"Don't you lie to me, boy," said Mal. He flung out a blurry arm toward the red edge of the sky. "We got women and children without a home tonight, and here you are with a wagon load of sulphur." He snorted, then spit.

The wad of phlegm landed on Lin's upturned forehead as he tried to climb to his feet.

Mal kicked him back down.

The man with the rifle moved his head around. Then said, "Looks to me like they pert'near burned themselves up."

A third man with long straw-colored hair slid off his horse and joined his friends. "How's about we finish the job, Mal?"

The rifleman grinned at his scarecrow friend. "I'd like the missy to myself for a while, first."

Scarecrow's face was a puffy orange moon in the flickering fire light. He gazed at Reece, shaking his head. "You'll have to wait your turn, Tom."

Instead of arguing, Tom bent over and picked up the Walch-Navy pistol from where Reece had dropped it. "What the hell kind of shooter is this?" He showed it to the scarecrow. "Two hammers, two triggers. You ever seen anything like this?"

"I never have," said Scarecrow. "How 'bout you, Mal? You ever seen such a gun?"

"Be...careful," Reece said, the pain in her shoulder making it hard to form words. The rifle slug had knocked her down, and it was impossible to know how bad she was hit. She might've sustained a glancing blow, she might be bleeding out on the green.

"What're you saying, dolly?" said Mal.

"Careful," she murmured, the men becoming little more than a blur. "Dammit...Klein...I told you to be... careful." Lost in the whirl of pain and smoke, her conversation with Klein came back to her.

"What if you shoot off a back load before you empty the front?"

"You don't."

"You might. And if you do it, you might not live to fire another shot."

Scarecrow giggled at his new idea. "You want to try the gun, Tom? How about you use it on her boyfriend?"

"Don't..."

"Shut-up, girl," said Mal.

She let her head loll to the side as the ghostly trio moved in on Lin. Tom gripped the heavy gun, and straddled Lin's unconscious form, standing at full height.

"Watch me now, boys, as I deliver some good old-fashioned Brushy Creek justice."

After a theatrical swoosh of his long coat, he pulled back the hammer.

The wrong hammer.

He pointed the gun at Lin's head. "For Quincy," he said.

And pulled the trigger.

EVER SINCE HE'D been a boy, Lin loved the open road. In his earliest Tennessee memories, he rode with his dad in the same saddle. He rode the bench beside Mom during a buggy trip to church.

When the Jarrets moved to Texas in the fall of the year, he reveled in the adventure, keeping a daily pencil journal of everything they saw on the way. Maple trees with their vivid gold leaves, cypress and sycamore and ash, every stop in the road offered a different abundance of trees.

As an adult, after his parents were gone, he'd worked briefly as a teamster, along with a score of other odd jobs. But the time behind the horses, with reins in hand, had enchanted him. Add to it, he liked people. Liked to learn what he could about them, find out how they reasoned and what they wanted out of life. He liked to talk to travelers he met on the road.

He imagined he might one day own a stage line, but then his uncle, Oscar Bruhn, stepped in to recruit him for the burgeoning return of the Los Diablos Tejanos, the Texas Devils under Rip Ford in 1857.

"Give you a chance to prove your metal," said Oscar, slapping him lustily on the back.

Oscar was a beefy man with a thick, bushy mustache the color of old iron.

In Lin's dreamy vision on the Brushy Creek prairie, Oscar bent over him, calling him by an old family slur, "Fight it, Slug. Fight the fog you boneheaded idiot. What? Are you planning to sleep your life away?"

Lin felt his eyelids flutter, and Oscar blew up with a scream and furious rending of steel.

Fully awake, his ears ringing with the explosion, Lin rolled to one side, then climbed to his feet in time to see the blond-haired Brushy Creek boy reel back in the firelight away from him. Frantic, screaming hysterically, Tom's right hand had been torn to bits and great gouts of blood spilled from his mangled wrist.

"Jesus and Mary," said Mal Billingsley, still on his horse.

Reece laid on the ground beneath him with her eyes closed. Lin ignored the Brushy Creek Boy's continuous cries of agony and came down beside Reece.

The left shoulder of her shirt was ripped and soaked with blood, but a quick inspection showed Lin the bullet wound was superficial. No doubt it hurt like hell.

Thank God she was still alive.

Turning over on his back, he saw the mangled smoking remains of the Walch-Navy 12-shooter on the ground and pieced together what must have happened. Lin had always warned Reece of the silly trick-gun's foibles.

"I guess nobody told the Brushy Creek Boys," he said.

As if in answer, Tom gave out another yell.

"Damn horseplay," said Mal, turning his attention back to Lin. "Enough is enough." He aimed his firearm and said, "Pick her up. Put her on my horse."

"What if I don't?"

"I'll drill you right between the eyes. And I promise, Mister, my gun will stay together."

As gently as he could with blistered hands, Lin got Reece to her feet and draped her right arm over his shoulders. Dazed and bleary-eyed, she let him support her weight.

Once she was positioned in the saddle with Mal, the bearded vigilante clucked his tongue. "You walk ahead of us, boy. One wrong move, I swear to God, I'll end you."

Then he put his tongue between his teeth and let out a whistle, long and shrill.

Once he had everybody's attention, he spoke to Scarecrow and the other two boys. "Bring the coach," he said.

He nodded at Tom. "We get back to town, you might want to look about the arm."

Then with a smirk, he called out loud and clear: "Homeward bound, Boys. We're taking these two to Quincy for the hanging."

13

FOR THE SECOND time in as many weeks, Lin Jarret woke up in jail with Reece hovering over him. The clear gray sky outside the open barred window told him it was still early morning, and the only sound from the adjoining room was the steady tick of a tall, grandfather clock. The dry air smelled of trail dust and fresh-sawed timber.

Compared to Rimrock Station, the cell in Quincy was luxurious with a straw-filled mattress and two feather pillows. Three of the walls were clean red brick and a wooden barrel of fresh water was accessible with a silver dipper on the other side of steel cage doors. A big oak desk watched over the front room beyond the jail, and the walls were fresh plaster washed in lemon yellow.

The building couldn't be more than a few months old.

A slight tugging drew Lin's attention to his hands. When he looked, he saw they had been cleaned and bandaged.

Reece wore a similar wrapping on her arm and shoulder.

"They're treating us a lot better now than they did last night," Lin said.

"I don't think the sheriff approves of the Brushy Creek Boys," Reece said. "At least it's not the impression I got."

Lin thought back to the night before when Mal Billingsley's gang had rousted the two of them on the lower reaches of Brushy Creek and announced their capture to the citizenry of Quincy. The assembled townsfolk had jeered them, tossing rocks and shoes and worse. The Concord wagon, driven by the vigilante named Tom, had taken an especially hard stoning.

After marching the bedraggled duo through the remains of a smoldering business district, Mal had delivered them into Sheriff Aggie Simms's custody.

Lin sneezed at the smell of putrid smoke and ash wafting in through the window.

"We're lucky to be alive," Lin said. "I thought sure the good Christians of Quincy were going to hoist us up by the throat."

"They still might."

"What do you suppose they did with the coach?" Lin said.

"I just woke up, Ranger. I don't know anything more than you do."

Lin patted his bandaged hands. "I don't remember them wrapping my hands."

"I barely recall it. It was awfully late, and we were both exhausted."

"If they were going to hang us, they would've done it then."

"Don't be so sure."

"Why keep us around? For the pretense of a trial?"

"Maybe. I found this beside the mattress when I woke up."

Reece handed Lin a folded-up newspaper. He unfurled it and read from the front page of The Quincy Times.

"Texas in Trouble: Abolitionists Torch More Towns."

"Read the letter they printed. It's by a Dallas man called Sperling."

Lin mouthed the words to himself as he read, increasing the volume when he got to one salient phrase: "The whole ingenious plan makes the blood run cold. These diabolical conspirators, these Hellbenders, desire nothing more than to destroy our cities, assassinate our leaders, and lay waste to our great nation..."

He lifted his head from the paper.

"Hellbenders? Us?"

"Looks like it, pard."

Lin chewed his lip and studied on their predicament. "Awfully convenient us freighting a load of matches across north Texas at the same time somebody starts lighting things up."

"Ain't it though?"

"We were set up. Your Vern Klein set us up."

"He's not my Vern Klein. Lambert suggested him. And don't forget, Klein's wagon burned too."

"All part of the set up," Lin said. "Making you sympathetic to his cause. I'll bet the whole story of Juarez and the Circle-B ponies was pretend. There aren't any Comancheros at Harbor Springs. The entire reason for this trip was to put us precisely where we are."

"At the end of a rope?"

"Exactly. Or shot full of lead. It's the conspiracy Jim Douglas told me about."

"I wouldn't jump to any conclusions. Jim Douglas barely got two words out before he died. He didn't tell you much at all."

"It's the only thing makes sense. He said there was a conspiracy."

"What about your Mountain Man friend?"

"I have no idea."

"But you think somebody put all these people out of their homes, in all these places, just to kill us off?"

"Not only us, no. I think the idea is turn everybody against the idea of us. Somebody has increased the heat, literally, on abolitionists and Union-sympathizers all over."

"Fire-eaters," mused Reece.

"Ironic nickname for the pro-slavery groups who probably instigated the arson in the first place."

"Yeah, but there's another possibility, too."

Lin raised his eyebrows. "An uprising?"

"Lots of abolitionists aren't as willing to work behind the scenes as we are."

Lin slapped the paper down on the mattress and paced back and forth.

In spite of what Reece suggested, things seemed clear now in a way it hadn't for several days. "I don't believe it's emancipators or slaves behind this thing," he said. "But it could be Lambert and his Chickasaw enforcers. They want to preserve the Union, sure—but they want to do it with slavery intact. What better way to sway the public than to make abolitionists and Africans look like an immediate threat?"

"I don't know," Reece said. "Somehow Lambert doesn't seem to fit."

"I don't suppose he does—by your way of thinking."

Reece's voice flared like hot coals in the wind. "My way of thinking?"

"I could tell you were sweet on him from the minute we met the ferry."

"You're jealous!"

Now it was Lin's turn to ignite. "So what if I am? The point is we can't trust Lambert any more than we can trust Bill Clay or Daniel Ray or these damn vigs who dragged us in here last night."

"Or your uncle."

Lin agreed with a loud affirmative. "Especially my uncle. You're damn right. Any one of them, or all of them, could be working for the Ivory Compass."

Reece sat back on the mattress and pulled her legs up under herself.

For a while Lin paced back and forth, muttering under his breath, making up theories, shooting them down. After a few minutes, he came around to Reece's argument and reluctantly agreed. "I think you're right about Lambert."

"What made you change your mind?"

Lin wasn't sure. "Maybe the way he handled himself on the ferry when the guideline snapped. The way he managed us and the men."

"Resolute, decisive."

"I just can't see such a man sneaking around, making plans in secret."

Just then, their reverie was interrupted by the sound of a latch being turned and the front door swung inward, striking a small chime, ringing in the appearance of a short, white-haired man dressed in coat, pants, and vest. Mal Billingsley followed directly behind carrying a pair of steaming mugs, one in each hand.

"If I were you, I'd say 'Good morning', or something equally innocuous and let it go," said the short man. He waited for Mal to cross the threshold, then closed the door behind him.

"Aw, you know how it is, Aggie," said Mal. "Cora's been sweet on me since I was in short pants. She almost lost her diner in the fire, and—"

"It's still no excuse for pitching woo over the breakfast table. I'd have had my coffee ten minutes sooner if you'd keep your romance private."

Sheriff Aggie Simms retrieved his coffee from Mal, took a messy slurp, put the cup down on the corner of his desk and dabbed at his vest. "Now see what I did. Hilda's gonna pitch a fit."

Mal let himself fall into a heavy wood chair in front of the sheriff's desk. "Sounds like I ain't the only one with female troubles."

"Hush," Aggie said, nodding toward the jail cell.

Mal greeted Lin and Reece with a jovial voice. "Happy day, Firebugs. I trust y'all slept well last night." Then he turned his attention back to Aggie. "Y'know, Sheriff, it occurs to me we're doing the community an immoral service letting these two live in sin under our roof."

Not paying attention, Aggie continued to pat at the coffee stain on his shirt. "Um-hmm," he murmured.

"No, I mean it." Mal let his tub gut fall forward, pushing his boots flat to the floor. Launched from the seat of his chair, he strode to the jail bar doors. "We can't have you two capitulating the same space."

"He means cohabitating," Lin said.

"How can you be so sure we're not married?" Reece said.

The thought had obviously never occurred to Mal. After a nervous heartbeat, he said, "Are you?" he said. "Married?"

"No," Reece said.

"See, well there you go, Sheriff. See what I told you? She admits they're sinners."

"I admit nothing."

Aggie looked at Mal like he was twice the idiot he already was. "We've only got one jail cell, ya bonehead.
"

Then Reece called out to Aggie. "When are you going to listen to our side of the story, Sheriff?"

For the first time since sloshing his coffee, Aggie turned his attention to his prisoners. The wide, flat forehead was unconcerned. The quirk of his mouth conveyed nonchalance. "I expect we'll hear enough of your side o' things at the trial."

"Y'all just wait—" began Mal.

"And when's our trial?" Lin said.

"Just before the hanging," Aggie said.

Mal tried to butt in. "Trial's gonna be something else—"

"Two-o'clock this afternoon," Aggie said.

Lin repeated the sheriff's words. "Just before the hanging. If you're so sure of the outcome, why bother with a trial?"

Aggie sipped his coffee and looked at the gold watch he removed from his vest. "We are a civilized society, sir." Flipping the watch cover closed, he stuck it back into its pocket. "We'll go by the letter of the law here."

During the interchange, Mal had clearly wanted to interrupt. Now he couldn't contain himself any longer. "We got us a special witness gonna speak."

Lin exchanged looks with Reece. "What special witness, Sheriff?"

"A fellow who just rode into town this morning," Aggie said.

"We met him over at Cora's breakfast this morning. Bald fella with a beard," said Mal. "Here he is now."

Aggie turned and the door chimed

A man dressed in dark wool walked in to grip his hand.

"Sheriff."

"Thank you for joining us, sir."

"Anything I can do to help."

Aggie turned to Lin and Reece. "Are these the folks you told us about?"

"Yes, sir. Sorry to say, they are. I had hoped never to lay eyes on these skunks for the rest of my life."

"And yet, here we are," Lin said.

"I believe, you both know Bill Clay from Rimrock, don't you?" said the sheriff.

"Unfortunately, we do," Reece said.

14

STEVE GARDNER USED his long steel blade to saw two thick steaks from the bloody haunch of the downed pronghorn. There wasn't a lot of meat on the critter, but when it had wandered past the cabin earlier in the morning, it had been easy to stick the old man's rifle through the front window and take the shot. Pronghorn never knew what hit him.

All day the carcass hung from a hackberry limb over the spring-fed creek behind the cabin, and Steve harvested what he could, calculating the number of meals he and the old man could make from the kill.

When they came to the cabin several weeks before, they hadn't planned on staying in one spot so long.

They wouldn't stay much longer.

Steve's injured ankle had pert'near healed, but the old man's temper was on a constant boil. A day more, two at most, and they would need to head east on the trail, Jim Douglas or no Jim Douglas.

Steve knelt down beside the gurgling stream and closed his eyes to breathe in the freshwater smell. He cleaned his blade, then sheathed it in the pouch on his belt.

Cleansing both hands in the cold spring, he thanked Manitou, the Comanche Great Spirit for the meat. Focused on his breathing, but listening attentively to the breeze, letting the air carry its messages to him, he kept his eyes closed and slowly stood.

The visitors had tried to creep up on him. Impossible to do on horseback. The sound gave them away, and so did the smell.

Equestrian lather, pipe smoke, the summertime sweat of two men who hadn't seen a bar of soap or bath in weeks.

He took a step toward the mesquite stump and his hammer polled tomahawk, its head half-buried in the wood.

The iron-fat cluck of a carbine hammer being pulled back.

"Hold it," said a young man's voice.

Familiar.

Him. The kid from before.

"Back for some more water?" Steve said.

He turned around, keeping both hands high, palms outward.

The young rider who had shared the newspaper with him had returned, this time with a long gun pointed straight at Steve's forehead and an older man on a second horse beside him. The second gent looked like he was carved from pale hickory, all jutting angles and wood-grain lines. Both men sat on a pair of itchy flea-bit mares, their tales twisting around, their ears flipping and twitching.

Dressed as before in a dark tunic with pants and a round kepi hat, the kid was a mirror image of the old man. Steve figured they were son and father. Or nephew and uncle. Definitely family.

Hickory wore a kepi hat, too.

"Reckon we'll have a drink, sure," said the kid. Then he nodded at the butchered antelope and the iron fry pan sitting beside the stump. "Got a couple steaks set up, do you?"

"Meager fare," Steve said, with an edge in his voice. "Only enough for one."

When the older man spoke, his tough leather voice matched his rough looks, but he addressed the boy. "You told me there was two of them out here."

"Guess I'm not sure. I could've been wrong," said the kid.

Steve addressed the old man with a casual air. "He was wrong. There's only just me."

"Check inside the cabin, anyway," said the old man.

Steve asked the kid, "You got a name?"

"You first. I don't think I caught it last time."

"Nick Bottom," Steve said.

"I thought so. Was telling my friend here you looked the ass."

Steve couldn't help but smile at the reference.

"You aren't the only one can read a book, Mr. Bottom."

"What's your name then?" Steve said.

"I'm Matthew," said the kid. "This is Mark."

"Soon to be followed by Luke and John?"

"Followed by a swift kick in your pants," said Mark.

"If you gentlemen plan on robbing me, you're bound to be disappointed. My wardrobe bespeaks my whole position."

Mark put a gnarled hand to his chin and scratched. Just as the first time Matthew had ridden past with the news about the Texas fires, Steve wore only a loin cloth. His long hair was pulled back in a twist, and his muscular frame coated in sweat from the hot after-noon's work. Around his neck, he wore a collection of Indian fetishes—a bird point, a smooth black rock, rattlers from the recently killed snakes.

His 10-bore scattergun was safe inside the cabin. Damn the luck.

"How about you throw the pig-sticker away," said Matthew. "Then maybe we'll all three walk in to the cabin and have an old fashioned palaver."

"What's there to talk about?"

"Drop the knife onto the ground. Real slow, with two fingers."

Steve put his hand to the butt of his long blade.

"I got an impatient finger, Mr. Bottom."

Steve did as he was told, and the blade fell on a bed of dry grass and leafy chaff.

Secure in its stump holster, Steve's tomahawk was less than two feet away. His only edge to fight off the intruders. Steve slid forward two inches. "You want to water your horses, go ahead."

The animals looked like they could use it.

When Mark spoke up, it was with the irate authority of a parent scolding a child. "Mr. Bottom, I shouldn't have to explain to you what's going on in this country. We've got more and more people trailing in here every day. People want to set up homes, communities."

Snakebite Canyon was quite a ways from the Texas road and its line of immigrants. Other than the two gents in front of him, Steve hadn't seen any other strangers during his entire tenure at the cabin. He figured since Matthew still had the shootin' iron pointing at him, he could concede the point.

"Let's say you're right. For the sake of argument," Steve said.

"The boy here says you're an abolitionist. Say's you're one of them Hellbenders."

"Don't know how he got such an idea."

He moved two inches closer to the tomahawk.

"You remember when I mentioned Harper's Ferry. When I mentioned the slave rebellion and you said it was inspirational to you."

"Sometimes words get taken out of context."

"But inspirational is the word you used?" said Mark.

"Reckon so."

"Sometimes words mean exactly what they mean." Now Mark dismounted from his horse. "I think we all know which way your words were going this time." He was a stout man with a regal, militaristic bearing. Toe to toe, Steve only had a couple inches on him, though the older man wore boots and Steve was barefoot.

"What else did Mister Bottom tell you, son?"

"The son-of-bitch barely glanced at the newspaper," said Matthew from his place still in the saddle. "It was like he already knew what it said. Plus, he argued with me about Arrowrock, like I hadn't seen it burn with my own eyes."

"Bastard probably set the fuses himself," said Mark.

Steve decided now wasn't the best time to get into a discussion on how he could possibly have started a fire a day's ride away and still be sitting on his porch in the canyon when the kid first rode up.

Logic obviously wasn't part of Matthew or Mark's repertoire.

Steve moved another two inches...

"Let's cut to the chase," he said. "You two men are...

what? Vigilantes of some kind? Here to see if I'm a troublemaker, a—what did you call it?"

"Hellbender. What some of these traitors are calling themselves."

"We're just men doing God's work," said Matthew.

"Just out proclaiming the gospel," said Mark.

One more inch…

"Preachin' the gospel," Steve said, putting his right hand to the cord around his neck. "Guess that means you're fixin' to go to heaven?"

Steve's left-handed grip on the tomahawk was sure. With a quick flip, he jerked the head out of the stump and spun to the side. As he moved, he shook the twin rattles at his throat with his right hand.

The instant Matthew's nervous, beleaguered horse heard the rattle, it reared back out of instinct.

"Well, now—"

Matthew uttered two words before falling back off-balance, unhanding the rifle. The carbine hit the ground between the two horses.

Mark's horse shied away from Steve too, momentarily cutting between the Mountain Man and its rider. Steve shook the rattles with one hand, spun the tomahawk around with the second.

The kid tumbled from his saddle, catching his bootheel in the stirrup. His horse reared, tossing Matthew like a ragdoll, slamming him to the ground again and again before dragging his limp body through the thorny mesquite bushes along the stream.

As Mark's horse turned tail to follow his partner, Mark picked up a spiked tree limb. The heavy bough was three feet long and solid throughout—the perfect club.

He swung it down overhead, attempting to split Steve's skull like a melon.

Instead, Steve thrust his arm high, flipped the heavy head of his tomahawk down and caught the hasty blow just under the weapon's heavy poll.

But the defensive move had forced him to go wide and move to the side.

As good an offensive weapon as the war axe was, defensive work had to consider the sharp edge opposite the chopping blade. As Mark's heavy stick landed, it forced the spear-like poll back toward Steve's torso.

Mark turned off, tried for another lunge.

Steve's nimble wrist spun and met the club's spike with the tomahawk handle, but damn—he was open to a fast second blow, so he moved his other arm up, snatching the end of the club in a steel grip. He cranked his arm down, jerking Mark off balance.

Then he spun in fast and hard with the limb-lopper.

Mark barely had time to bring the club back up and check the blow.

The impact sent the older man back on his heels, close to the spot where Matthew's lost carbine waited in the grass.

Steve couldn't risk Mark retrieving the gun.

Whirling like a cyclone, he pressed in, hacking air, thrusting through Mark's defense.

Suddenly, the man of hickory found two inches of axe head embedded in his sternum. Blood quickly bubbled up around his tongue to spill over his lips and down his chin. A deadly spring, gurgling over.

As Mark slumped over and made a slow slide from his saddle, Matthew came from the woods with an explosion of oaths. The kid had a six-shooter in hand and lobbed off a deafening shot, filling the air with blue powder smoke.

But Steve wasn't a sitting target.

As fast as his healing ankle allowed, he darted behind the remains of the pronghorn, then, as the carcass shuddered with the impact of a lead slug, he rolled down and into the shallow bank of the creek.

Flustered with surprise and struck with sudden grief at the loss of his friend, Matthew lobbed another blast over Steve's head, popping up leaves and chaff from the opposite bank.

Belly to the rough grass, Steve struggled with the sandy clay mud as briars and thorns tore at his hide.

Dammit.

One day he'd learn to wear a set of proper outdoor clothes.

The next bullet crashed into a flint rock less than a foot away from Steve's face. Sparks and a hail of airborne sediment rained down to obscure his vision. The kid had a couple shots left, but one shot was all he needed to stop Steve's heart from pounding.

The Mountain Man rolled into the creek basin.

The spring-fed pool was hardly more than knee deep, but if he could lay thrash across with enough force, he might send up enough water to spoil the kid's aim.

"You won't get away with it, damn you," said Matthew from the edge of the creek bank.

Heart racing and running out of hope, Steve churned through the frigid water, sending up massive geysers. A last-ditch attempt at survival bound for failure.

Matthew stood firmly rooted ten feet away, gun held at arm's length.

He pulled back the hammer.

There was a tremendous blast, and Matthew tumbled over into the water, cut in half as surely as the pronghorn on the hackberry.

Teeth chattering with the cold, Steve hauled himself up. As the water spilled from his shoulders and back, the old man spoke from the leafy flat esplanade beside the antelope.

The scatter gun he'd used to kill Matthew still smoked like a chimney.

"Been waitin' on supper," he said. "You figure you're about done horsin' around? I'm hungry."

15

THE TRIAL LASTED a total of ten minutes and four of those rotations of the clock were spent setting up wood folding chairs in Aggie's office and swearing in the jury. Sheriff Simms was sworn in as judge-in-lieu of the current circuit court rider, and then Mal Billingsley had his say.

Crowing over the circumstantial evidence of the Concord's cargo and being sure to point out Lin's blistered hands, he forgot to mention the blond man who attempted Lin's murder with the 12-shooter or why Reece had a wound dressing on her shoulder under her shirt.

Will Clay's testimony took up even less time and consisted of two sentences.

Judge Simms: "Are the two people who left Rimrock Station with a wagon load of matches and the intention of committing arson seated in this courtroom?"

Will Clay: "Yes, your honor, the two arsonists are right there." (Witness points out Lin Jarret and Reece Sinclair.)

Sentencing took all of thirty seconds. "At six o'clock this evening the defendants will hang by the neck from the Baynard tree outside town until dead. A light supper and refreshments to follow at the Congregational Church."

The gavel came down on the mahogany desk. Court dismissed.

Half the town had been razed the day before, but tonight there was cake and lemonade. Whoopie!

At least the people from Quincy had their priorities straight.

"I have an idea," Reece told Lin once Aggie had locked them behind the jail bars. "Maybe a way we can get out of this."

"Keep your voice down." Lin glanced over his shoulder at the sheriff. "What is it?"

"You're not gonna like it."

"I'll like hanging even less."

"No, I mean, this is worse than meeting up with Comancheros at a deserted spring or even hoofing through Snakebite Canyon. When I say you won't like it, I mean—"

Lin gently covered Reece's mouth with his hand, then leaned back with a reassuring look of affection. "Just...tell me."

She did.

And she was right. He didn't like. As far as plans went, it was awful.

But it was the only plan they had.

Ten minutes later, Reece grabbed the jail doors with her hands and writhed with pain.

"Oooooh no," she sighed. "Oh...gods..."

Tears poured down the sides of her face, and she clawed weakly at the bandaged shoulder beneath her tight-fitting shirt, pulling the front a little bit tighter across her chest. "Sheriff Aggie, I need help, huh? Puuhh-leeease?"

Lin knew Reece's discomfort was an act, but even so it tugged at his insides to see her pretend such agony. "It's my...shoulder, Aggie. It's a festering up something fierce."

If Aggie ignored the commotion, Reece's plan would never work. Even worse—what if the lawman got overly irritated and simply left the building until the six o'clock deadline? After all, why should he care about the aching shoulder wound of a woman condemned to die in a few hours?

"What is it, Miss Sinclair?"

"I need a doctor, Aggie. Where's Bill Clay?"

Aggie rose from his desk and straightened his vest.

When Aggie responded as they had hoped, Lin felt a weight fly off his shoulders. It felt good to be pushing the action rather than waiting for the other guys to make all the moves.

Aggie met Reece at the bars of the jail, and Lin made an obscene gesture for the sheriff's benefit. Then he crossed to the back right corner of the cell and sat on the mattress with his knees pulled up to his chin and his face toward the bricks—the picture of petulance.

At the front left corner of the cell, under the window and closest to the outside wall, Reece waited until Aggie was just out of arm's reach. When she addressed him this time, she put a seductive purr into her voice as phony as anything Lin had ever heard this side of a Kansas City brothel.

Her voice brimmed with tears.

"I know you don't owe me nothin', Sheriff, but, like I say, this shoulder is goin' bad fast."

Aggie looked over his shoulder at the big grandfather clock.

Two-thirty.

"I can't see how your shoulder matters much."

"I sure would be obliged if you could arrange a private audience with me and Mr. Bill Clay."

Surprised by the request, Aggie put a fist to his hip. "Clay? Why Clay?"

"I'm sure he would never brag, but back at Rimrock, Bill Clay worked as a medic. He's not an official doctor, you understand."

"I see…"

"But even though he betrayed me on the stand… which I now see was his legal duty…I trust him with doctoring." Reece raised a gentle hand to her injured shoulder. "Oh, it hurts so bad…"

Aggie's face was lined with unspoken reluctance.

Reece pushed ahead with an obligatory sob. "I…I wanted to compliment you on how well you handled yourself at our trial. My gosh, you're a well-spoken fellow."

Cringing at the delivery, Lin closed his eyes tight and tried not to listen. He'd laugh if the situation weren't a matter of life and death.

Reece was no actor. Aggie and Bill Clay both would have to be pretty damn stupid to fall for their plan.

Reece soldiered on. "Your suit is simply scrumptious, Sheriff."

"Do you really think so?" Aggie said. "I mean…the coffee stain wasn't too visible, was it?"

"Not visible at all from where I sat."

"I do like to look professional in these, ah, types of settings."

"You make Mrs. Simms quite proud, I'm sure."

Aggie blushed. "Ah...um, I'm afraid there is no Mrs. Simms."

"You poor, poor dear," Reece said, fluttering her eyelashes.

"Where did you say your shoulder hurt, Miss Sinclair?"

Lin let out a second sigh of relief.

One down, one to go.

———

REECE WAITED behind a closed door in Aggie's private room adjoining the sheriff office.

Partially reclined on a long, velvet covered daybed, she loosened the top three buttons of her shirt, uncovering a seductive dose of cleavage, and waited for Bill Clay.

Her plan was full of holes. A lot of things might still go wrong, but for the time being, she was out of the jail cell.

The hook had been baited. Now if Clay would only just bite.

And she believed he would. Something Klein had said back in Rimrock gave her the idea.

"Maybe if you had the eyes of a sharpshooter you'd know where my hidey holes were. Otherwise, nobody else knows."

Eyes of a sharpshooter.

At the time, Reece had let the figurative expression pass, but what if Klein had meant it literally? Reece was betting her and Lin's life on Bill Clay being the sharpshooter Klein referred to. Maybe he was a partner in Klein's business? Maybe he was the one who'd convinced Klein to reconsider talking to Reece back in Rimrock.

If he knew about the supposed conspiracy of fires, he certainly might be the one behind framing the Hellbenders for the crime. What better way to do it?

Plenty of people wanted to silence Reece's ongoing mission to abolish slavery.

There was no denying Clay had silenced Jim Douglas.

The door cracked open with a rough query from the office side.

"You wanted to see me, Sinclair?"

Time to go into her act.

"Oh, my, yes, Mr. Clay."

"You decent?"

Reece answered huskily. "No. But don't let it stop you."

Clay poked his head into the room, took a quick gander around, then walked in.

He closed the door behind himself.

His expression was a mixture of annoyance and curiosity. Puzzlement and lust. He wore the same clothes as before, during the trial, a cotton shirt with a darkq wool, military-style coat and trousers.

But he'd cleaned up for her. Lin wouldn't notice, nor would the sheriff. But a woman knows.

Fresh lashings of bay rum exuded from his pores, and his beard had been trimmed since earlier in the day. His hands washed and fingernails cut.

Clay held his cavalry-style hat in hand and cleared his throat. "What's this about me being a doctor?"

Reece saw his attention flicker down, past her neck and back up. She pursed her lips. "You've never played doctor?"

Clay squeezed the brim of his hat ever so slightly, and once more cleared his throat. "I don't know where

119

you heard such a thing, but I can't help you. And I wouldn't even if I could."

"But you came, didn't you?" Reece kept her voice flirtatious. Teasing. His reluctance wasn't unexpected. She'd cracked harder nuts than Bill Clay.

"Came to find out what you were up to."

She beckoned him with a bent finger. "Now you're here, it wouldn't hurt to have a look?" She unhooked another button, and let her shirt drop away from her shoulders. Turning her chin toward her bandage, she said, "Look at my injury, I meant."

Clay took three quick strides to the side of the daybed. Now he didn't bother to avert his lascivious gaze away from her chest. As he took in the view, his breath came quick, his voice husky and full. "Tell me what you want."

She almost had him.

Reece continued with a voice hurried, passionate—she was a woman in trouble. With only one way out. "You need to help me, Bill. Help me get away from the noose. From the awful predicament Jarret got me into."

"I heard you and Lin Jarret were sweet on each other."

"Lin Jarret's a filthy piece of gopher scat," Reece said, pleased with Clay's abrupt reaction at her rough language. She put some music back into her voice, "Don't you think he is?"

Clay nodded, dumbstruck, as Reece stood up and caressed his bruised cheek. "After all, Bill—can I call you Bill? Look what he did to you. Your jawline. Your poor nose." She bent forward and kissed the tip—

Quick as a rattlesnake, Clay grabbed Reece by the wrist and bent her arm behind her back. He leaned over her, his breath hot and rotten with stale coffee and tobacco. Pressing her backwards, he spoke between clenched teeth, and she felt his spittle mist across her face. "Listen, sweetie, I don't know what kind of trick you're trying to pull, but Bill Clay ain't nobody's fool."

She closed her eyes and rubbed her arm, whispering, "This...ain't no...trick. Proposition...business only. Or more...if you like."

Clay put his mouth next to her ear, and she could smell the rancid decay of his teeth. "You know damn well I like. You tell me. You tell me everything...and we'll go from there."

Reece swallowed hard willing herself not to think about the agony of his grip on her arm and focus on what she needed to do. "There are Comancheros...at Harbor Springs...waiting to buy Klein's matches. If you get me out of here, we'll go there together, and you can have the split instead of Jarret."

Clay's laugh was deafening.

"Comancheros? You stupid bitch." He shoved her back down to the daybed. "Are you talking about the Juarez family, by chance?"

Reece shrunk away from Clay's gloating.

"Maybe you'll be looking for the Circle-B horses they ride?" Clay smirked. "Would it surprise you to know I made the story up myself?" Nodding, he continued with his confession. "It's true. After Klein turned you down the first time, I told the old fool to come back to you with the story about Juarez and Harbor Springs. There aren't any Comancheros! They only live in my imagination. I just wanted you two out here in the middle of a hundred burning villages."

"Freighting a bunch of matches," Reece said. "Naïve as a pair of newborn calves led off to make into veal."

Clay stood triumphant, as if waiting for applause. "Maybe I should take a bow?"

"Maybe you should."

He spread his arms wide, filling the room with body odor and smug satisfaction.

But now it was Reece's turn to laugh.

She put every ounce of grit she had into her voice and replied, "Don't you think I know all about your foolish plan? I've known since we left Rimrock."

Clay shook his head. "I doubt it," he said.

"It's your turn to play baby calf. There's a lot more going on than you realize."

"Uh-uh. I don't think so."

Reece countered his argument with a financial figure. "A thousand dollars."

Clay let out a long breath.

Talk of money always got their attention.

"Go ahead. Enlighten me."

Reece continued with her act, poking her lower lip out into a pout. "You called me a stupid bitch." Then she smiled. "Maybe Klein played us both?"

There it was again. The flicker of curiosity across Clay's face. "Go on."

"What you don't know is there really are Comancheros at Harbor Springs. I've been there as recently as last month and seen them myself. But the man's name isn't Juarez. It's Paco. And while they don't have any real interest in matches, they're paying an awful lot for...information."

Clay seemed skeptical, but the haughty tone was gone from his voice. "What kind of information?"

"Information about the cotton trade. About the Cotton Grower's plans for the coming years. About the future of the Union." Reece took one last leap of faith. "About the Order of the Ivory Compass."

"What do you know about the Order Ivory Compass?"

Reece stood up, and this time she put both arms around his shoulders, pressing her breasts into his shirt. He didn't resist.

"It's not what I know about the Ivory Compass. It's about what we can sell them."

Clay inhaled deeply.

"Truth or fiction, it makes no difference if we can sell it," Reece said. "Klein agreed with me. I know Harbor Springs. I know the Comancheros. They trust me. I figure there's a thousand dollars in it for us."

She kissed him passionately on the mouth. When she pulled away, she said, "Do you trust me, Bill?"

His features flared like a wolf, and he answered her. "Not a damn bit. But I'm gonna take you to Harbor Springs. Once we get there, guess I'll find out whether you're talking true or not. Either way, I figure I'll get something out of the deal...right?"

Reece calmed the ache in her gut and forced a grin.

"Oh, don't worry. You'll for sure get something. I'll be seeing to it, personally."

16

ALONE IN THE sheriff's office, Lin pressed his forehead on the cold steel of the jail bars lining the front of his cell and watched the clock tick away the remaining seconds of his life. Less than an hour until his appointment with the Baynard Tree, and there was no sign Reece had succeeded in wooing Bill Clay to accompany her to Harbor Springs on the Concord.

On the positive side, Lin told himself, there was no sign she'd failed. For the time being he did his best not to lose hope. He'd been in worse spots before. At least this time he didn't actually have a noose around his neck.

Pushing off the jail bars, he turned and paced to the rear of the cell. Lin leaned in to stand on tiptoe, craning his neck to peer through the window.

The back of the jail faced the open range, brush-spackled prairie with an easy loping sense of luxury about it. Restful and quiet, it was preferrable to the town noise bleeding in around the edges of his view. He heard male conversation from the saloon across the way and the cackling of old women, the clatter of horse and buggy, the softer tread of boardwalk customers. The Quincy air still reeked of smoke and desecration, but Lin couldn't see it from his window.

All he could see was a clear blue sky and the vast serenity of the Texas landscape.

For now, he told himself. How long until another wispy column of black smoke rose from the horizon? How long until another fire? Another ruined town?

If there was a conspiracy, Texas was in trouble for sure.

If only Lin knew who was behind it.

Somewhere out there, in Snakebite Canyon, Mountain Man Steve Gardner might know the answer.

The grandfather clock chimed the half-hour, and Lin glanced over his shoulder.

Right now, he had bigger problems than finding his old friend.

The truth was, he might never make it farther than the damned tree on the edge of Quincy.

Turning his attention back to the view outside his window, he played out Reece's plan over and over in his mind.

Despite what Reece and Lin believed to be true— that there were no Comancheros at Harbor Springs, she had to convince Bill Clay otherwise. If she made him believe there truly were Mexican Indian-traders at Harbor Springs, she could get him to secure the Concord with whatever remained of its flammable cargo and go there.

If Reece disappeared from Quincy, Lin had a chance with Mal and the sheriff.

If Reece couldn't convince Clay to go to Harbor Springs, she'd end up with Lin at the Baynard Tree, a swinging buffet for the buzzards.

Reece could be darned persuasive. Especially if she got her patented pitiful look on her face. If she put just the right sob in her voice.

If she kissed a man.

Lin tried hard not to think about the more infuriating parts of the plan.

At six o'clock, the office door burst open, sending Aggie's little chimes into a tornado spin before they tumbled down to the floor.

"Gol-dammit, I knew it," said Sheriff Aggie Simms. "I knew you two were up to no good, and now Bill Clay is gone with Miss Sinclair. The two of 'em took off in your Concord wagon when nobody was looking."

Lin could barely contain his smile. Clay had taken the bait.

But, gol-dammit, he hoped she hadn't kissed him.

Instead of showing off his relief, he recited the lines of a jilted suitor. "I'm heart broke, Aggie. How could she do it to me?"

Aggie closed one eye and leveled his index finger at the jail cell. "I'm not so sure you weren't in on this, Jarret."

"How could I be in on it? You think I'd willingly allow the woman I love to go off with a man who lied about me in open court? A man who figuratively put a noose around our necks?"

"I don't know. Would you?"

"My God, man, if you think I could go along with such a thing, then you don't know me at all."

"It certainly proves I didn't know Bill Clay." The old man was honestly puzzled. "What kind of man does his Christian duty in court, only to turn around and take to the owlhoot trail with the gal he incriminated."

"Don't be too hard on yourself, Aggie. Reece Sinclair is a tough woman to disagree with."

Aggie brushed his upper lip with a nervous forefinger and eyed the clock. "Yes...yes, I guess you're right." Then he said, "It's a damn shame. We've got folks lining up down by the Baynard Tree to watch the two of you swing."

"Don't forget the cake and lemonade after," Lin said.

"Shame for all of it to go to waste."

Aggie tapped his fingers on his desk. Then he shook his head. Nothing to be done.

"Looks like it's going to be you alone, Jarret."

"What a disappointment to the folks," Lin said.

"If only we knew where they went. Hell, we could hang all three of you."

Lin snapped his fingers.

"Now, there's a helluva point, Sheriff. Three for the price of one—I've got an idea where they went."

The sheriff looked at him through the bars with helpless anticipation.

"Well, spit it out..."

"Hell, Aggie, I ain't gonna just tell you. If it's worth anything to you all, you'll postpone the hanging until we get them back."

"I could postpone the hanging until morning. Twelve hours."

"How about you postpone it indefinitely?"

"No...no, I'd say twelve hours is the best I can do. A hanging at sunup."

"It'll be cutting it pretty tight if they went where I think they went."

"Tell me where."

"Let me go with you to get her?"

"Out of the question."

"Just you and me? I promise to behave." Lin showed Aggie his wrists. "You can even keep me tied up if you want."

"I don't know."

"C'mon, Aggie. Imagine the possibilities. Texas is in a time of crisis. If you capture all three of us and hang us as firebugs? Next election season, Texas might be willing to send you to Washington DC."

Lin could tell Aggie liked the sound of it.

"Do you promise you'll behave?"

"Of course."

Aggie retrieved the keys from his desk.

————

THE CONCORD COVERED half the distance from Quincy to Harbor Springs before sundown. The team of grulla horses Clay had commissioned was healthy and mature, and the coach wasn't as damaged as Reece previously believed.

The previous night's misadventure at Brushy Creek had left the undercarriage and suspension intact—despite some ominous creaks while crossing the cottonwood roots. Other than a patch of singed paint around one of the cabin doors and some burnt interior upholstery, the matches had likewise done little damage upon ignition.

At camp on the open prairie, Bill Clay set up a shelter from the wind. First, he drove two-yard-long oak sticks into the ground, then slung a measure of rope between them. Over the rope he draped a blanket.

As Reece raided the coach's front boot for their supper, Clay staked back the corners of the blanket and put together a pile of kindling.

"We're makin' good time," he said from his spot crouched over the smoldering pyramid of grass and twigs. "One thing about it—with these matches we're carrying, it doesn't take long to get a fire going." He laughed a little too long at the observation, and Reece decided he was trying to be affable.

"If we continue to push on overnight, we'll make Harbor Springs before daybreak," Reece said.

Clay offered an evasive grunt, fanning his hat over the smoke.

"I'd say we're about three hours away," Reece said.

"I'd say, why hurry?"

Reece hadn't figured on Clay covering any more ground after supper. Once the two of them left Quincy, it had been all the man could do to restrain himself on the seat next to her. Twice he'd put his hand on her leg above the knee, and once, he brushed his arm against hers and kissed her on the jaw for no reason.

As soon as they finished eating, she expected him to make moves of a more intimate nature.

"Did you forget where you put the grub?" Clay said.

"Just getting it all pulled together," Reece said.

The wood-paneled storage boot immediately under the Concord's bench seat was covered in front with a leather tarp and filled with essentials for the trip. Jerked beef, canned fruit, dry beans and other provisions had come from Lambert's larder at Rimrock, and Clay added a few things in Quincy.

Clay was impatient. "Hurry up, will you?"

Reece reached under the bench and tapped the boot's false ceiling.

A spring-loaded lid fell open.

All her life, Reece had been fascinated with hidden rooms and hidey-holes. The Hellbenders' Concord was riddled with custom compartments and secret storage nooks. Inside this one was a Walker-Colt identical to the one Lin Jarret carried.

Or it was supposed to be.

The pigeonhole was empty.

"By the way," Clay said. "If you're looking for the six-shooter, I've got it down here with me. Nice little niche for it there under the seat."

So as not to let her spirits sink too far, she settled for the next best weapon she could grab: a heavy six-inch wide iron frying pan.

17

STANDING outside the jail bars in the tidy sheriff's office, Lin thanked Aggie for his hospitality, then debated on whether to bop the man in the nose or let himself be tied up.

In good faith, Aggie had given him a reprieve from the hangman.

Of course, it had been Aggie who sent him to the gallows in the first place.

Lin's crisis of conscience lasted all of twenty seconds.

He put everything he had into one fast, sledge-hammer blow to Aggie's face. The old fellow folded up like a spring tulip caught in a late April freeze.

Lin lost no time dragging the sheriff into the jail cell, binding him with his ribbon tie and gagging with his twisted bandanna. Then he locked the bars and made a fast search of the office.

Once he'd retrieved his Colt, he was ready to ride for Harbor Springs.

With one problem.

He didn't have a ride. Aggie had said Clay and Reece took the Concord, which was part of the overall plan. And as a condemned man, Lin couldn't exactly walk into the streets and procure a horse.

He walked through the room where Reece had taken her interview with Bill Clay, then out the back door where they had presumably escaped together.

A tall buckskin horse was tacked up there with its reins wound round a hitching post. It was outfitted with a woven Indian blanket and burnished Mexican saddle.

Lin figured it for Aggie's horse.

Once more, Lin's biggest qualm was taking advantage of a fellow lawman, no matter how misguided Aggie might be. Plus, horse thieving in Texas truly was a hanging offense.

For the time being, he shoved his scruples aside even as he mounted the stirrup and slipped behind the horn.

Nothing to be done about it.

Quincy was a half-decimated ember on the plains, and Lin left it in a cloud of ash and dust.

He made it two miles before he heard the first pursuing gunshot.

ON THE NORTH Texas prairie between Quincy and Harbor Springs, the orange band of sunset faded to a soft pink stripe behind a far rocky butte, and the wind announced itself with a hollow whistle, cold and sharp. Stars broke through the deepening blue as Reece cooked up a pan of beans and boiled a tin pot of coffee.

Bill Clay had rolled his heavy wool coat into a pillow and used it to prop up his elbow while watching her. Reece's Colt-Walker dangled by the trigger guard from his fingers.

After they ate, the moon rose into the vast indigo sky like a glowing copper penny, and Clay stretched out on the flat earth, his head propped on his coat. He patted the dusty sod beside him. "Hey, cute thing— how 'bout you rein in beside me, here?"

Reece held up her cup. "How about you let a girl finish her coffee?"

Clay chewed on her response for a while, then hoisted himself up on one elbow. He clucked his tongue. "I just don't figure you, girl."

"What's to figure?"

"Girl as purty as you, wasting her life away with this emancipation business."

"I don't know what you mean."

"You act like I don't know who you are. Shucks, girl, everything I said at your trial today was pretty much gospel truth. You and Jarret are making a name for yourselves all over Texas. Lots of folks know about the Hellbenders. Most of them know where your sympathies lay."

"Most of them might be wrong."

"Don't try and deny it. You two conspire every damn day to undermine everything generations of good Texas people have built."

"Generations of good Texas people might differ with you."

"See, I don't think so. I don't think you understand what emancipation truly means. It's a loaded word, as dangerous as this here Colt. Not so much to you and me, maybe, but especially dangerous to the Cotton growers. What's even more ironic is it's dangerous to the good, Christian, black folks you're trying to help. You just don't realize it."

Clay held the pistol up to emphasize his point. "It's a kind of hornet's nest you're kicking up here."

"Why don't you tell me about it?"

Rising to the challenge, Clay said, "Remember when I asked you about the Ivory Compass?"

Reece nodded.

"I kinda got some influence there. Been a member a long time."

"Fighting for secession?"

"I'm fighting for order."

Reece eyed the six-shooter, knew she had to tread lightly. She chose her words with caution.

"I can respect your decision, Bill, I truly can."

"I'm surprised you and Jarret can't see clear enough to join us."

Still playing her part, Reece told him, "Jarret's a fool. I have my own plans for the future."

He nodded. "It's one of the things I like about you. I knew you had wheels turning in your head. I could see it in Aggie's office. What I couldn't decide was who you were planning to betray, Jarret...or me."

"Have you decided yet?"

He ignored the question and carried on with his appeal. "The Order would enjoy having you, Reece. Tough as you are, you'd make a good asset for us in the coming empire."

"Empire? Talk about loaded words. Aren't you counting your chickens a little early?"

"How so? The world we envision isn't some kind of pretend dream. It's a civilization existing here and now, in spiritual alignment with the natural order of science and history."

He recited the words like memorized scripture. For all Reece knew, it was.

Clay continued with his diatribe. "The Compass points in one direction—no matter who reads it, and one direction only. A glorious empire of feudal kings, a nation of cotton, gold, and spices carved from Mexico, the tropical islands, parts of Central and South America. A proper nation to usher in the Second Coming."

The nation Clay was helping to birth was horrendous and built on the backs of a renewed African Slave Trade and the subjugation of everybody except the wealthiest plantation owners.

It was a nation she and Lin hoped to see stillborn.

She continued to play her part. "I'll give you credit, it sounds like you're doing the Lord's work, Bill. How do y'all hope to achieve so much in so short a time?"

"All will be thoroughly revealed, once everybody gets the proper guidance."

Behind her back, Reece relaxed her grip on the handle of her frypan. She hadn't pegged Clay for a fanatic.

She certainly hadn't expected a philosophical conversation at this time of night.

She welcomed both over the lecherous alternative.

After a few more minutes of sermonizing, Clay said, "You got any idea what kind of information we can give these Comancheros? Anything worth so much money?"

"Just what we're talking about right now," Reece said. "Comancheros like guns and trinkets, but they like to know what's coming around the bend, too. They appreciate getting in on business deals. Political intrigues. I'm sure they would appreciate being in on any conspiracies or plans the Order might have in the works."

He picked his teeth, then said, "Maybe I do have something, after all."

"Tell me."

"You ever heard of the Dalton Company?" Clay said.

———

LIN PUSHED Aggie's buckskin along the banks of Brushy Creek toward the Brazos, zigzagging around leg-snapping gopher holes and mole mounds, ducking through the creek bed wherever access allowed.

Under different circumstances, the horse would be a joy to ride, agile and good at following his lead. As it was, the reins bit deep into his injured, bandaged hands, and he squeezed the horse's ribs, steering mostly with his legs.

Another boom echoed from behind, and Lin laid low as a hot slug whistled overhead.

No way a six-shooter had the range. They were pelting him with rifle fire.

A flash of movement caught his eye, and Lin inadvertently took the horse in the same direction.

A coyote.

Scrawny with a flea-bit mangy coat, the yellow cur slunk down along the edge of the crick bank, then froze when it saw him, front paw in the air, its nostrils at a continuous twitch.

A tremor rippled through Lin's gut like white corn whiskey.

The coyote was a bad omen.

The Mountain Man had taught Lin about it, saying most Indians felt the same way, but especially the

Navajo people of the southwest. Whenever Coyote appeared, sudden mischief was at hand.

Lin hadn't believed it until he and Steve were riding together one day under a clear blue sky. No way the coyote they saw should've been out in daylight. But instead of napping in a rock depression or dugout den, it pranced ahead of them as if deliberately coaxing them into danger.

Five minutes later, the two friends had been attacked by a swarming band of Comanche braves. Nobody knew the Comanche better than Steve, and yet they had surprised even him.

Damned coyote.

Lin rubbed his shoulder, remembering the arrow which chipped off a piece of bone.

He and Steve had been lucky to survive the encounter.

Lin swung around through a draw of cedar trees, temporarily obscuring his pursuers' view. If only he could get around them, learn who they were, and how many.

The hard ride was ruining Lin's hands, and he pampered his blisters as much as possible.

He steered the horse up a slight incline and was able to peer above the treetops for an instant, long enough to make out the trio of riders thundering along the creek toward him.

His heart stood still in his chest, missed a beat, then whirred like a kid's windup toy.

They were closer than he thought.

The lead man's tall boney frame swayed over a paint-horse saddle under a too-big hat, and Lin was sure it was Mal Billingsley. Beside him, the beanpole blonde was the Scarecrow from the night before. Lin couldn't see the third man's features for the dust they were raising.

Gigging his horse through the sparse woods, he stopped to get his bearings. If he wasn't extremely careful during the next few minutes, he was going to die.

It was just that simple.

18

"WHAT A SORRY-ASS PREDICAMENT," Lin said, biting through the bandage knot on his burned palm, ripping the dirty cloth, spitting fiber.

The buckskin moved its head around and snorted in agreement.

Lin figured Reece must have been the one to doctor him the night before because whoever was in charge had done a fine job. The wrappings were tight, and when he pulled them away, he discovered an orange salve greased his right palm.

"I'm sorry to get you into this, old hoss. You're a fine mount, and it's been my privilege to go for a run with you."

The horse flicked its ears, softly nickering as if he understood perfectly.

Next, Lin unraveled the bandage on his left hand and tossed it away.

His red, raw fingers looked like something he ought to be frying up with onions on a grill. They smelled like something he ought to toss in the gut

139

bucket. Hesitant, he tried an experimental flexing of joints and knuckles.

Pain shot up through both wrists.

With a clenched jaw and trembling grip, he pulled his gun from the holster, wrapped his index finger around the trigger and bit back a whimper. The buck-skin swung its head around in sympathy.

No doubt about it, the burns were bad. He didn't regret pulling the flaming packages from inside the Concord, but he was sorry he hadn't first donned the gloves they carried in the front boot or even stripped off his shirt to cover his fingers.

What had Reece said?

"If I've learned one thing this past year, it's when violence comes a callin', ain't nobody ready."

When the matches sparked to life, there hadn't been time to think.

Lin's grip relaxed into a tumultuous shaking he couldn't control. Propping the gun on the saddle in front of him, he struggled to stay focused. Through the sun dappled cedars, on the other side of the creek, Mal and his vigilante boys were closing in, the smell of cigarette smoke heralding their imminent arrival.

A thin sweat broke out along the brim of Lin's cap, and he licked his lips.

He could barely hold the shooting iron, let alone cock the hammer and pull the trigger.

What to do?

He needed a trick of some kind, a distraction to buy himself time to get away.

The sheriff's horse carried a fine blanket and saddle, but no rifle boot. A heavy loop of maguey rope swung free behind Lin's left leg, and a canteen full of fresh water was strapped over the horn.

He reached down and let his aching fingers brush the smooth, expertly wound rope.

Lin Jarret had worked a wide swath of jobs during his life, from smith's assistant to farmhand, from hostler to vaquero. He could heel a calf with the best of 'em.

He wondered if he could grip the rope for a longer time than he was able to hold the gun?

Then the first rider came around the bend of cedars and there wasn't time to play around.

All Lin could do was try.

———

HE SCREAMED down on the blond rifleman, twirling the wide lariat, bucking Mal and the third-man's double lancing of gunfire.

One of the slugs slapped through the crown of Lin's hat while its partner was lost to the wind.

The buckskin's hooves chewed up the crumbling turf like sweat-soaked hardtack.

Lin's hands complained with the abuse as he tossed the loop at just the right angle, but the rope fell true around Scarecrow's chest and shoulders. Once the rope stretched tight from Lin's saddle horn, it jerked Scarecrow off his horse, rifle in hand, directly into the path of Mal's nervous paint horse.

Scarecrow rolled under the flurry of the paint's hard-driving hooves and bounced like a rubber ball once, then twice, before careening off into the clearing, his body kicking and twitching.

Urging Aggie's horse into a flat-out gallop and letting the rope spin free behind him, Lin continued on a straight-ahead course at the side of the Brushy.

Ignoring the fate of his friend, Mal tried to draw a

bead on Lin with his pistol, popping off a smokey crack. Then another. But Lin had soon pulled out of range, the rope trick had improved his odds.

Now he only faced two men armed with cap and ball shooters, instead of three and a carbine. But he'd lost the rope, his hands were a bloody, painful mess, and shooting the Colt now would be more impossible than before.

The only things keeping Lin alive were his superior cowboy skills and Aggie's fine horse.

And even those were beginning to fade. The horse was balking at every turn, and Lin's arms and legs ached with exhaustion.

Well outside the range of Mal's gun, he angled around another bosquecillo, driving into the creek at the last second.

Up to his fetlocks in water, the buckskin slowed to a meandering trot, arguing with Lin's intent.

The water was cold, but it felt good.

Splashing up his pant-legs and side, the shower was invigorating. Shocked out of his stupor, Lin began to think more clearly, began taking in his surroundings with all his senses.

Now there was more variety to the lightly timbered plain. A stand of hay showed dark green in the distance and rock outcroppings dotted the terrain. He rode along the stream bed under a clear sky and pinpoints of twinkling light appeared with each footfall.

The horse stopped to dip his nose into the water, and Lin saw a series of tracks scurrying up and down the muddy wall of the creek. Ground squirrel and prairie dog, racoon and skunk. The hollow was a well of life, unseen and hidden except for what it left behind.

Lin needed to hide.

Night was coming on fast, and two men still hunted him, each of them armed with guns like his Colt. Nursing a pair of sore hands, and with only half their firepower, Lin definitely had the disadvantage.

And then from the corner of his eye, Lin caught a glance of the coyote.

This time it was springing out of the creek ahead of him on the right, loping across the patchy grass landscape. Lin spurred the buckskin up and over the bank of the crick onto flat ground, keeping a careful watch on the coyote's retreat. He didn't want to look behind, but he couldn't not know, so he took a quick squint over his shoulder.

If the vigs were there, he couldn't see them.

Back to the coyote.

The creature's shadow darted left, then slowed to a walk before it finally stopped. In the full copper moon rising from the eastern horizon, the coyote looked back in Lin's direction before padding to the right— and disappearing completely.

Impossible.

The Natives called Coyote the trickster.

Aptly named, this trickster had vanished.

Lin caught a whiff of cigarette smoke, spun his horse in a full circle and gauged the wind. The landscape behind was devoid of life, but for a buzzard winging up from the dark slash of the Brushy. Mal and his vigilante pal were coming up the creek bed, covering the same territory he had.

Within minutes they'd be in sight and, guns blazing, on his heels.

Lin turned back to where the coyote had disappeared, fleeing in the same direction.

"Go on, gidd-yap," he said, and the buckskin did as

it was told, but just barely, trotting forward with a reluctant attitude.

A hundred yards down range, the road plunged into a hollow, and horse and rider almost went ass over teakettle. Grabbing hold of the gelding's dark mane, Lin stayed upright, managing to steer the horse into the natural depression, a rocky lowland which because of its odd contour, hadn't been visible until they were directly upon it.

A jagged rut plowed through the sod here, a minor tributary of the brushy with dry crumbling sidewalls and clusters of thorn and wildflowers. In one spot a hollow had been cleared away and a pile of fresh dirt showed.

Lin figured the spot for the coyote's den, but there was no time to ponder it.

This was his only chance.

Leaping from the back of his horse, he doffed his hat, gave the buckskin a slap on the rump and told him to carry on alone. As if sensing the urgency in Lin's voice, the horse cantered along the thin branch and up the slope out of the depression without a backwards glance.

Lin fumbled the hat and let it land in a heap on the ground.

Steeling himself, counting to three, he grabbed his pistol. Holding it with both hands to compensate for the searing pain, he ran to the dugout and fell to his knees. Then lowering himself to his elbows, he wormed his way backwards through the weeds and dirt into the smooth depression, feet first, until he was relatively hidden from view.

Best of all, he had heard no rattles as he belly-crawled into the hidey hole.

Lin hated snakes with a passion.

Doing his best to breathe easy, he cursed the stinging sweat trickling into his eyes. In daylight, the meager cover of the branch depression and stand of weeds would be laughable. At dusk, he had a chance.

A few seconds, maybe half a minute if the men weren't looking too hard, but he had a chance.

Then the sun winked out, slipping down behind the western horizon and dusk settled in beside Lin to wait.

They appeared ten minutes later.

Mal Billingsley, tall and boney in the saddle, his gun arm held up at the ready in a right angle. His partner, a barrel-chested hombre with furry Mexican chaps. The two came over the brow of the rise bold as brass, but slow, at a deliberate pace.

Hunting. Patient.

Chaps saw Lin's hat resting in the dirt and led the way toward it. Mal followed.

There was no indication either of the men had spotted Lin.

Side by side, the men dismounted and stood over the hat, cranking their heads around to the left and right. After what seemed ages, Chaps bent over, picked up the headgear and slapped dust from it.

Lin peered down the short barrel of his Colt, fighting the shakes, and gritting his teeth in response to the agony in his hands.

He concentrated on taking the shot.

It was the kind of shot he'd made a thousand times. A few days before, he could've taken both men with one lead ball.

He had any number of options—through the legs, through the ribs.

Anticipating the explosion, his hand trembled all

the harder, and he sucked in his breath, making a faint whistle.

Mal Billingsley turned.

Had Lin given himself away?

He held his breath. Finger tight on the trigger. Do it, he thought. Kill or be killed.

Then Mal took out the makings for a smoke. He shared the tobacco with his friend. The two men chewed the fat and toed the dust. At one point, Mal gestured back toward the way they had come. The other man nodded.

Could Lin cut them down in cold blood?

Given the chance, it was no more than they would do to him.

But to slaughter them outright...to watch them kick and cough blood into the evening dust?

Reece would advise him to pull the trigger and be done with them. But Reece wasn't here, and she didn't have to live with his conscience. Something about cutting the unsuspecting men down seemed wrong.

Maybe because, in some ways, Mal Billingsley and the Brushy Creek boys were only doing what Lin or any good man would do if he believed his home and family were threatened.

Such favorable thoughts didn't forgive all they'd done...but Lin's consideration saved them from an immediate death sentence.

He watched Mal drop the remnants of the smoldering butt to the ground. Then the two men walked back to the top of the rise, mounted up, and turned their horses around.

Lin waited a full ten minutes before crawling out from the coyote's den. He rose to his full stature, dropping his gun mercifully into its holster.

Regaining the high ground, Lin peered across the

range and saw the two men riding back toward Quincy. Satisfied the Brushy Creek gang had given up, Lin walked close to retrieve his hat, then traipsed across the range to retrieve Aggie's horse.

He meant to make Harbor Springs by morning.

19

OF COURSE, there were no Comancheros at Harbor Springs.

Under the watchful morning sun, Reece pulled in at the festering grove of fat cypress, oak, and maple trees just off the Brazos trail. Clumps of leafy weeds and prickly mulberry bushes threatened to engulf two wood shacks and the sagging corpse of a split-rail fence. The air was stagnant with clouds of gnats and smell of rotting wood, and one thing was clear.

"The goddamn place is abandoned," Clay said.

The irritation in his voice was as plain as the truth of his declaration.

Clearly undisturbed during the weeks leading into summer, the weeds were tall, the moss-covered structures moldering in place. The silence was broken only by the buzz of the occasional fat horsefly.

Reece surveyed the foreboding patch of woods with its brush-covered cow trail path. Deceptively serene, Harbor Springs was a place of sudden, unforeseen danger.

But not for the reasons Bill Clay assumed.

"Ain't nobody here," he said. "What do you say now, sweetie?"

Reece was ready with an answer. After all, she'd had plenty of time to work on her story.

The night before had been an ordeal—but not in the way Reece originally imagined. After hours of droning on about the Ivory Compass and its plans, Clay had talked himself to sleep with his verbal meanderings, and Reece had time to herself to cogitate on a course of action.

Once the coach reached its destination, she planned to come into the woods at Harbor Springs from the south, close to a couple rickety shacks where they could park the coach.

From there, they could pick their way through the forest to the springs on foot. As for the Comancheros...

"They've learned the art of concealment from the Comanche," she explained. "You've never heard about it?"

Her answer exuded confidence, and Clay was briefly taken aback. He chewed his lower lip before nodding.

"I could believe it," he said, half-way convinced. "Ain't nobody sneaky as a Comanch."

"Now you're catching on."

From his spot on the bench beside her, he motioned toward the thicket. "You're saying they might be in there? We just can't see 'em 'cause of the shadows?"

"Oh, they're in there, alright. I know the signs."

He motioned her down from the wagon.

"You first, missy. And if nobody's in there, you and me are going to have a real interesting morning."

With a mocking sneer, Reece flipped her braid over

her shoulder. "I declare, Mr. Clay, you are proving yourself to be the most tiresome man I know."

"It's one way I've managed to stay alive all these years," he said. She watched while he removed his six-shooter from its holster and motioned toward her. "Now move."

Reece climbed down from the wagon and led Clay into the weeds.

His gun wouldn't do him any good now. He wasn't fighting that kind of enemy...only he didn't know that.

In fact, the only weapon currently in play was Reece's passing familiarity with the place and her unerring sense of direction.

She kept to the path and felt a sense of calm as he moved toward her goal as if it were his idea in the first place.

The foot trail she navigated was as ancient as the gypsum and limestone foundations of the topsoil here, a worn rut winding between crumbling sinkholes and man-made cisterns. Secretive and reluctant to share its wealth, Harbor Springs offered life to the cautious and death to the reckless. Unexpected in the region, the karst geography had been well-known, but little documented, by natives and Spanish explorers alike. Like so much of Texas, it was a treasure guarded with whispers, and filled with traps for the unwary.

"Do stay on the path," Reece said. "Don't wander off."

Pushing aside the tall stickers and iron weed, they passed the first shack and moved deeper into the shadows. Here the ground cover was viny and short, a carpet strewn over chunks of limestone rock and red mud. Ahead in the distance, a long ridge wall of earth rose up several feet to run next to the path, and the bubbling trickle of water became an audible backdrop to the chirp of small birds and drone of stinging insects.

"My father brought me here when I was little," Reece said. "Even before the fort was built."

Wiping his brow with the back of hand and swatting away the bugs, Clay grunted. "Indian lover, was he?"

"In his own way, yes, he was. My father would trade with any man of good character. Or any woman too."

"Sounds like your father was the Comanchero."

"My father was many things, but no—not a Comanchero in the way you mean it."

They trekked the uneven ground with slow, careful steps. Near a series of white rocks embedded in the ground, almost like steppingstones, Reece pointed out a particular pattern. "See the markings there? A recent sign."

"Where?" Clay said, "I don't see it?"

"Just off the path, there's a line of stones. There and there." Reece pointed out the rock placement.

Clay turned his back to her and sauntered over for a closer view of the area Reece had indicated.

"I don't see it."

"You will."

"All's I know is we better not have come all this way to—"

Charging forward, Reece put all her weight into one flying bodycheck, catching Clay in the small of the back with her shoulder, driving him forward and down.

"Gaaah!"

Slammed off-balance, he tossed his arms into the air, fingers spread wide, and lost the gun.

Tumbling over frontwards, his feet slipped out

from under him, and he twisted to the side. Passing through a soft web of morning dew, he smashed into the clover and vines, breaking through the paper-thin cap of rotten wood planking into an endless dank hole.

For an instant, Clay was poised over the old cistern in perfect repose, arms and legs lifted up and out, shards of broken wood decking still holding him out of the maw.

Disbelieving, his eyes locked onto Reece. "Thought...we had an...agreement."

"I lied."

The wood cracked under Clay's weight and his mouth worked, struggled at the words.

"You...you gotta help me."

Creeeeeak.

"How about this?" Reece bent over and pulled a heavy rock loose from the soil.

"What? No...don't! It ain't fair!"

"More fair than you treated Jim Douglas," she said, tossing the rock up in the air with both hands. "I'm just adding a little weight to the scales of justice."

She watched the rock crash down on Bill Clay's chest, punching his body through the last resistance of wood over the cistern. And then he was gone.

Reece stood on the edge, counting the seconds, listening to the scream.

Clay fell a long time before she heard a sloppy wet thud.

———

LIN JARRET FOUND Reece sitting at a welcome campfire not too far away from their Concord coach. But far enough to keep inadvertent sparks from igniting the load of matches still ensconced there.

Well rested and adorned with a clean blouse, canvas pants and boots, she seemed completely at ease and utterly careless. A book lay next to her on the ground, its pages spread open, and a tin of coffee gurgled above the flames on a tripod pot hanger.

Lin brought Aggie's tired horse to a standstill, grinning down at her with a mix of so many emotions, he couldn't form any words.

He practically fell out of the saddle into her arms.

"Aw, Contessa, I don't have the words...," he said, pressing his face into her shoulder, inhaling everything she was to him, feeling his heart explode.

"You don't have to say anything, Ranger."

He took her into his arms.

She ran her fingers through his hair. "We don't have to say a word."

And for a while, they didn't.

20

THE DAYS PASSED, and before too long Lin Jarret had
been too long on the wagon bench.

Much as he loved the open road, he was ready for a
breather.

The long ride from Harbor Springs to Snakebite
Canyon had every muscle, bone, and joint
complaining.

The gently undulating earth had flattened back out,
like a tablecloth pulled taut, and the green grass went
brown with thirst.

From her spot next to him on the bench, Reece
commented on his progress. "This drive's got you red
as a summer tomato and twice as sour. At least you can
hold the reins now."

Grudgingly, he had to admit she was right.

After three days on the road and many applications
of medicinal salve, his burns were healing, albeit not as
fast as he'd like.

Reece said staying free of infection was a flat-out
gift from the Almighty.

Lin had to agree. He'd seen men initially survive a blaze, only to sicken and die days later.

"Thing is, Contessa—I've relied on you too much. I'm not a child." Along the road, she became chief cook, shotgun rider, part-time driver, mechanic, and conversationalist.

If her shoulder injury bothered, she didn't let on.

"Need a drink?" she asked, handing over their shared canteen.

"Obliged." He took a sip but thrust the can back at her. "Dammit, there's just the thing I'm talking about."

"You'd do the same for me," Reece said, quietly, and Lin let the conversation drop.

They had traveled many roads together since acquiring the coach, but more than any other, the sunbaked venture they were on now had forged them into something damn-neared invincible.

He was flour, she was water. Together, they were hard tack—able to see through the rough times and last damn near forever.

As long as they didn't do themselves in.

"We don't have much farther to go," he said.

Ahead, like a painter's brush had dragged brick red across the horizon, the Caprock Escarpment blocked their forward way, and a series of snaky trails led to a series of ridges and uphill slopes.

Nearly 200 miles long, the imposing caliche façade which, in some places, rose to 1000 feet above the rolling eastern plains, was a hard divider between the high plains of the Llano Estacado and east Texas. The road they followed broke up into a dozen whiplash trails along the ridge and into the myriad gaps where scrub trees and dry brown tumbleweeds clustered.

Lin stood up on the coach and picked a route.

"Let's wander south-west up the grade over there," he said. "There's a series of outcroppings…we can follow those until the brow of the first ridge, and into the arroyo leading to Snakebite Canyon. Might be a tad bumpy, but at least we don't have those damn matches anymore."

They had agreed to leave the cargo at Harbor Springs, stashing it inside one of the broke down shacks.

"Damn things are more trouble than they're worth," Lin said. He pulled the makings of a smoke out of his shirt pocket. After sprinkling out a fat portion of leaf, rolling the paper and licking it tight, he took out a match and scratched it on his holster. "'Course I'm glad to have kept a few."

Lin breathed in the smoke and smell of phosphor, gave the reins a swish, and the team pulled in the direction he wanted.

After a while, Reece ventured a question Lin hoped she wouldn't ask.

"You haven't said much about Clay. Don't you want to know what happened?"

He took a long, last drag of his cigarette and flicked it out over the prairie. "He's dead ain't he? You said so."

"Clay's dead at the bottom of a deep well," she confirmed. "I heard him hit bottom."

"It's all I need to know."

After an awkward silence, she said. "I wanted you to know. I didn't…he didn't. The night he and were in camp together. He didn't even try."

"Okay."

"You don't care?"

"We both did what we had to do. We're together now. That's what matters."

"But you believe me—"

"Near as I can figure, everything turned out for the good. Ain't no reason to stir the pot now."

"It's important to me you believe me."

"It's more important we move on with the business at hand. You want me to say I believe you, okay—I believe you. Like I said, we both did what we had to do."

They rode a while in a companionable silence. Finally, Reece said, "How do we know this friend of yours will be home in the canyon?"

Up until now the tranquil morning air had rested cool on Lin's neck, but the impatient sun was climbing its ladder into the sky, threatening to roast him alive.

"I have no idea if Steve will be at the cabin or not," he said. "But there will be water and shade. What's most important is getting the horses a drink and out of this heat."

Lin had swapped the wagon team out at Gruber's way station the day before, but kept Aggie's buckskin trailing behind. He had every intent of returning the horse to Sheriff Aggie Simms of Quincy.

The new horses were relatively fresh, but with limited water rations, Lin didn't want to push them. Pulling the Concord over increasingly rugged ground was a sure way to break a hoof or worse. Rolling through the middle of nowhere, they couldn't risk a break down.

"There's no telling when we'll cross paths with anybody out here, friend or otherwise. Could be a couple days, could be a couple months. In case you haven't noticed, we're all alone."

They hadn't met a single, solitary soul since leaving the way station.

"If we can find Steve's cabin, we can stay there, even if he's not about," Lin said.

"You're sure there will be water?" Reece said. "What about food?"

"Plenty of water. There's a spring out back. Not sure about food. It depends who's been staying there. But there's always game in the area, so we won't starve."

"You told me it was a shared space?"

Lin nodded, fishing around for the right words to describe it. "No one person owns the place. And there's a bunch of us who know about it. Call it...a retreat."

"Who built it?"

"Who knows? Steve found it first and fixed up on it. Me and Jim stayed there a full week once."

"Sort of a hunting lodge?"

Lin acknowledged the similarity. "Except we were hunting men."

———

IN FRONT of the cabin at Snakebite Canyon, Steve Gardner firmed up the cinch of Romeo's saddle. He double-checked a pair of leather saddle pouches, making sure they were buttoned up, then thought better of it. Flinging open one of the satchels, he removed a thick twist of tobacco and put it between his front teeth to soften the leaves.

The gospel riders, Matthew and Mark, hadn't been wise men, or even polite company, but they came bearing gifts. The bags with wheat bread and bacon, the pouch of leaf tobacco and the twist had made the recent days a touch more pleasant. The guns and ammunition the riders carried were welcome, doubling the cabin's arsenal, and now he wore the kid's six-shooter on his hip.

After removing the saddles and blankets, Steve had secured the two company horses in his sorry broke down corral where they had miraculously remained.

Once he and the old man set out for the east, he had a mind to set the animals free.

The two of them would be suspect enough to anyone they encountered.

No sense adding a pair of company-branded horses to the mix.

Hopefully, they wouldn't meet anybody.

Steve closed the satchel, making double sure it was buttoned shut. When he did, he couldn't help but read the company name stamped into the lip of the leather flap. The same company who had branded the horses.

The Dalton Company.

They had already dawdled too long at the cabin. What was supposed to have been a pleasant couple of weeks sitting tight, waiting for Jim Douglas to return from Rimrock with the Hellbenders, had turned into a tense, endless ordeal.

The days kept adding up, one after another.

The old man had an appointment to keep, and if he was to make it, Steve decided they had to leave today.

This morning.

Add to it the fact they'd given themselves away. Somewhere, somebody waited on Matthew and Mark. When the two didn't return from investigating the cabin, another team would appear. Then another, and another.

After these last two, there was no reason to think more men wouldn't come.

If only Jim Douglas had gotten through to Lin Jarret. The longer Steve waited the more convinced he was Jim hadn't made contact.

The Hellbenders should have been here by now.

Steve sighed, continuing to work the twist over between his lips. The hard, dry leaf tasted of apples and smoke, and it softened as he chewed. The morning was warm on his skin and smelled of sage and sunshine, the wind from the north, cool in contrast to the mid-summer heat sure to follow by afternoon. The empty landscape beyond the canyon rock beckoned, and there was nothing to be done about it but mount up and go.

The urge to move, to travel, had been tamped down long enough.

Steve's ankle was healed, and the old man agreed—it was past time to move.

"Looks to be good weather for it," Steve said.

"Guess it don't matter a good goddamn if it is or if it isn't." The old man stepped down from the porch, letting his weight settle with each step before moving on to the next. Under his arm, he carried a copy of Homer's Iliad. "Been waiting on your confounded ankle to heal up so we can get under-way. If we don't leave now, you're liable to bung it up, and we'll be stuck on this island of earth for an eternity."

Romeo nickered at the approach and side-stepped back and forth, eager to stretch after too long without traveling. The old man dropped his book into a leather bag on the side.

Steve patted Romeo's saddle.

"Let me help you up."

"Hell with you. The day I can't mount up by myself is they day you leave me behind. Not that your horse is worth a damn. I wouldn't take three like him for one of my old Saracen."

Romeo remained stoic in the face of such unwarranted criticism while Steve bit his tobacco in two and rolled the softened wad into his cheek. The dry remains of the twist he put back into the saddle bag.

"Each his own," he said.

He watched the old man lift his foot to the stirrup. Trying not to worry.

For one, the old man had been injured years before in a battle with the Creek Indians, and the wound never truly healed. During the past few days, it had pained him considerably.

For another thing, the septuagenarian was dressed too warm in a heavy, long-sleeved shirt topped with a blue silk cravat, wool vest and gray suit coat. "I think your coat weighs more than you do," Steve said.

"Some of us prefer the civil practice of wearing clothes."

Steve slapped his bare chest, causing the rattles on his leather cord to stutter. "I'm a man of the elements."

"If you say so."

"Don't forget your hat. Sun's gonna get brutal 'fore noon."

The old man put his foot back on the ground. Worked to catch his breath.

"I got my hat here...somewhere."

"Back in the cabin," Steve said. "I'll get it. You put yourself in the saddle." He snapped his fingers. "And we still need to open the gate on those Dalton horses."

As Steve brushed past to retrieve the hat, the old man grabbed his arm in a blue-veined grasp. Behind the hold was more strength than might be expected, and Steve appreciated the will driving it forward.

"I want you to know. No matter what happens, I appreciate all you've done."

Frozen by the clear eyes, Steve felt his chest swell and his breath caught in his throat.

Damned old guy still had a lot of charisma.

"We ain't beat yet," Steve said, giving a wink, trying to signal a confidence he didn't feel.

He patted the wrinkled hand and jogged into the house. When he carried the hat back outside, his friend was atop the horse.

But an ominous cloud had appeared on the trail. "Visitors," he announced.

Damn.

Steve had hoped to get away before Luke and John followed on the heels of the prior gospel boys.

Fast as anything, the old man had his scatter gun out of its boot and leveled at the approach.

Steve handed over the hat and tugged his tomahawk free, preferring its heft over the Colt six-shooter on his opposite hip.

The scarf of dust trailing on the horizon carried the sound of many hooves—at least four horses and the rattle of a wagon followed behind.

There was no reason to believe the newcomers were friendly, thought Steve, not after the last go-round.

Luke and John with all the other disciples in tow.

Expecting anything, the Mountain Man waved Romeo and his friend off behind the cabin. "Take cover on the north side," he said. "I'll stay to the south over by the corral and watch their approach. If they're not friendly, I'll buy some time, and you ride hell for leather out of here."

"You're awful cock-sure of yourself this morning."

"And you're awful surely."

The old man considered it. "Guess we both been cooped up too long."

THE TRAIL to the cabin was full of switchbacks and the
grade left no way for the Concord to arrive unde-
tected. Lin didn't figure Steve for shooting strangers
off the bench, but he didn't know if Steve was inhab-
iting the cabin, did he?

"For all we know, the place could've been taken
over by a gang of those vigilantes."

"What do you suggest?" Reece said.

"I'll drive the wagon within a few hundred feet and
park it. From there on, we hoof it around the perimeter, use rocks and brush for cover. I'd like to give the
property a good eyeballing before we announce
ourselves."

"You said the cabin would see us coming for the
dust."

"They'll know where the wagon is, sure. They
won't be sure about us."

Reece understood.

Lin navigated the final approach from memory,
and the cabin appeared around the last bend, low, flat
and sun-bleached gray. A quiet house, nearly invisible

as it hugged a backdrop of scanty woods and scattered rock formations. The chimney was inactive, the air dead still. To the left, a broken-down corral peered out from a hairy overgrowth of weeds. Two horses stood unafraid near an open gate. *Domesticated steeds* thought Lin. Ponies in a corral meant people.

Somebody's been feeding them.

Lin left his team of horses hitched to a scruffy mesquite bush and padded over to a high pile of rocks. At his approach, a dun-colored rabbit broke away from one of the rocks and loped away.

Jacking himself up to the first layer, Lin risked being seen, surveying the seemingly abandoned spread.

From here, the creek behind the cabin was visible, a garish wound plowed through the sod.

Lin told Reece, "You stay here. I'll slip around back."

"See if you can do it without scaring up any more rabbits," she said. "Or snakes."

He slipped between the rocks and made a fast run for the corral fence, dropping to his haunches when he arrived, keeping a moldering corner post and its attendant thistle patch between himself and the cabin.

He sniffed the air, picked up a lingering scent of fried meat and tobacco. Somebody had been staying here alright. Recently as this morning, if his sniffer was to be believed.

Lin strained his senses—just in time to hear a snap of grass behind him. He flexed his knees and reached for his gun and felt a hard, cold poke in his back.

In the corner of his eye, the ground cover seemed to shift and levitate, and a figure rose up from the corral earth. Dust and weeds tumbled from the form, and a man's voice said, "Hold real still, partner."

Before Lin could reply, a heavy-set old-timer came around the front side of the cabin on a traveling horse. The animal carried bedrolls and saddle bags. The codger carried a shotgun, its muzzle lined up with Lin's chest. "Throw down your sidearm," he said, "or sure as God is my witness, I'll put you into the ground."

Something in the man's voice demanded immediate compliance. Lin couldn't decide if it was the militaristic tone or almost regal bearing. Either way, the smug expectancy on the man's face showed he was used to giving orders.

The pressure in Lin's back helped cinch the deal. Lin picked his gun from its holster with a finger and thumb. Dropped it to the ground.

And then Reece evened things up by stepping into the scene from behind the cabin. Both arms outstretched, she held her Colt-Walker at an angle guaranteed to take off the top of the old man's head. "Lose the shotgun."

The old man ignored her. But neither did he pull his trigger.

Then to Lin's assailant, Reece said. "You, too. Throw down your gun."

The voice behind Lin was suddenly full of mirth. "Ain't got a gun," he said.

The prod came away from Lin's back and he spun around.

Face to face with a duck's head on the end of a tomahawk.

The man who held it wore his hair long over his bare shoulders. Covered with dirt, he'd buried himself under a layer of rock and soil to surprise Lin and Reece. Now he stood tall and muscular wearing only a loin cloth.

"How's about I drop my duck?" Steve said, holding up the war axe with its carved handle.

Reece hesitated, then with some confusion said. "Yeah...go ahead and drop your...duck."

Mountain Man Steve winked at Lin. "I don't think I've ever had a gal ask me to do that before. How about you, Jarret?"

Recognizing his friend, Lin felt the smile grow on his cheeks even as he wound up his fist. "You god-forsaken wild man," he said, tossing off a punch at Steve's chin. The mountain man slipped past the friendly clout and landed a jab on Lin's shoulder.

"You damn Ranger."

"Glory be, Reece, we made it," Lin said.

The two men fell into a rough and tumble manly embrace sending Lin's hat skittering into the dust. Retrieving it, he gave Steve a swat and flung his arm around a broad shoulder. "Damn, but it's good to see you, Steve," he said. "I didn't think we'd find you."

"Is Jim with you?"

"One thing at a time."

"Is this your woman?"

"She's a beaut, ain't she?"

"I will say she is. Como esta, señorita?"

"I'm Reece Sinclair, and I'm nobody's woman but my own."

"Beg 'pardon, ma'am," Steve said. Then to Lin: "She's a feisty one?"

"My partner in business. C'mon and say howdy, Reece."

Reece stayed where she was, arms folded, with one hand on the Colt still pointed at the old man. "Howdy," she said.

"Damn," Lin repeated. "It's good to see you."

Steve nodded, then said to Lin. "Jim Douglas is with you, isn't he?"

"Steve, I..."

All the driving time in the world couldn't have prepared Lin for breaking the news about their mutual friend's killing. He'd had days and days to figure out what to say when the time came. Plenty of time to find the words.

When they mattered most, they weren't there for him.

"Let's talk later," Lin said, but he saw a sense of understanding creep across Steve's face. The news wasn't welcome, but maybe not completely unexpected.

From the back of the traveling horse, the old man spoke up, "Who the hell is this, Steve?"

The old man cocked his head and the blue eyes cut Lin to the bone.

Lin was struck by the deep baritone voice. Together with the shock of white hair, the twin muttonchops, and the excessive clothing, it projected an air of authority not to be denied.

Lin could have ignored a lesser man asking the question. Instead, he felt compelled to stand up straighter and answer quickly. "Lin Jarret, sir. The gal there is Miss Reece Sinclair."

Steve turned to the old man. "They're the Hellbenders I told you about."

"Where's Jim Douglas?"

"These are the folks I sent Jim Douglas to fetch back here for us."

Lin piped up. "You did?"

"Didn't Jim tell you?"

"He didn't...we didn't talk as much as I hoped we would before...," began Lin.

"Dammit," Steve said, reading the sorrow in Lin's face. "I knew something went wrong. Jim didn't tell you anything?" Steve said.

"Not much. He didn't get a chance," Lin said.

Steve took the news with stoic resignation.

"If these are your people, we ought to be on our way," said the old man.

"On our way? To where?" Reece said.

"Back the way you came."

"But, sir...who are you?" Reece said.

"I apologize," Steve said. "Being too long away from society has made me a poor host. This is Governor Sam Houston. He's in trouble, and he needs a ride back to Rimrock Station."

The breath caught in Lin's throat.

22

INSIDE THE CABIN, Reece and Lin stood beside a tall counter, filling their plates with cowboy caviar and strips of peppered bacon.

On the opposite side of the cabin, close to the door, Steve Gardner filled four mugs with hot coffee from the cook stove and added dollops from an open can of milk.

"Does he always go around naked?" Reece said under her breath.

"Steve has his own sensibilities about these things. You'll get used to him," Lin said.

"Like hell," Reece said.

She crossed the kitchen space to take her cup of coffee. Careful to keep her eyes above Steve's waist, she smiled her thanks.

Steve nodded. "Hope you'll forgive this rugged bachelor. I'm not much for making coffee, ma'am."

"It also appears you're not much for wearing clothes," Reece said.

"I dress like my brothers, the wind and the rain," he

said. Then: "If you like the caviar, I'll write out the recipe."

"Black beans, dried corn, peppers, tomato, and onion," Reece said.

"Plus, vinegar and cilantro," Steve said. "And one additional ingredient I'll let you guess. Patented, 1858."

"I ain't much for cooking," Reece said, "but I'm right handy opening a can of peaches."

She carried the salad to a time-worn table at the far end of the cabin situated between two weather beat benches. "May I join you, Governor?"

Houston finished his mouthful of bacon and nodded. "Please do," he said, cordially rising as she sat down.

At least one of the three men was a gentleman.

Normally ambivalent about such chivalrous actions, Reece felt herself inexplicably drawn in by this aged fellow, who seemed so incredibly out of place in the canyon shack, but still so comfortably at home.

Houston handed her a heavy napkin as he sat down to resume his meal.

After the past week's exertions, the hominess of the surroundings was more than welcome.

Houston waved his fork toward the half-dressed Mountain Man. "You see what I've had to deal with. It's good to dine with a pretty face for a change."

"How long have you known Steve Gardner?"

Houston had to think about it. "Fifteen…no, closer to twenty years this fall." He swallowed some coffee and reassured her. "Don't take my teasing the wrong way. He's a good man. Jim Douglas too. Good as they come."

"How do you know them?"

Houston shrugged. "Call them my guardian angels. Damn fools took it upon themselves to nanny me during the past few years. Steve even put clothes on so he could follow me out to Baltimore for the Constitutional Union Party convention, came back home with me. Had a scrap of trouble at the Capitol, now I'm holed up out here for the duration."

"We read about the convention in the paper. You were a candidate for president."

"I lost."

More than this, he didn't seem to want to say and changed the subject.

"I had hoped to be halfway to Lambert's Ferry by this time," Houston said. "I told Steve and Jim we might just as well undertake the venture alone, the three of us, but they were determined to commission your services. For we do not wrestle against flesh and blood, but against principalities, against powers, against the rulers of the darkness of this age, against spiritual hosts of wickedness in the heavenly places. Ephesians, 6:12."

"I never took you as one to quote scripture, sir."

"I am many things, and please call me Sam, dear."

"Still…"

Houston patted Reece's hand. "You have my lovely Margaret Lea to thank for taming this old bear. I was carried into the faith in a cold river where my sins were washed away…and God help the fish down below."

"You said you sent for us?"

"Steve did the sending. Or rather, they drew straws for it. Jim won and galloped away to Lambert's Ferry to find you."

"How did Steve know we would be there?"

"You carried Dale Hemlock there for the Cotton Growers' meeting, didn't you? Word gets around. The Dalton Company…" He let his words fade, shook his head, and sipped from his cup. "We'd be better served to go back to Bible talk than speak of the Dalton Company—rotten bastards. If you'll pardon me, ma'am."

Houston gave Reece's fingers a squeeze, and she got the feeling he enjoyed touching her hand.

"And here we are now with poor Jim lost," he said. "Nevertheless, I mightily appreciate your making the journey."

"And I appreciate your willingness to wait until evening to leave," Reece said.

Initially after the Hellbenders' appearance, Houston had been eager to depart for the east. Impatient and suffering a wearisome dose of cabin fever, he wanted nothing more than to lead the charge to Rimrock Station where he was due in less than ten days to deliver a speech to the Cotton Growers.

Thankfully, Steve had managed to convince him a few extra hours—long enough for Lin and Reece to fill their bellies with lunch and plan the trip—wouldn't matter.

"What will you say to the Cotton Growers?"

"It wouldn't interest you." Then, after studying her face, he said, "Or maybe it would. Either way, there's time enough to talk about it later. We have a long journey ahead of us."

"Hopefully the worst is behind us."

"You've got a strong team there," Houston said, motioning outside the window with his fork. "Hard to find good animals these days."

"We'll keep 'em good by replacing two with the mares you've got in the corral."

Houston agreed.

"About those horses," began Reece.

"Dalton Company horses."

"How did they come to be here?"

He told her about the young rider and his newspaper, then about how the man had come back on a Dalton-branded horse, bringing his older friend with him. He told her about them calling themselves Matthew and Mark and how the gospel they spread was incredibly dark.

"Mercenaries for the Dalton Company," Reece said.

"You don't sound surprised."

"I got quite an earful from a man named Bill Clay."

"Who's Clay to tell you about the Daltons?"

Deciding it would lead to a variety of hard-to-answer questions, Reece refrained from identifying Clay as the sharpshooter who killed Jim Douglas.

As the governor himself had stated—there would be time for all of it later.

And Lin Jarret should be the one to bring it out.

"Of course, you know about the Order of the Ivory Compass," Reece said. "Bill Clay is a member. He told me the Daltons help finance the organization and have big plans for the future of Texas."

"Big plan for Texas—over my dead body," Houston said. Apparently, she was only saying what he already knew.

Houston immediately confirmed her suspicions. "It's a conspiracy Jim and Steve discovered back in San Antonio."

"Conspiracy?" The specific word Jim Douglas had used.

But Reece didn't get an answer because just as Houston started to talk, Lin spoke up from his place at the counter beside Mountain Man Steve.

"Us two have been comparing notes, and there's no easy way to say it. The truth is, there's no shortage of folks out there who seem determined to see the four of us dead. If we're to cover the distance between here and Rimrock Station and arrive in sound mind and body, we'll need to be well stocked with food and supplies, but also with armaments."

"Suppose we take inventory?" Houston said, slapping the table good naturedly. Leaning back on his bench seat as far as he could without toppling over, he stretched out an arm and picked up the ten-bore percussion shotgun he and Steve shared. "Thirty-two-inch barrel, a Walnut stock, with engraved silver fittings. When we were out in Baltimore, I bought this gun personally from Brownson, Slocum & Hopkins, an east-coast dealer. I carried it along when Jim and Steve brought me here."

Reece interrupted the show-and-tell with a question. "Tell us more about this conspiracy Jim and Steve discovered? Conspiracy is the reason they brought you here?"

Steve answered for the governor. "It's precisely why he's here, Miss, and why we wanted you two to escort us back east. Word is, the Hellbenders will protect whatever and whoever they carry. And they protect them with their lives."

"I think you're all acting like a bunch of mother hens. I may be getting older, but I don't need to be looked after like a child."

Steve shook his head. "I think with Lin Jarret's gun on our side, we've just improved our odds of survival by a wide margin."

"I appreciate the vote of confidence," Lin said.

Houston continued down the list of weapons, counting on his fingers. "I've got the shotgun; Steve has access to a pair of Remington pistols as well as a couple Colts we picked up from the Dalton boys. And of course, his Comanche duck."

"Not the most efficient weapon in the world," Reece said.

"You'd be surprised," Steve said.

Lin spoke up. "Reece and I each have a Colt-Walker, and we're carrying plenty of balls, caps, and powder in the coach."

For an instant, Reece thought to mention the Walch 12-shooter, before remembering its final fate on the banks of Brushy Creek. The trick gun had served her well for a long time, and now she missed it. "We've got a couple carbines in the coach as well," she added.

Then she said, "I still want to hear more about this conspiracy. Lin and I saw the newspaper headlines about the fires. We saw your conspiracy play out as we crossed the state: smoke from the fires all along the horizon. Quincy is nothing but burnt ruins."

"Whoa there, Miss Reece," Steve said. "We're talking two different things for sure."

Reece raised her eyebrows at the revelation.

"How so?"

"The plot Jim and I discovered in San Antonio is more personal in nature, and more specific. Not saying the fires aren't being set by the same folks or their followers—but it isn't why we're out here."

"Then why are you out here?"

Houston was impatient with the topic. "To put it simply, the Order of the Ivory Compass has put a price on my head. A million dollars to the man who ends my life." Houston looked at the three of them, one after another. "With Jim gone, the only person I trust right now is Steve Gardner." He put his palm on Reece's hand. "You'll forgive me if I hurt your feelings, dear."

"He's willing to let you earn his trust on my word alone," Steve said.

Reece could see Lin felt flattered by the dubious honor.

"So you and Jim learned of the plot and spirited the governor away," he said.

"Until we could find out more."

"Did you find out more?"

Steve shook his head. "Just what you already know. The Daltons are tied up in it, and with what Lin's told me about Jim being killed at Rimrock, I have to imagine they're planning to take their shot at the governor there."

Reece had an easy solution for the Governor. "Don't go to Rimrock," she told him. "Politely decline your speech to the Cotton Growers."

"I agree," Lin said. "How important is giving an agricultural talk to a bunch of farmers?"

"More important than you know," Houston said, clearing his throat. "You all may know I stand against the Disunionists who would tear our nation in two. The true fact of the matter is, it's only been 15 years, and I would see the Republic of Texas go it alone like it was rather than be carried away by the other Southern states."

He cleared his throat. "With that said, cotton is the foundation of our economy here in Texas, and the Cotton Growers Association holds great clout. In turn, the Daltons hold great clout with the Cotton Growers. Daltons are planning a merger with another plantation group from South Carolina. In fact, they're meeting with them in Arkansas after the conference in Rimrock."

"And certainly the South Carolina plantation does not side with the Union," Reece said.

"Naturally," Houston said. "The plantation has

enormous contracts with Britain and France to supply the European textile mills."

Reece saw the dilemma. "If Texas stays with the Union, the Dalton-Carolina confederacy is in jeopardy. They stand to lose—"

"A fortune times ten," Houston said.

"You're going to address the Cotton Growers in Rimrock…"

"And try to convince them to see reason," Houston said. "To stay our course and reject the southern states."

"No wonder the Dalton Company wants you dead."

"What about Dale Hemlock?" Lin said. "He's the head of the Cotton Growers. Where does he stand?"

"Dale's an old curmudgeon," Houston said, "and oftentimes a sizable pain in the neck. But I believe he stands with me. He wants nothing to do with secession."

"Then his life is in danger, too."

"Almost assuredly," Houston said. "If he's not dead already."

23

BROTHER LAMBERT TOSSED a napkin down to his supper plate and adjourned to his front porch for a smoke. The fat cigar he positioned between two fingers was a delight, and the acrid flavor of the tobacco mixed with the smell of the river and honeysuckle calmed his nerves.

He hadn't slept well these past few nights, and it wasn't because of the summertime heat and sultry nights.

Odd, especially since Rimrock Station had been quieter than usual. The calm before a storm? Excitement about the recent spate of fires across the river had trickled away to background chatter, and the Cotton Growers were at the end of their third week of meetings and deliberations.

What new trouble might be on the rise?

Because, in spite of the peace, his constable, Daniel Martin Ray, seemed increasingly more agitated. Ray had stopped in before supper to offer his daily report, which included nothing out of the ordinary—yet his speech was abrupt, the nervous tic in his cheek, a sign of hidden strain.

Now Lambert watched Ray ride up and dismount in front of his house for a second time in the same day.

"Nice night, Mr. Ray."

Ignoring the pleasantries, Ray joined his boss on the porch. "Bill Clay has disappeared," he said.

Lambert chewed a leaf from his cigar tip and spit it to the porch. "I should hope so. Mr. Clay and I parted company weeks ago. And if he understood me correctly before he left, I would be surprised if he came back this way."

"Some of the men were hoping to convince him to come back to Rimrock."

"I'm sorry to hear it, Daniel. Clay burned that bridge, and I wouldn't employ him on a bet. Not after the street display he and Jarret put on. The fact is both of those men are banned from Rimrock Station for life."

"Jarret was the problem. Not Clay."

"Perhaps," Lambert said. "I'm not giving either of them the chance at redemption."

Ray shifted from one boot to the other, and his fingers played a fife-and-drum rhythm on his pants leg.

"What is it you're so worked up about?" Lambert said.

Ray took a slow, deep breath and willed himself to relax. "Is it so obvious?"

"You're positively breathless, man."

"His disappearance is a mystery. I don't like mysteries."

"Tell me why you think he's disappeared. I told him to git and stay gone, and he did."

"Bill Clay was supposed to meet me and some of the Indian police across the river earlier today. I was prepared to offer him a handsome fee to come back for the last week of the Cotton meeting."

Before Lambert could interject, Ray held up his hand. "As added security for Sam Houston's speech, you understand. That's all—just added security."

Lambert thought it made sense. Clay was a crack shot with his Sharps and had an eagle's eye for trouble. But Lambert also believed Rimrock's Chickasaw force was up to protecting the governor from any sudden mischief, and Clay would always be a wild card.

"I don't appreciate your going behind my back, Dan."

Ray's scowl was openly contemptuous. "The fact is, sir, you never liked Clay. He was scheduled to meet us today, and now—for all we know—he might be dead."

"Clay's a crack shot with a lot of…shall we say, contracts, under his belt. Men like him…they carry a certain reputation. They invite vengeance."

"You're saying he was gunned down by a rival?"

"It's certainly not outside the realm of possibility."

"Gods, let's hope not."

Lambert wondered at Ray's concern. It was unlike the big Indian to show so much emotion.

"Well, I just thought you should know," Ray said.

"He'll show up one of these days."

"I hope so."

"Regardless, I have faith in your ability to protect the governor whenever he arrives."

Ray wore an odd expression on his face. "As you say." He turned and marched down the steps.

Lambert watched him go. Watched him mount up and ride away up the street.

Even his horse was in a lather.

Such things shouldn't be, thought Lambert.

The dog days of summer were here, and with them came a slow, relaxed pace. The number of mischievous "accidents"—like Klein's wagon fire—had decreased during the past few weeks.

Time to relax into a wide wicker chair and try to smoke away his worries.

A week from today, Houston was scheduled to arrive and deliver the convention's closing speech. Then the Dalton Company, along with the rest of them, would pack up and follow the Overland Road northeast to Fort Smith.

Word was they were pressing for some kind of big business confederation with another cotton growing concern out of South Carolina.

Lambert didn't care.

He was just ready for them to be gone and his life to return to normal. Ferrying the steady flow of eager immigrants across the river every day was enough to roil blood. He didn't need anything more.

"Ah, another visitor," he said, tapping a long cylinder of gray ash from the end of his cigar.

He watched Dale Hemlock advance along the boardwalk across the street.

To Lambert, Hemlock had seemed like a dry, shriveled husk of a man, and he'd only shrunk more since arriving on the Hellbender's express. The evening was warm and muggy with steam rising off the river and mosquitos squalling in mid-air, but Hemlock wore a heavy dark coat and fur-lined cap.

He spied Lambert on the porch of his hacienda and shuffled across the street. He coughed before his greeting. "Evening, Brother."

"Beautiful summer evening, Mr. Hemlock."

"There's a chill in the breeze."

"How are your deliberations going?"

"Your guest house is turning into a pig sty." Hemlock made a shooing motion with his long, ivory fingers. "Too many men gathered for too long in one place. The accommodations are splendid, mind you, but the house is beginning to smell."

"I'll have some of the women come over if you'd like."

"Too many of those too. Every night. All night long."

"I don't think we're talking about the same kind of women," Lambert said.

"I know we're not," Hemlock said with disgust.

He stood in the street, shifting his weight from one foot to the other. Like he had something more to say but wasn't sure how to say it. Instead, he asked to be invited to the porch.

"By all means," Lambert said, standing to offer the older man his chair. "May I get you something to drink? A cigar?"

Hemlock coughed. "No, no," he said. "I'm not here to make a fuss."

With considerable effort he mounted the front steps and dragged himself into the wicker chair. Once there, he unbuttoned the top two buttons of his coat and exhaled long and loud.

Lambert turned and took a puff off his cigar. "Something on your mind, Mr. Hemlock?"

"Yes…yes, there is."

Lambert waited with the patience of Job, maintaining faith in his ability to deal with any paltry troubles the man might have.

"Food not to your liking? Perhaps the water…?"

After more than three weeks, Lambert had no idea

what was bothering the old devil this time. Seemed like he always had something to grouse about.

"Matches," Hemlock said.

"Gads," Lambert said. "Those damned lucifer sticks. What about them?"

"They say this man, Vern Klein, deals in matches."

"Yes, he does. Among many other things."

"But he does have a reputation for supplying the area with the new phosphorescent match?"

"Indeed, he does." Lambert's curiosity was piqued.

"What else? What other things does he deal in?"

"Oh, various paper products, I suppose. Tin cups. Laundry soap. Sundries. I can't say I'm exactly privy to details," Lambert said. "Why do you ask?"

"Some of my colleagues have been meeting with him at odd hours of the night. Strange comings and goings."

"I see," Lambert said. "Have you asked them about it? Have you asked Klein?"

"Oh, no. No, no—such a thing wouldn't do. I'm not one to pry into a man's private dealings, especially not his personal business."

"Then why tell me about it?"

Hemlock seemed unsure of his answer. He raised a weak hand and it fluttered in the air as he flailed for the words. Then he said, "Why...I suppose just so you would know. In case..."

"In case?"

"Of an accident, I suppose."

Lambert took the information in and thanked Hemlock for telling him. "Would you be willing to share which of your colleagues are dealing with Klein? Who is it you're talking about?"

Hemlock took even less time to answer than he had

before. "I don't think I should say," he said. "It doesn't seem...prudent."

The tremor in his voice convinced Lambert of something he'd suspected all along.

"If you don't mind me saying so, sir—you don't get along especially well with the men in your association, do you?"

Hemlock kept his attention focused on a horse fly perched on his knee and answered weakly, "Not especially, no."

Hemlock's cough was a dry, nagging bark, and Lambert decided it wasn't his imagination. The man's pallor matched the gray of the river, and his stamina was half of what it was when he arrived.

When he tried to stand, he reached out to Lambert for support.

"I...guess I'm getting old."

"We all are," Lambert said. "But it beats—"

"—the alternative, yes, I suppose it does."

Slow but sure, Hemlock went down the steps, but stopped at the bottom to turn and say one more thing.

"You asked about the water," Hemlock said.

"Yes, what of it?"

"Since you brought it up, I will complain after all. Your spring's gone bad. Or somebody's been giving us river water," he said. "When we first showed up, it tasted fine. Now the water I'm given has an odd, chalky taste. Not so bad I can't drink it. But different from before."

Lambert puffed his cigar. "I hadn't noticed anything out of the ordinary."

"It tastes chalky. Not good at all. Not healthy." The old man doddered away, and Lambert studied his sickly stride.

"No," he agreed. "Not healthy at all."

Something was wrong with the old man.

And something was wrong with Daniel Martin Ray.

And Lambert, for the life of him, couldn't decide if possibly the two problems were connected.

24

THEY SET out for Gruber's way station under the stars, and as they rolled along, Reece Sinclair made room for Sam Houston on the Concord's bench seat. With Steve riding Romeo on the left and Lin riding Aggie's Buckskin on the right, the long dark wall of the escarpment was left far behind, and the rock-strewn hardpack gave way to low cut hills. A shallow curving slope brought them around to due east, and with the reins in her control, Reece preferred a quiet drive with a chance to enjoy the star-studded sky.

Houston, snug under a heavy quilt blanket with a flask in hand wasn't about to give her silence or space either one.

"It was during my time living with the Cherokee when I received a tribal name. Raven they called me, which means good fortune, but also wanderer. Both appellations would seem applicable to this old soul in today's circumstances, wouldn't you say so, my dear?"

Reece didn't comment either way, and Houston continued to drone on.

On and on and on.

"After I was the governor of Tennessee, I moved to Texas. This was…oh, round about 1832. I imagine you were little more than a sparkle in your papa's eye, honey." He stretched out his legs as far as he could and took a drink from the flask. "Ah, Lord. Incredible to think I've been a Texan longer than a pretty thing like you has been alive."

My Dear. Honey. Pretty thing.

"You can call me Miss Sinclair, Governor."

"Yes, yes, and you can call me Sam," he said, not taking the hint. "I imagine it's disconcerting for you to suddenly become involved in a scenario of such gravity with personages such as myself. But you must excuse me, a great many of the stories about me are nonsense. I'm no legend. I'm a simple man."

Which prompted a bit of song, "The honest man, tho' e'er sae poor, is king o' men for a that." Houston smiled. "From the poet, Robert Burns," he said. "I like to think of myself as an honest man."

With sour breath and an unstoppable ego, thought Reece.

Houston moved his hand to her knee. "I do appreciate all you're doing for me," he said.

And there he was with the touching.

Reece politely picked up the old man's hand and put it back into his lap. His wide blue eyes showed amusement in the moonlight.

"You're something of a legend yourself, you know," Houston told her. "You and this Concord. Between the two of us, tell me how you lured Ranger Jarret into your abolitionist cause?"

"Ranger Lin Jarret can think and speak for himself."

"Most times, I imagine it's true. But in the presence of a lovely damsel like yourself, I'm afraid the best of us would find our faculties, uh…challenged."

Reece feigned embarrassment. "To say such a thing. And you, a married man."

"Don't misunderstand me, Reece. My Margaret is my life. My children are the future. I would bend heaven and hell for them."

"Then you already know our motivation. It's the same with Lin and me."

"You have children?"

"No, of course not. But we're working for the future. A place where all men and women are free."

Houston let out a long exhale and situated himself more comfortably under his blanket.

"I'm working every day to preserve the Union."

"But not emancipation."

"You may not have noticed, my dear, but I'm not a young man anymore. I have only so much energy for contentious issues. I'll take them one at a time."

"Then you're only half right." Reece not so gently pushed away his wandering hand. "And half wrong."

"You have no idea the hornet's nest you're stirring up with your running about. If it wasn't for Steve Gardner and Jim Douglas speaking up for you as they have..."

"What?"

Houston waved the query away, but Reece pressed him.

"What would have happened if it wasn't for Gardner and Douglas speaking up for me?"

"Dear heart, there's very little goes on in Texas I'm not aware of. The blood of this place rushes through my own veins. The whispers of her every wind pass my ears."

Reece was confused. "If you know so much about us, you must know you can trust us? Especially Lin Jarret. He's one of your Texas Rangers."

"But his uncle is Oscar Bruhn. Hardly a trust-worthy gentleman."

"Lin is nothing like his uncle."

"Whatever the case may be," Houston said. "I pardoned the man just before we adjourned to the cabin."

"You pardoned Oscar Bruhn? What in God's green earth were you thinking?"

Reece almost stopped the team in its tracks. The man who almost single-handedly conspired with a Cortinista to topple her father's rancho...was free?

Reece could barely contain her anger...or her voice. "Lin and I were almost killed bringing his uncle to justice. We sat at his trial and saw him dragged away to jail. Now you tell me he's been pardoned?"

Houston patted her leg. Then he took a long pull from his flask and offered it to her. "Here you go, sweet thing. You may need this more than me."

Reece shoved the flask away.

"It contains deer hoof shavings. Guaranteed to help prevent influenza and rheumatism."

"You do know Oscar Bruhn works for the Ivory Compass?"

Houston took another nip and stuck out his lower lip. "Compromises might have been made. Favors exchanged."

"Favors?"

"Well, it didn't do me any good, I can tell you as much." Now it was Houston's turn to spread his arms and raise his voice. "You see where making deals got me. You see where it got all of us. People put out of their homes. Towns burned."

"You knew about the fires? About the Daltons and their plans to sow terror in North Texas?"

"I knew there was the potential for mischief. We

did our best to waylay these ruffians' plans. I conceded to certain demands—"

"Freeing Oscar Bruhn."

"And in return, the Dalton Company assured us a peaceful summer." He laughed bitterly and the chuckle became a cough. "Instead, we find out there's a plot to kill me. We had no idea about it until the first attempt —a grubby little man with a derringer pistol.

"Gardner intervened, and it was then he whisked us away to our cabin to strategize."

"After Bruhn had been pardoned," Reece said.

Houston nodded. "These men are not to be trusted."

"Fancy the thought."

"I had hoped otherwise."

Reece wanted to smack the old man across the head.

That the Hero of San Jacinto could be so...so...

"Naïve?" Houston said. "You need to work on your poker face, missy. I can see what you're thinking. How could a veteran of my experience be hoodwinked by a gaggle of foolish young idealists? If it makes you feel better, I stay awake at night wondering the same thing myself."

Reece let the team pull them eastward through a long, lonely valley. She chose her words carefully before answering.

"A quarter century ago, you defeated Santa Anna on a plain beside the San Jacinto River. The Mexicans made a strategic blunder. You took advantage of it. Remember the Alamo, you said. Remember La Bahia. My father was there."

"He was one of my men?"

"Under Captain Billingsley."

190

"The spineless worm-skinned rascal," Houston said. "Er...Billingsley, I mean. Not your father."

"I was brought up to believe in the Hero of San Jacinto."

Houston laughed bitterly. "As was I."

"You said before, you aren't a legend. Understand, sir, you were once. To me. To my father."

"We seem to have traded places. Now you're the legend, Miss Sinclair."

"If it's true, I can only hope to live up to it."

Houston put the flask to his lips, then took it away without taking a drink. He thrust it under his blanket. "We all need hope," he said.

Ahead, Lin Jarret waved in the pre-dawn light and circled the buckskin around, back to the Concord. When he got close enough to converse, Reece pulled up on the reins, slowing the team.

As dawn approached, the Ranger rode straight and tall in his saddle, inspiring confidence. Whether Governor Sam Houston trusted Lin or not, Reece would give up her life for the Ranger. And he would do the same for her.

She wondered if Sam, for all his haughty pronouncements, would do the same?

"You been drivin' for a couple hours. Looks to be a bit more hilly ahead. I'll take over if you want."

Ha! He wanted his turn at riding beside the Governor.

"I'd appreciate the rest," she said, with an irony he wouldn't understand.

She had hoped to ride beside a legend.

Apparently, the Hero of San Jacinto was missing in action.

LIN JARRET WATCHED the predawn sky fade from gray to orange to blue.

Reins in hand, it was where he'd always wanted to be, atop the bench, a strong team in front of him. Reece riding shotgun by his side.

Only a short way ahead, alert and straight in the saddle, Steve Gardner rode point. During the night he'd occasionally forayed a mile or two ahead, surveyed the way, returned with news of the route. Avoid the swale here, take the left fork there.

They made good time traveling at night, and if Sam Houston's ride was uncomfortable enough to force him into the cabin for a nap, Lin couldn't help it.

"I had hoped to chat with the old badger," he told Reece. "You spent some time with him. What's he like?"

Reece ground her back teeth together and tried to think of a polite answer.

"Exasperating," was the best she could come up with. "Not what I expected," was her way of being polite.

Cresting the arid ridge above Gruber's three frame structures, Lin pulled down the brim of his hat to block the rising sun. He drew the animals to a stop, waiting as Steve approached in rapid gallop. Romeo wheeled around and drew his rider into a parallel position with the Concord.

The sun reflected off the tomahawk on his belt and lit his long, raven hair from behind.

"All's quiet," Steve said in response to Lin's wordless query. "The way it appears, everybody's sleeping."

The side door of the coach popped open, and Houston stepped out of the cabin in shirtsleeves and braces. Sans coat, vest, and cravat, he looked twenty pounds lighter and ten years younger.

The morning sun highlighted his ruddy complexion, and he stroked the whiskers on his chin. "What do we know?"

"You seem well rested, Governor," Lin said.

Houston motioned toward Reece. "Miss Sinclair gave me some new things to think about," he said. "A fresh perspective."

"She'll keep you on the straight and narrow," Lin said.

"It's what I gathered. Not a woman to trifle with."

"Yes, well…"

"Steve's just back from inspecting the way station," Reece said.

"Quiet as a saloon on Sunday morning," Steve said.

A warning tingle crawled along the base of Lin's skull. "I can't imagine such a thing," he said. "Not on a Saturday, especially. Gruber's runs a mercantile here along with the stage service."

"Lin's right," Houston said. "Settlers from all around ought to be stocking up for the week."

"Something's not right."

After trading horses, Lin and Reece had left Gruber's Station a day and a half ago under a dusky, evening-star dotted sky. Even as total darkness approached, the place had been a bustling den of activity. The Grubers, Zeke and Nelda, catered to customers while the three Gruber kids ran back and forth after the horses. The place employed two or three additional men. At least one of them would've been out of bed before the sun.

They stared down into the settlement, and Lin thought he saw a flicker of movement at the door of a long, one-story pole barn. "Looks like Nelda Gruber."

While they watched, a short woman with a long dress tramped across the open dirt yard from the structure to the two-story frame dining room stagecoach station which doubled as the Gruber's residence. She held the front of her dress up, waist-high to create a hollow basket.

"Bringing in eggs?" Houston said.

"Appears so," Lin said.

"Nothing out of the ordinary there," Reece said.

"Something...," Steve said.

Lin waited in the vast silence.

Nelda Gruber went inside, shutting the door behind her. Everything remained quiet.

"Too quiet," Steve said. "If she's getting eggs...why no chickens clucking? No rooster crowing?"

"There were chickens the other night. Around a dozen. More."

"Where are they now?"

Lin turned the question over in his mind. Possessing a healthy brood, nobody in these parts would rid themselves of their chickens. Good laying hens were worth their keep times two, for eggs and for chicks. Plus, the old hens made for good stews.

But Steve was right. There was no sound.

And when he and Reece had stopped before, the chickens had free rein of the dirt yard. Now the space was empty.

Houston shrugged. "It's your call, boys. But frankly, I'm an hour past my breakfast time as it is." He stroked his chin, and the bristly whiskers made a noise. "And I could use a shave."

"I don't like it," Lin said.

"We can go around the place," Steve said. "I don't think anybody's seen us."

"Too late," Reece said.

While they were talking, a lone figure had come from the house and stood watching them from the yard.

"One of the kids," Lin said.

The boy waved.

"In for a penny, in for a pound," Houston said. "Let's go get some breakfast."

The boy was more animated now, waving them in, jumping up and down.

"Too eager?" Steve said.

"Too eager."

Houston's good-natured chuckle had a bit of the knife's edge. "I know you two think you're responsible for my safety, but I'll be damned if you'll talk about me—"

"Not you, sir, you misunderstand us," Lin said. "It's the boy. The boy's too eager for us to roll in."

"Let's go around," Reece said.

Lin had hitched the Dalton Company mares in the lead. Crossing in front of the team on Romeo, Steve cut a perpendicular course away from Gruber's Station. "We'll navigate toward the hills yonder and cut through the brush there to the east. I figure the route will take us closer to the Brazos anyway. We can camp somewhere along one of the tributary creeks tonight and get water. Then on past Quincy and up to Lambert's Ferry."

"Not too close to Quincy," Lin said.

Having heard all about Lin's adventures with the Brushy Creek gang, Steve grinned. "No, we'll keep a wide berth around the Brushy."

Lin agreed to the plan and, once the governor was back inside the coach, he steered the horses from the Gruber trail and cut cross-country behind Romeo.

They were in higher country here, leaving the depression with Gruber's place behind. Ahead, the landscape flattened out to an anemic beige plain with dapples of dark brush and gnarled trees. Except for one final slope, the way was clear all the way to the horizon.

Lin followed Steve's lead but couldn't shake the nagging feeling at the base of his spine. Something was off. Was there a faint whiff of tobacco smoke or horse flop, a murmur of voices or extra set of hooves on the sod?

Several times, he spun to the left or right on the bench, his head on full alert swivel.

Once he thought he saw a shadow duck behind a ridge.

Twice, he saw startled birds take flight for no discernable reason.

The next time Steve glanced over his shoulder Lin signaled him back to the Concord.

"You get the impression we're not alone out here?"

Steve nodded. "Wondered how long it would take you to notice. I figure there's ten or twelve of them— back less than half a mile." He gestured off toward the hills behind them. "They'll need to make their move soon. Not much cover left now that we're back in flat country."

"Comanche?"

"Not like you mean. Not Indians."

"Comancheros," Reece said.

Then Romeo kicked up a ribbon of dust, and Steve veered hard to the right as a gunshot pierced the sky ahead.

A whirling cloud of dust rolled around the base of the hill ahead, and the roar of a cyclone rose into the air.

"Horses and riders," yelled Reece, loud enough for Houston to hear.

"Ambush," Lin said, hauling back on the four-in-hand. "Get your scattergun ready."

There was at least a dozen of them, dressed in sombreros and brightly colored serapes with fringes. A few of the men wore furry Mexican chapels.

They all carried carbines or wheel-guns held high. One of the men pulled his trigger, launching a lead ball toward the moon.

The lead Comanchero wore all black: an ebony outfit with silver conchos on the side of his pants and a dark cape with a flat, wide-brimmed hat. No less dark was his steed, a fire-eyed stallion whose hooves slashed into the sod and pitched dust high into the air.

Steve pounded back around the coach, coming back alongside to position himself beside Lin. He gripped a Remington .44 caliber pistol. "I know this one," he said. "Robin Alexander."

"Probably been trailing us since Gruber's place," Lin said.

"Waiting for an opportunity to jump us," Reece said.

Houston poked his head out of the coach. "I'd say we're outnumbered, folks."

"We can't outrun 'em," Lin said. "Or outshoot 'em."

All they could do was wait on the side of the hill as the thundering horde spread out around them, guns gleaming in the morning light.

Lin and Reece rose from the bench, weapons at the ready, and Steve kept one hand on his tomahawk, the other holding his pistol across his heart.

The man in black rode his rambunctious horse forward, jarring Lin's team into a prancing sidestep.

"Whoa, Meg," he said, slapping at them lightly with the leathers, "quiet now. Quiet."

The Comanchero was ruggedly handsome with a square, clean shaven jaw and eyebrows so dark they appeared to be drawn with grease paint. His teeth were exceptionally white, and he wore his hat askew on the back of his head. A charming rogue, with venomous, deadly eyes.

"*Hola, amigos,*" he said. "*¿Como estas esta hermosa manana?*"

How are you, this beautiful morning?

Now positioned ahead of the team by several yards, Steve paused a beat before answering. Then he launched a stream of tobacco into the dust.

"*Quien quiere saber?*" Who wants to know?

"*Tu respondes primero.*" You first.

"No," Steve said.

The rogue laughed out loud, and Steve asked, "*¿Ustedes son comancheros?*"

"Why do you say so?" said the rogue, switching to English.

"You're familiar to me. Dressing in black. Your cape. You are Robin Alexander?"

"My name has preceded me." His smile was mocking. "But I don't know you, amigo."

"No, you don't."

"I'm asking who you are."

"I'm asking you to move aside so we can be on our way."

Alexander remained still while his men fidgeted behind him.

Lin thought the Comanchero leader was too content. Too sure of himself.

"We have no business with you," Lin said.

Alexander seemed to notice Reece for the first time, and he sat up a bit straighter. "I wouldn't be so sure," he said. Turning back to Steve, he said, "We thought you might be looking for Gruber's station."

"Reckon not."

"Didn't you see our boy waving you in?"

"Your boy?"

"You would decline a polite invitation?"

"You don't mind me saying so," Steve said, "y'all don't look so polite."

Robin Alexander's laugh was longer and louder than before, but when it stopped, there wasn't a trace of mirth in his tone.

"You will follow us to Gruber's station, amigo. Once there, we can break bread, drink a toast." He let his eyes wander over Reece's tight-fitting shirt, "We may find many things to do together."

"We'd prefer to be on our way."

Alexander's tone cut off all further conversation. "Come with me. Or my men will cut the three of you to ribbons."

"Not before we take at least half of you with us," Lin said.

Steve agreed, and his smile was malicious. "And you'll go first, Robin."

Alexander nodded. "So it will be," he said. "But…ah, one thing."

The Comanchero held up his finger.

"Yeah? What one thing?" Steve said.

Through those damned snow-white teeth, Alexander said, "You and I might sleep with the dead tonight, amigo, but while we slumber, my men will have no choice but to roast your Governor Sam Houston on a spit."

The morning sun climbed over the hill behind him, and Alexander said, "Shall we go?"

26

GRUBER'S STATION was quiet all day.

The normal Saturday routine had been disrupted, commandeered by Robin Alexander's traders, and the Gruber family showed no backbone whatsoever. Everybody knew a ruckus might soon ensue, but for the time being, everybody peacefully made ready in their own way.

Nelda Gruber continued to stock shelves behind the mercantile counter. The three kids were kept busy sweeping the floor and polishing the counters and table. At the cook stove, the oldest Gruber girl served lunch, then tended a fire and boiling water.

Zeke Gruber mostly moped around with his shoulders hunched and his hands thrust deep in his pockets.

Lin understood the man's reluctance to fight, but he felt sick at his fake, professed remorse.

"I am so sorry, friend, so sorry indeed," said Gruber with his tufts of cotton white hair poking out underneath his cap and his fat nose purple with booze-broke veins. "The Comancheros showed here around midnight looking for you. Alexander threatened my children. He threatened my wife. There was nothing I could do, you understand. Nothing at all."

"You said it all before," Steve said.

"You told them Reece and I had stopped here on our way to Snakebite Canyon," Lin said.

"Ah-yuh. He was especially interested in where you were going. Why you were passing through. He likes the buckskin you left—the one belonging to the sheriff in Quincy."

"I'll bet he does," Lin said. "Do you still have the horse?"

"Yes, out in the corral."

"Alexander's probably figuring out a way to sell it back to Aggie," Reece said.

Lin braced Gruber with another question. "You told Alexander we were going to Snakebite Canyon, and you told him we'd be back through."

"Yes. But you gotta believe me, Jarret, I had no choice at all. Why, you shoulda heard the outright nasty language the dirty skunk used around my Nelda."

From her place behind the counter, Nelda stopped stocking shelves long enough to look up with an embarrassed face. "He's telling you the truth, Mr. Jarret."

"Otherwise, I never woulda uttered a word about you," said Gruber.

Lin brushed past the whining tub of lard to pull back a chair in the middle of the shadowy dining room. The day had wasted away and there was no sign of Alexander. Only his soldiers stood outside, guarding over the building's door and windows.

Outside, the morning sun was climbing toward noon.

The wait was interminable.

Letting himself fall in behind the long central table, Lin said, "Save your excuses, Zeke. You have no idea what you've done."

"I expect I don't," he said. "I mean, didn't. I mean...I do now. Now I see you sittin' here, Mr. Governor, sir."

Across the table from Lin, Sam Houston held his tongue.

Reece walked from the back of the room, past Steve Gardner who was pacing back and forth, and pulled out a chair next to Lin. Houston partially stood in deference to her, then sat back down.

Gruber stood by the wall and picked at the faded pink wallpaper with an itchy finger. "I guess I've always been seventy-eleven kinds of stupid."

If Lin was impatient with the station keeper, Steve Gardner was outright furious. Coming forward he flipped one of the three-legged stools over, then brought the seat down on the tabletop with a crash. "No, sir," Steve hollered. "Stupid is newborn calves or squirrels on the road. Stupid is in the head and can be forgiven. What you got lives in the guts. It's sick and yellow and is never forgiven."

"You're a coward, Mr. Gruber," Reece said. The accusation cut the musty store smell like a gunshot and forced Nelda to suck in her breath behind the counter.

Lin noticed the old lady didn't defend Zeke.

"I oughta pound the worthless out of you," Steve threatened.

Lin assured Gruber, "He would too, if he thought it would get us back on the road."

"I swear to God, I didn't know you all were carrying the governor."

"But just to keep things straight, you have no problem weaseling on your friends and customers?"

For the first time since Alexander had led them to the station dining room and store, Houston spoke, "You all are fishing in water already gone bad. We need to look ahead to the future."

Lin shook his head. "You're right, sir, of course. All this belly-achin' ain't getting us nowhere."

"We're open to ideas," Reece said. "You got any?"

Thinking back to earlier this morning, Lin remembered immediately upon pulling into Gruber's yard, the kid they'd seen before ran out to meet them. As Robin Alexander had declared, it was his own boy. "Follow me," he'd said. "You stay here until we come get you."

The four Hellbenders had ignored the summons until Robin dismounted and approached the Concord, twin Remington pistols in hand. "You listen to Paco," he said. "Get down off there and into the station."

Nothing had changed since Lin and Reece had been there before.

Gruber's place was a simple compound of four low-slung frame buildings, each in various states of disrepair, but no worse for the Comancheros having been there.

Having missed the Overland Route by several miles, Gruber's was a secondary stop on a seldom used highway. The main station and store, home to the Gruber family, was the longest structure, measuring more than 30 feet by 20 with three rooms inside. Behind, and to the west, were a storage shed, and pole barn for the horses. Perpendicular to these was another, shorter version of the main building, with glass windows and a heavy door.

Once he'd ushered the travelers into the dark, cool interior of the station, Paco and the other Comancheros vanished, leaving Lin and the others alone with the Gruber family for the remainder of the day.

Now Lin stood up and braced Gruber with a question. "Where's Alexander now? What're they planning to do with us?"

The fat man's jowls wagged, and his voice rose an octave. "How would I know?"

Steve pulled the tomahawk from his belt and carried it to Lin. "Sounds like tubby needs some incentive to answer the question."

Gruber shook his head. "Keep this maniac away from me," he told Lin.

"I don't think so," Lin said. "Not unless you start to talk. I'll ask you one last time, where's Robin Alexander?"

Gruber started to blubber, and Steve put the axe-head directly under his chin, pressing into the fat layers surrounding his neck. "You got ten seconds."

"Pellum," he stammered. "Small settlement about five miles north."

"I've heard of it."

"They've got wire there to and from the east. A telegraph."

"You think Alexander is up there talking to somebody?"

"C-could be."

"What are they going to do with us?"

Gruber began to openly weep.

"Enough, Steven. Enough." Houston's voice was firm and controlling. "It's obvious the fellow had no more idea of our fate than his own."

With visible reluctance the Mountain Man backed away from Gruber, nailing him to the wall with an awful glare.

In spite of Houston's pronouncement, Gruber

talked. "I-I guess maybe I do have some idea about all this after all," he began. "Th-there's rumor you all had Mr. Houston out this way. S-some folks said it was a joke, but some took it serious, knowing the Daltons were after you."

"Sounds like the secret conspiracy isn't so secret," Houston said.

"Depends on the kinds of people you mean," said Gruber. "It ain't no secret to the bad men. The Daltons want your head on a stick."

Lin said, "And you're just the one to give it to them, eh, Gruber?"

"The good Lord knows I had nothing to do with it. Alexander knew all about you and the Daltons before he ever showed up here."

"So he plans to ransom me off to the Dalton Company? He's up in Pellum right now making the deal. Sorta sum things up for you?"

"I-I s-spose it does," said Gruber. "But I don't think they'll hurt you none. Mr. Alexander has never been about hurting anybody. It's mostly about the money with him."

"You sound pretty chummy, the two of you," Reece said.

"We've traded with Mr. Alexander a good many times," said Nelda. "He's never gone so far as to lock us up in our own home." Her voice carried more than a little bit of irritation. "I'm not thinking we'll do business with him in the future."

Houston spoke, "Once Mr. Alexander has made his arrangements to deliver me to the Daltons, I'm sure he'll return with his demands. Until then, I for one would enjoy a cup of coffee. Ma'am?"

Nelda Gruber straightened at the query and sent an imploring wave to the girl at the stove.

"Now, if everyone would join me here for some further discussion—reasoned discussion, I'd appreciate it." Lin figured he was speaking mostly to Steve and Reece.

Houston's calm demeanor had defused some of the room's explosive tension. Steve put the stool upright on the floor and sat down with a heavy sigh.

Before long, the Gruber girl carried four steaming mugs of coffee to the table.

"We've seen more difficult action than this, you and me," Houston told Steve. "I'll wager Jarret and Miss Sinclair have been in equally dire straits."

"We told you about our turn of events in Quincy," Lin said.

"At least there's not a hang rope waiting outside," Reece said.

"Only a crazed gun-horde guarding every exit," Steve said.

"Instead of emoting, we ought to take action," Houston said. "Miss Sinclair and I had a fine, long talk during our overnight ride, and she opened my eyes to a few things. Mostly, she reminded me sitting around and waiting wasn't much of a strategy."

"We did plenty of waiting around back at the cabin," Steve said.

"Precisely," Houston said. "Neither will we compromise."

Reece smiled at Houston's declaration as he continued.

"I shouldn't think a sunbaked gun horde—as you call them—has any more cunning than the four of us."

"Agreed," Lin said. "What do you propose?"

"As we were being led in here, Alexander's men parked the stagecoach over beside the pole barn. Unless they're more ambitious than they seem, I'll wager the team is still hitched up, the wagon is probably ready to go."

Houston was right. It was hard to imagine the Comancheros bothering to unhook the horses or give them any more than the most superficial care at this point.

"First, they need to deal with me," Houston said. He sipped his coffee and asked Zeke Gruber to join them.

Gruber dragged his boots across the floor. "I-I want to apologize for my actions, sir. I haven't been a good host—"

"Yes, yes," Houston said, impatiently. "Hush now, Gruber. We need your help."

"We do?" Steve said.

"Indeed, we do," Houston said. "If we're going to get out of this scrape, we'll need every hand on deck, and a good dose of luck." He stood up next to Gruber and examined him up and down, side to side. "The station master and I are roughly the same size, wouldn't you say, Miss Sinclair?"

Reece said so.

"I believe we might share the same tailor, Mr. Gruber."

Lin understood what Houston intended to do. "Alexander will see through such a ruse immediately. You are not switching clothes with Gruber."

Houston ignored the outburst and turned to Reece.

Whatever truths they shared riding together on the Concord had forged an alliance of equals between them. Houston's trust, previously reserved only for Steve Gardner, now firmly extended to include Reece. The governor's eyes sparkled when he talked to her.

"Isn't it true you have employed your Concord wagon in...ah, certain activities which might be deemed undesirable by our government?"

"I'm an abolitionist, sir. If you're asking whether or not I've carried runaway slaves in my coach, I will not confirm nor deny."

"Under normal circumstances, a man in my office might be pressured to act on such an admission," Houston said. "But these are far from normal circumstances."

Lin understood the banter was more for the benefit of the Grubers than anybody else.

Reece seemed happy enough to join the old man's theatrics.

"What in blazes are you two talking about, sir?" said Gruber.

"I've been led to understand Miss Sinclair's Concord has some special attributes. Custom built cubby holes…"

"There are hidden compartments in the floor of the Concord," Reece said. "You're suggesting we spirit you away inside such a compartment?"

"If I can get out to the coach, disguised as Gruber. You'll go with me."

"Dressed as Nelda," Reece said.

"What about us?" Lin said.

Houston queried Gruber. "How many men would you estimate are with Alexander, and how many are here?"

"He usually rides with no fewer than five men."

"Looks to me like we only have five or six here, watching us," Houston said. Then to Lin and Steve: "Are you men up to such odds?"

"We are indeed," Lin said.

Houston removed his coat and handed it to Gruber. "Then let's get cracking."

GRUBER'S STATION was like a church before a wedding.

Quiet, peaceful, a ruckus soon in the offing.

Lin and Steve sat peaceably at the long table, calmly anticipating their part in Houston's plan of escape. Between them, Zeke Gruber slouched without a word in Sam Houston's hat and coat. The coffee in their cups was cold.

Sitting on a stool at the mercantile counter, Nelda Gruber, visibly uncomfortable in Reece Sinclair's shirt and pants, hushed the children playing in the corner of the room.

As soon as evening fell, Reece and Houston, dressed as Nelda and Zeke, had successfully exited the station under the cover of darkness.

They had been fortunate.

Robin Alexander and his side men had yet to return from Pellum.

Lin figured it would take Reece ten minutes to check the horses and get the Governor ensconced in the floor's hidden compartment.

It had already been five minutes too long.

As he eyed his pocket watch, he ticked off dozens of things which might have gone wrong.

At any moment, Alexander could appear and uncover the deceit before Reece set out with the wagon.

Or maybe the Comancheros had disabled the wagon in some fashion.

Maybe they had already discovered the false floor in the bottom of the coach and ruined it.

Getting away from Gruber's Station was only part of the victory. Escape still wasn't assured.

Even if Reece made it back to the trail, the coach might be stopped—and not just by Comancheros. There were plenty of other owlhoots out roaming around. Indians, vigilante gangs, and plain, old-fashioned road agents were continually on the prowl.

If it came to such a thing, Lin hoped the seemingly empty coach would be allowed to continue with the governor well tucked away under the false floor.

But maybe not.

While he waited, Lin made a casual stroll around the interior walls of the three-room station for the tenth time. Walking helped burn off tension, and it allowed him to keep track of the five men watching over them.

Outside the front door, the guards were two burly middle-aged men who seemed fairly drowsy. This sleepiness had worked to Reece and Houston's advantage in sneaking out to the Concord.

When the wagon rolled away, the guards' attention would be split. Lin didn't figure those two to be much trouble to outshoot.

Additionally, there were three more guards.

Those men were Steve's problem.

One man stood beside each window at opposite

ends of the structure, and one covered the rear of the building. Standing inside one of the back windows, in a room the Grubers used for sleeping, Lin watched the slender young Comanchero stride back and forth at attention.

He hoped they wouldn't be forced to kill the man because this fellow took his job a lot more seriously than the two out front. Lin admired his dedication—if little else.

Lin took out his watch and held it near a lantern to read. Twenty minutes had passed, yet there was no sound from the pole barn.

Even as he snapped the lid shut on the timepiece, a clattering of hoofs and the familiar turn of the Concord's wheels sounded from outside.

Success!

Now for action.

Lin bounded to the rear window in time to see the slender guard cut around the house to the left. Launching himself forward into the dining room, Lin saw Steve was already at the front door.

They escaped the house together and faced four guards in the splash of lantern light fanning out across the threshold. "I've got the duffers," Lin said, immediately drawing a bead on a Comanchero who lifted a rifle to his shoulder.

The single-shot percussion carbine was unwieldy in the big man's hands, and it was clear he wasn't overly experienced with it. Lin pressed the trigger on his Colt, blowing a chunk of the guard's shoulder apart, forcing him to drop the gun with a scream.

"You'll live," Lin said, under his breath. "Maybe."

There was no time for guilt, he told himself. These men were out to kill him.

From the corner of his eye, Lin watched his friend confront more attackers.

As the two younger guards ran parallel with the front of the house, Steve swung his Remington into place and slammed a lead ball home into the first guard's chest.

"Like shootin' coyotes in a trap," Steve said.

At the same time, the second guard, the slender one from behind the house, popped off a shot, catching Steve across the scalp. Lin saw a sizzling line of blood appear and the Mountain Man staggered.

"But which one of us is the coyote?" Lin said, drilling his second attacker between the eyes.

Then a shadow flashed between them, and Steve's young guard was struggling with his tunic.

The guard fell to his side with a wailing, scrabbling appeal to his chest. Lin saw Steve's tomahawk half-buried there and said a silent prayer.

Lin caught a glimpse of the Concord's lantern-lit outline at the edge of the road, pounding away from them, hell bent for leather with Reece at the reins.

Then an obscene oath forced him to whirl around and fire the Colt point blank into the fifth guard. In a cloud of blue smoke, the man fell over flat on his back, kicked once, and died without a whimper.

Lin stepped back, feeling the rush of energy spur him on.

All five guards were on the ground. One of them, the one Lin shot in the shoulder, was still alive and rolling about. He pitched to one side, then another, reaching for a dropped carbine.

Lin stepped into the fuzzy darkness just as the wounded man got his hand on the rifle.

He brought it up and around, but not fast enough

to avoid Lin's vicious kick to his jaw. With a soft moan, he succumbed to unconsciousness.

Lin dusted his hands and looked around.

With nothing more to shoot at, he ran away from the house toward the road, watching the Concord escape with Sam Houston hidden away in its guts.

A wave of emotion rushed over him.

They'd done it.

Reece had escaped with Houston. He and Steve had survived.

Now they had only to mount up on a pair of horses and rejoin the Concord further up the road. Steve said he knew a couple Comanche trails they could follow to the Red River—trails Alexander hopefully wouldn't know about.

Lin rejoined the Mountain Man in front of the station house, but he wasn't alone.

"Oh, my, my, my," said Nelda Gruber, over and over as she surveyed the quintet of bodies sprawled out in the cabin light.

Three bodies were twisted in violent repose. With bloody holes in their torso or heads, they lay with eyes open and pained expressions. The gruesome victim of Steve's axe had a grisly gash in the front of his tunic and, though the only survivor of the melee was still breathing, his shoulder looked like chopped meat.

A sorry scene to add to the legacy of Gruber Station.

"Children, no," said Zeke. "Get back inside. You don't need to see this." Then, dressed in Sam Houston's coat, he looked directly at Lin. "Goddamn you for bringing this terror to our household."

Steve dabbed at the blood on his forehead with a handkerchief and laughed out loud as Lin snarled up his lip.

"Goddamn me?" Lin said. "Goddamn you! If you had kept your mouth shut, none of this would've happened. You're the..." Lin couldn't make the words come out. He turned to Steve. "Can you believe this man?"

Steve responded with a short, derisive laugh. "Yellow-bellies are always mad because they get the clean-up detail." He pressed the hanky to his forehead.

"Are you alright?"

"Yeah. I'll live."

Gruber pushed into the conversation. "More than you can say for these men."

Lin stepped into the heavy man's personal space. "Don't you see what happened here, man? You're damn lucky this isn't your children laying here. If you don't wise up, next time it will be."

"More likely it will be if we can't get Houston back to Rimrock to deliver his speech," Steve said. "Everybody knows war is coming. Some of us are doing all we can to stop it."

"Stop it?" said Gruber. "Seems to me you bastards are starting it."

"You butchers," said Nelda. "If I had known you were going to—"

Nelda's mouth clapped shut when Lin punched her husband straight in the nose. "Both of you shut the hell up," he said.

"She's right about one thing," Steve said. "These cadavers make for rotten decoration."

"Somebody's liable to be upset when he sees 'em," Lin said.

"We better get moving."

"Sheriff Aggie's buckskin is in the barn. I'll take him, you take one of the Gruber mounts."

"Damn horse thieves," muttered Gruber through a bubbling of blood.

"You want another sock?" Lin said.

Gruber's silence indicated he did not.

Lin and Steve rushed toward the barn.

"Let's hurry," Lin said. "We don't want Reece getting too far ahead of us."

"Not much chance of it will happen," a voice said, and they both whirled at the sound.

Sitting beside the cold, flaking wood of the barn was Reece Sinclair.

"Somebody was hiding inside the barn," she explained, "laying for us, I guess. As soon as I got the governor secured in the secret compartment, they knocked me over the head."

"But we saw you drive out of here," Lin said.

Reece shook her head and put a palm to her temple. "Owtch," she said, sinking down into a seated position on the ground.

She placed a hand on the barn to steady herself and said, "No, you saw somebody drive out of here. It wasn't me."

"But the governor?"

"Was inside the Concord. Yeah."

"Aw, damn," Steve said.

"You mean, Sam Houston—"

Reece gave a sleepy nod as she massaged her scalp. "Yeah. He's been taken away."

EVEN BY MOONLIGHT, the trail wasn't hard to follow.

No one else had traversed the open range above Gruber's Station since the Concord had spirited away the governor, and the iron-rimmed wheels left a distinctive impression in the soft topsoil.

Having shucked the station-master's shirt, coat, and trousers, Steve again wore a belted loin cloth and boots. His long hair was loose on his shoulders, and the Indian beads and twin snake rattles he wore around his neck clicked together as he knelt to the ground.

"They're headed north and east, all right," Steve said, squeezing up a pinch of moonlit silver road dust to toss in the air for a barometer. He watched the cloud dissipate on the breeze and clapped his hands together. "And the driver's got the wind with him. They've got a good head start. If we waited until morning, we'd never catch 'em."

He climbed onto the back of Gruber's roan mare, saying, "My bet is they're headed for Pellum."

Beside him, Reece was snippy in the saddle of a

dun-colored gelding. "Your Cherokee tracking skills tell you that?" She too was dressed in her own clothes, but short-tempered since losing Houston to the imposter on the Concord.

Steve didn't know Reece well, but he knew enough about women to keep his mouth shut.

"Gruber said it's where Alexander went," Lin said. "I reckon the Comancheros had already planned to meet up in Pellum with Houston in tow."

Steve nodded. "Gruber also said Alexander went ahead to use the telegraph. To make things ready—but with who? Who was he contactin'?"

"Only name keeps popping up," Lin said. "The Dalton Company."

"Back at the station, Gruber has a map of the region around the Brazos and north," Reece said. "I had a chance to study it yesterday. The Daltons have a plantation not far from here. Just east of Pellum."

"Seems reasonable to expect the Comancheros might take Houston there," Lin said.

Reece offered another opinion. "Or they'll meet the Daltons in Pellum to make their deal. Alexander won't let go of a valuable commodity like Sam Houston without having some gold tickle his palms."

"I'll agree with Reece on this one," Steve said.

"I appreciate the gesture," Reece said.

Steve shrugged with a mischievous grin. "Just givin' the devil her due."

She shot him a dirty look. His return expression said he couldn't help himself.

Reece turned her attention to Lin. "What do you say, Ranger? Do we make a run for Pellum?"

Before he agreed, Lin considered the wheel ruts and the direction they pointed. The air was warm and dry, but the stars glimmered with cold. The column of blue-white smoke rising from the far horizon stood in stark contrast to the blackness of the night sky. What sort of danger were they riding into?

"You smell it?" he said. "Looks like another one of those fires off in the direction we're headed. Wonder if the Concord got caught up in it."

"Maybe the Concord driver started it," Steve said.

"After looking at the map, I'm guessing the smoke is coming from Sunderman's plantation. It's only a couple miles outside Pellum."

Lin said he'd heard of the place. "One of the bigger spreads this side of Quincy."

He held the buckskin's reins lightly. His hands were on the mend, but his fingers and palms were sore after the earlier gunwork. He felt lucky to have Aggie's horse. Assuming they both survived the next few days, Lin was committed to returning the horse to the Quincy sheriff.

They'd promised Gruber the same courtesy. Naturally the fat man had complained about the loan of the dun and the roan, but when invited along to keep track of them, he declined the invitation.

Lin couldn't imagine why.

In readying himself for the journey, it had taken all the dexterity Lin could muster to charge each of the six cylinders in his Colt with black powder and prime the firing nipples with percussion caps.

Reece and the Mountain Man were likewise armed, her with a second Colt, and Steve with his Remy and tomahawk.

The image of the young soldier with that damned axe buried in his sternum slid through Lin's mind, and he shuddered.

As had always been the case, there was a side to

Steve Gardner wilder than Lin imagined. The Comanche side. The Cherokee side.

Probably also true of Sam Houston, who had also lived with the Indians. Maybe the reason the old man and Steve got along so well.

Lin wondered how the old man was holding up out there. Wherever he was.

One thing was sure. Houston would need all the wild strength he could muster for this ordeal.

They all would.

"We're agreed then," Lin said. "We're well-armed, we've got water, and we know where we're going. Let's not waste any more time getting the governor back on the road to Rimrock."

Spurring the buckskin into a gallop, he led Reece and Steve toward the tower of smoke.

THEY FOLLOWED the trail of the carriage wheels and when they arrived at Sunderman's plantation they found a burned-out disaster lined with broke down, tangled fencing.

A bottom land swath of cotton was nothing but a choked spread of shriveled, black polyps and horizontal tapestries of moonlit fog settled over the rough, crackling surface.

The scorched remains of a once-prosperous crop.

The rancid thick stink of ruined vegetation and charred earth stuck in Lin's throat, and even the cooperative buckskin balked when Lin gigged him along the hacienda's pea-gravel covered lane.

Two stories tall, with a grand wrap-around porch, the house appeared to have escaped the worst of the fires, but two nearby sheds were reduced to smoldering skeletons, and a red-orange blaze still churned in the adjacent orchard.

"Hey, there! Hup. Get on!" Voices sounded through the night from a dozen beleaguered men with buckets, picks, and shovels. "We need men at the mulberry trees."

Smoke blotted out the starlight, and the moon was a frail lamp behind a hazy lens.

If anybody noticed the Hellbenders' approach, they didn't let on. Busy with the business of preserving what was left of the home place, Sunderman plantation ignored its visitors until they were past the house.

Lin steered his horse toward a pull-off under a pair of cottonwood trees where a young African girl sat on a stump, cradling a cat in her lap. Reece and Steve came behind. When the three dismounted, the cat stiffened in the girl's grasp, but didn't jump away.

"Looks like you had some trouble here," Lin said, by way of greeting. "How can we help?"

The girl's face was blank as she studied each of them in turn. Then she tossed the cat to the ground and stood up. Brushing her long dress out, she rose to a stature just under five feet, but confidence made her seem taller.

Her voice was warmly deep and calm, but indifferent. "And who might you be to offer help?"

Lin introduced himself, Reece, and Steve. "What's your name?"

"Ernestine Bell," she said.

"Tell us what happened?" Reece said.

"Ain't nothin' you can't see," said Ernestine. "Fire done took the place."

"How did it start?"

"Beg pardon, ma'am?"

Reece repeated the query.

Ernestine couldn't hide the mocking tone of her voice. "How'd you think it start?"

"I don't understand."

"You think lightnin' come down out of the clear night sky? You think maybe the devil shot up a mountain?" She put a hand on her hip and shook her head. "Or do you think maybe somebody done started it on purpose."

"Did you see somebody start it?"

"Naw," she said. "But I know what's goin' on. I know we all got troubles."

"What about Pellum?"

Ernestine turned to the east, nodding. "I guess Pellum been burnin' up too."

Lin caught Reece's worried expression and held it for a beat. If Pellum had burned, there was a chance the Comanchero's plan had been foiled. What if they couldn't reach the Daltons by wire? What would happen to Sam Houston? Where would they take him?

"Ernestine," Lin said, addressing the girl, "Did you see a stagecoach pass through here?"

She ignored the question.

"They sayin' we doin' this. They blamin' me and my people. My family. Ain't nobody in my family want to see nobody burned up."

"I've heard those stories too," Reece said.

"They sayin' it in the newspaper."

Steve said to Lin, "She means the story I showed you. The one written by the reporter, Sperling. It blamed the fires on abolitionists and slaves."

"Ain't nobody in my family," Ernestine repeated.

Reece looked around the pull off, at the little creek branch behind the cottonwoods and the open meadow beyond. Smoke drifted in hazy waves over the surface of the world like the foamy tops of the sea.

"Where's your family now, Ernestine?"

Her eyes were wide and damp, but her voice remained clear and steady when she said, "They burned up, ma'am. They done burned up and went to heaven."

"Oh, Lord. Sweetie, I'm so sorry." Instinctively, she reached for Ernestine's hands, but the girl flinched away.

"No need to be sorry. You want to be sorry, you be sorry for me. Mama and Papa, they free to sing and dance, now. They free to go where they want. I'm still here."

"I think I understand."

This time when Reece put out her hands, Ernestine didn't pull away.

"I need to ask you," Lin said. "Did you see a stage-coach pull through here earlier tonight? During the fire?"

"I seen Elijah carry mama to heaven in his flamin' chariot."

"No, no," Lin said. "I mean a real chariot. A coach. A stagecoach!"

"Ease up, man," Steve said, putting his hand on Lin's shoulder. "The kid's had a rough go of it. Let her breathe a little."

Lin was momentarily chagrined for his impatience, but only for a moment. With the fire there's no trail to follow now. When he shrugged off Steve's grip, he complained, "We don't know for sure the Concord came this way. For all we know they cut off before Pellum and went around the fire."

"Or got caught up in it?" Reece said. "You think they were waylaid?"

"I don't know."

"Stagecoach got no business on this road, anyway," said Ernestine.

"This one does," Lin said. "It's carrying an important man."

"How important could he be? Sneakin' around in the night."

Lin moved to mount up. "We need to go."

"Tell me about your important man," said Ernestine. "Was he more important than my papa?"

Lin stepped into the stirrup and flung a leg over the cantle.

"Was he more important than Mr. Sunderman?"

"What about Sunderman?" Steve said.

"He burned up too. Tryin' to save my papa and mama."

Reece drew the girl into her arms, but Ernestine stood stock still, her arms by her sides.

"We have to go," Lin said.

Steve mounted up on the roan. "Ask her if she wants to come along with us," he said.

But Ernestine shied away from the suggestion.

"I got to stay here for my kitty," she said.

"Bring the cat along," Steve said.

"We don't have time," Lin said.

Reece stepped away, her eyes filling with tears.

The orchard fire had doubled in size, and the house was clearly in danger. More shouting from the men across the road, and a heavy-set fellow dressed in long underwear trundled past.

"We can take you to a better place?" Reece said.

"Ain't no better place." Ernestine jerked her arms away.

"Oh, honey, there is. There is a better place."

"I got to find my kitty. You got to go find your man."

"Reece," Lin said.

"You go, ma'am," said Ernestine.

Reece rested her forehead on Ernestine's scalp, then, after a pause, turned away and got into the saddle.

"Yeah," she said. "We've got to find our important man."

"Reece, wait—" Lin said.

She spurred the dun away from Lin, and he watched her go, back onto the road toward Pellum where more fire flickered through the trees.

29

THE ROAD into Pellum exhibited the same destruction as Sunderman's plantation. Perpetual smoke drifted in layers over singed grass, and burned-out shacks littered the scorched woods. At the edge of town, a gathering of weary men loitered around a single bonfire, and the air tasted of ruin.

The town appeared to be roughly the same size as Quincy, a few hundred hardy souls banded together to fight the frontier.

Tonight, buildings on the south side of the main street were blackened and razed while the north side crouched in the shadows of destruction, bashful and ashamed. Behind the smoking ruin, a drowsy pastureland spread to the horizon, and whitewashed homes gleamed innocently in the moonlit distance as if unaware of their neighbors' plight.

The scene weighed on Reece's heart, Lin could tell by the way she carried herself in the saddle, and even Steve seemed to have lost his usual zest for life.

Cheated out of their livelihoods, grieving men and

women loitered in the remains of Pellum, and newly orphaned children sobbed.

Lin counted a line of five cadavers stretched out in a row at the side of the road. An old man knelt beside the first one, arranging the dead hands, tidying the corpse's clothes.

The human toll of these new troubles staggered Lin.

"If this is what the new decade has in store for Texas—for America...," Lin said.

"How will any of us survive?" Reece said.

They slowly made their way past the group of men, down the gutted business district with the horses flinching at every pop and snap of flying embers and brazened wood.

Unlike Sunderman's plantation, the conflagration in Pellum had been mostly tamed, and the men who weren't actively taking stock of their families were resting. Sitting on a bench outside the saloon as the barkeep poured from a bottle into their cups or propped up against the foundation of the town's post office, their legs flat out in front of them.

Lin rode up to the honest little building, its stars and stripes flying proud on a wooden pole out front. He held up a gloved hand and offered a quiet greeting.

Obviously exhausted, the lead man didn't bother to stand, but instead tipped back his soot covered hat and gave a nod.

Lin said, "I wonder if you've seen a Concord stagecoach come through here? Say a little more than an hour ago?"

At first the man acted as if he hadn't heard the question.

Lin was about to repeat himself when he got an answer from the second man.

"Yes, sir. There was a coach. Can't say I paid much never mind to it."

Reece sat beside Lin on her horse and asked the man, "Was it green?"

"Didn't notice."

"Did it pass on through? Did it roll out of town?"

"Missy, you might have noticed we've been a tad bit busy tonight," said the first man.

"The Concord rolled through during the worst of it," said the second man. "Like to be driven by a madman the way it was tearing through."

"Who the hell are you, anyway?" said a third man. Then, with a snarl in his lip, he pointed as Steve rode up close. "Who the hell's he supposed to be?"

"Doesn't matter," Lin said.

"He looks like an Indian to me."

"Didn't you recognize him, Mike?" said the second man, mockingly. "He's old Chief Bullshit."

All the men laughed, but it was a bitter, angry sound.

There wasn't much more to be gained here, thought Lin. The Pellum men were worn-out and on edge. They weren't in the mood for questions. Especially from a woman and a half-naked savage wearing beads around his neck.

Lin tipped his hat. "Much obliged for the information. We'll be on our way."

"I s'pect you will," said the third man. "You take your 'breed and your Mex gal and get outta town 'fore we run you out. 'All we know, you're the ones started this awful thing in the first place."

Lin took the man's anger in stride but denied the accusation. "It wasn't us, mister. I'd like to know who's behind all this just as much as you would." Then he turned the buckskin back in the direction of the street.

"You find out," said the second man, "you let us know."

"Likewise," Lin said.

He signaled to the others, but before they could move away, another loud voice came at them from a trio of figures crossing the street. The three were dressed like cowboys in long slickers and tall hats. The shiny spurs they wore glinted in the moonlight and clinked on the gravel road as they approached.

"Ah, holy hell," Lin said.

"What'd you say, Jarret? I don't think I heard you right. Jarret's who you are, isn't it? Lin Jarret? Firebug, escaped convict, and horse thief?"

"Horse thief?" Reece said. "Not too many people around would call you a horse thief, except—"

"Mal Billingsley," Lin said.

"Y'all get down off them steeds," said Mal.

Instead of making small talk, Lin spurred Sheriff Aggie's buckskin head on into the blustering vigilante and his men, brushing Mal aside, making way for Reece and Steve.

They made it to the end of the burned-out block before the first round of gunfire boomed, smacking bullets into the clump of trees ahead.

The road curved here and ran out of town alongside a tired little tributary of the Brazos. "Bet the crick's getting a workout tonight," Lin said as they thundered past.

"Ain't we all," Steve said, ducking another round of flying lead. "Who the devil's shootin' at us?"

"Tell you later."

"I resent bein' run out of town."

Lin didn't answer, his attention drawn by the wreck of a wagon turned over in the woods. Was it the Concord?

"Reece," he called, motioned at the carnage in the trees even as another barrage cracked through the night, and then broke away up the road.

Lead balls sang past Lin ears with holy purpose, a choir of sudden death he intended to avoid. Time enough to examine the wreck later on.

Reece and Steve drew alongside Aggie's horse, ducking as the shots from behind continued overhead. "We're lucky they're not better marksmen," Steve said.

"They're drunk," Lin said, "but even a stumblebum can get lucky."

As if to punctuate his observation, he felt a tug at his pants as a ball skimmed the surface.

Too damned close!

And in the moonlit meadow there was no cover available.

With the observation came another discouraging sight. Four more riders circling around in front of them from the right, pulling into the road ahead. Lin's only choice was to breakaway across the grass and wave his friends to do likewise.

"Or we surrender," he said, lifting his hands high, squeezing his legs tight against the buckskin's barrel. Signaling a slow down…a stop.

Lin, Reece, and Steve waited with their arms wide, away from their weapons.

The posse of four approached from the road ahead with weapons drawn while Mal and his two cronies came up from behind.

"I didn't come all this way to be stopped by a crowd of drunken townies," Steve said.

"Did you come all this way to die?" Reece said.

"If need be."

Lin berated him with a harsh tone. "Too soon. You wanna die, we do it when it counts for something. Out here our lives would just be wasted. And be damned if I'll give my life to Mal Billingsley."

"You gonna tell me who this bastard is?" Steve said.

Mal and his men braced the three of them.

"Brushy Creek vigilantes," Lin said. "You're a long way from home."

"Farther than you expected," said Mal. "But not too far."

"This here crick is part of the Brushy," said a brawny man wearing furry Mexican chaps on Mal's left. Lin recognized him as the fellow whose life he had spared when hiding in the coyote's dugout.

Had he shot the man and his boss right then and there when he had the chance...

The other horseman filled in the circle. It was the tired quartet from the post office in Pellum. The men still looked tired. If they weren't armed, with firearms pointed straight at Lin's chest, he might've given some thought to taking them on.

As it was, those temperamental trigger fingers were more itchy than ever.

"Smart thing, giving up like you did," said Mal. "I'm a law and order man. You know it. Things will be easier for you at the end of a rope then what the men would do to you if I turned 'em loose. Some of them lost their homes tonight. Some their business."

One of the Pellum men spoke up. This was the first man Lin had initially addressed, the most genial of the four. "Are you saying these are the ones who started the fires?"

"It's what I'm saying."

"Because I don't think they are, Mal. There was a different man, earlier who I saw—"

"Shut up, Jensen."

"Thing is, these folks weren't even—"

"I said put a cork in it."

Lin chuckled out loud, speaking to his defender. "Don't pester him with the truth, Jensen. Mal Billingsley has a grudge as big as the Palo aAlto range. If anybody around here loses so much as a penny, you can bet where Mal will put the blame."

"I oughta kill you where you sit," said Mal.

Steve put his hand on his tomahawk, and Lin shot him a negative glance.

It was enough to draw Mal's attention to the Mountain Man.

"Looks like you're ready to go with him? Well, it suits me."

Mal's hand moved, but before he could lift his weapon, Lin drew his Colt and held it at arm's length, less than three feet from Mal's left ear.

"Don't," he said.

"Holy Christmas you're fast," said Jensen.

Mal carefully lowered his gun and peered at Lin through hooded eyes. "I want you to turn around and ride back to town with us."

But he didn't order them to throw down their weapons.

"Once we get there, we'll go to the saloon and have a drink," said Mal.

"Like civilized folks," Lin said.

"Like civilized folks." Mal agreed. "But you're still under arrest by order of the Brushy Creek vigilance committee. In fact, I think—"

But he never finished the sentence.

Instead, his face turned ashen gray as he gazed over Lin's shoulder. The other men were equally mesmerized.

Lin spun around to see Sam Houston walk out of the trees and up to the road.

Disheveled, his suitcoat in a state of severe disrepair, but apparently uninjured.

Doddering, but still dignified.

The governor's slow approach allowed everyone the opportunity to suck in their breath and wonder if they weren't witnesses to something almost supernatural.

As always, Houston had his feet firmly planted on earth. "Don't you all stop talking on my account." He took in the circle of acquaintances and grinned. Hooking a thumb over his shoulder he told Lin, "The Comanchero jasper who absconded with your Concord and me is dead. Killed in the wreckage."

Lin felt is stomach sink. "Wreckage?"

"I'm afraid he missed the turn in the road. Too busy watching the fires, though I believe he'd had more than a snootful of the old rotgut before we left Gruber's Station."

Houston continued to brush at his coat as he took in the dumbfounded faces of the riders surrounding him.

Lin put his hand on the governor's arm. "You're not hurt?"

"No, no…scraped up a bit. I'll ache like a broke steer tomorrow." He bent backwards and pressed a hand to his side. "Or maybe today." Lin offered Houston a steady hand, and the governor noticed somebody he knew.

"Get down off the horse, Billingsley, and let me ride," he said.

For once, Mal had nothing to say. His mouth formed silent letters and his jaw cranked open and shut, but no sound came out. He slid from the saddle and landed on the ground with a thud.

Billingsley saluted without a word.

With Lin's help, Houston crawled onto Mal's horse. When he saw Reece, he winked. "I was worried plum crazy about you, gal," he said. "After you got me situated under the wagon floorboards, I heard you whistling. Then...well, then I'm not quite sure what I heard."

"You heard my skull getting cracked."

"You're sure you're unhurt now?"

"I'm fine, Sam."

"Sam?" said Mal.

"Miss Sinclair and I are old friends," Houston said. "Mr. Jarret is one of my Rangers."

"Y-you are?" said Mal. "I mean—of course you are."

"Now pipe down, Billingsley." Houston shook his head. "Just like your damn uncle, can't shut your pie hole."

"My apologies, sir," said Mal.

"Billingsley served with me alongside his uncle at San Jacinto." Houston made himself more comfortable in the saddle and grumbled. "Like I needed another thorn in my paw."

"Goddammit," Steve said, slapping his bare thigh and wheeling his horse around. "Damned if the rotten sonuvabitch didn't pull my fat out of the fryer one more time." He jerked a thumb at the governor and railed on about him to Lin. "He's always showin' me up," Steve said.

Houston winked at Steve and chuckled. "Gets a little old, doesn't it?" he said.

FROM THE BACK of Mal's steed, Houston addressed the assemblage. "You all know who I am. You all know what kind of evil is being unleashed tonight on the good people of Texas. Quincy, Sunderman's, Pellum, you all have seen and experienced the first flickers of a new war, a skirmish on the horizon which may define the remaining course of your life."

He cleared his throat, spit on the ground, and continued. "We know who's behind this latest incursion. The threads of terror have led you all here tonight. The threads of an extraordinary, highly personal plot to end my life—they lead here too. Here, tonight, these threads have combined to lead us only in one, final direction: Dalton Farm. Are we ready to get to the bottom of this once and for all? Will you march with me in the morning? Will you follow me as I lay siege to Dalton Farm?"

The audience cheered.

Houston held up his arms. "We ride in six hours. Who's with me?"

A dozen men rushed forward, tripping over their boots, tripping over each other.

Then another dozen. And a half dozen more.

"First thing to do," Houston shouted over the martial din of cheers and whistles. "Somebody cut the damn telegraph wire between here and the Daltons. We don't need somebody sneaking over there and tapping out our intent."

Immediately four men ran in the direction of the post office.

Reece followed their progress, then said to Lin, "Have you seen any sign of the Comancheros?"

"I haven't. Robin Alexander and his pinto horse are awful recognizable. If I saw them, or any of the others —I'd know."

"You think maybe they moved on to Dalton Farm?"

"We didn't meet them on the road here. I s'spect it's a good bet they went on ahead to the Dalton's place to await delivery. Whoever the man was who hit you and crashed the stagecoach was likely scheduled to carry Houston over in the morning."

Reece pulled a long face. "About the Concord. We ought to see what's left to salvage."

"One more price the Daltons have to pay."

"Their tab does seem awful steep."

Lin tipped back his hat and hitched up his gun belt. "Between you and me, Contessa, they can't afford the bill."

30

IT WAS after midnight when they reached the stage-coach wreckage.

Shining an oil lantern on the scene, Lin and Reece found the Concord a broken ruin laid over sideways in the ditch weeds. Both wheels on the left side were broken and the passenger cabin had collapsed in on itself.

Lin pointed out the steel tire skid marks in the dirt road. "The driver didn't see the curve. Those horses must've been kicking up the dirt in a lather."

The team miraculously broke free according to Houston, and one of the Pellum men found them less than a mile away, dragging what was left of the trace.

The only loss of life had been the driver, crushed under the rig like a porcelain doll, still smelling of cheap whiskey.

"He probably spent all day in the barn at Gruber's waiting for the word to go. When you and Houston came outside, he couldn't pass up the opportunity to race off with his prize."

Two of Mal Billingsley's men spirited the corpse

quickly away, while the Hellbenders got to work saving whatever supplies they found.

Lin carried a bedroll and change of clothes away from the split rear boot. Reece rolled a ten-pound barrel of powder from under a busted panel and followed him to the buckboard parked at the side of the road.

In the time they had, they saved what they could.

Reece said, "We're finished here. Whatever's left underneath isn't worth the effort to find."

Lin agreed with her. "As long as we got the powder and percussion caps."

She held up a package wrapped in oil cloth, "And a hunk of salt pork."

"Ought to make a good breakfast."

They met Sam Houston and the others in the Pellum café, already tucking into a meal of eggs and ham, beans, biscuits and sorghum with hot coffee.

The long, single-story room was kitchen, dining room, hospital, medical dispensary, nursery, and refugee camp.

The hardy people of Pellum doing what they always did. Pulling together, working to make things better. Now welcoming in denizens of Sunderman's as those weary souls sought out water, food, and shelter.

Everywhere Lin turned, he saw hope mixed in with the sorrow. Gratitude winning out over worry.

Mostly in the eyes of the men he saw a desire for revenge.

He planned to help give it to them.

Dalton's Farm was a two-hour ride to the northeast. Two hours closer to the Red River, and it too a community hub for neighboring families, passing immigrants, and dozens of laboring slaves.

"If we leave presently, we'll be there at sunup,"

Houston said, looking for a napkin to wipe his mouth, settling for the sleeve of his jacket. His expression was sheepish. "I can't tell you how good it is to be outside of polite company for a change."

"Hell of a compliment," Reece said, "but we'll take it."

"If we lay siege to these devils," Lin said, "what happens to the families who rely on the place? The laborers?"

Houston poured hot coffee into his saucer to let it cool. He paused to consider the question before answering.

"It's a question I might ask you and Miss Sinclair."

Reece put down her cup and pushed away her breakfast plate.

"I don't understand."

"Simple question." Houston picked up his saucer and slurped. "You're an abolitionist. It's not something we'd talk about in polite company, but was we just said..."

"Enlighten me, sir."

"When slaves are freed, what does one do with them?"

"What does one do with anybody? The point of freedom is people aren't yours to command."

"But to take away their livelihood is to leave them at a great deficit."

"Greater than what they currently face?"

Houston was taken off guard by the comment and saved from answering when a young girl with spectacles stopped by the bale with an iron skillet and spatula. "More ginger cakes? More cider?"

"None for us," Lin said.

When the girl returned to the kitchen, Reece addressed the question.

"Your point is taken. Perhaps one of us might stay behind at the Dalton place for a time to make sure everybody has adequate care. Assuming your plan is a success, General."

Lin grinned. Reece wasn't the only one who'd started referring to the old man in military terms since the late-night briefing.

He still had the gift of gab, but did the old man retain his keen strategic mind? Did he have the big picture vision with attention to details needed to take on a well-armed foe?

Houston knew the importance of terrain, of using geography and architecture to win battles. With uncanny precision he'd drawn a bird's eye view of Dalton Farm on the back of a flour sack, and every one of his followers had been asked to memorize the battle plan.

But it was hastily conceived, with virtually no reconnaissance ahead of time.

"I'll let you organize a team of women and older children who might occupy Dalton Farm after our victory," Houston said.

Success was a foregone conclusion in the general's mind.

Lin wasn't so sure.

Before Reece could argue further, one of Mal Billingsley's men rushed up to the table. "Excuse the interruption, General."

"What is it, son?"

"The wagon you asked for. It's outside for your inspection."

Houston's eyes sparkled. "Come see."

Lin and Reece followed him out of the busy dining room into the smokey street where a second buckboard wagon was parked with a covered load. The

Brushy Creek vig threw Houston a salute which the old man ignored while he reached for a corner of canvas.

"Give me a hand with the cover, Jarret."

Together, Lin and Houston pulled back the canvas to reveal a stack of heavy square wooden crates, seven long, three wide and two deep.

The construction was familiar to Lin.

The red painted label on the side even more so.

Phosphorescent matches.

"Good Lord."

Houston laughed out loud. "Some of the boys from Pellum uncovered them tonight in an abandoned shed just over west. Seems the place was used for storage by a quirky old drummer from across the river."

The description caught Lin's attention. "What did you say?"

"A quirky old drummer?"

"Did the man's name happen to be Klein?"

"Yes, I believe it was. Why?"

"This man Klein is reputed to have hidey holes of matches and powder all over the area."

Houston took the news in stride. "Sounds like a man preparing for war."

"Aren't we all?" Lin said.

Two hours and fifteen minutes later, Lin Jarret crept through the early morning underbrush, wearing a round brimmed hat, tough canvas shirt, and britches with two guns strapped to his hips. He parted a prickly bush with a gloved hand to reveal Dalton Farm's white plantation style mansion.

Two stories tall with red shingles and a wrap-around porch supported by smooth, white-washed pillars and dotted with wicker furniture, the house seemed to glare at him from its perch on a small clay rise surrounded by dry yellow grass, patches of tall weeds, and a black iron palisade. Beyond the house, a vertical series of stacked lofts made an open-air barn half full of cotton bales and hanging tobacco leaves. A broken-down buggy rested at a precarious angle near the western wall, and the dirt yard in front swarmed with chickens.

A tall wooden pole, maybe ten feet high protruded from the crab grass holding high a strand of cable which led inside the house.

Lin traced the telegraph line to the back of the

242

house where another pole cropped up, then into the trees where it continued on, presumably all the way to Pellum.

"Aside from the sheer size of the house, it's far from the magnificence I expected," Lin said.

Beside him, Steve Gardner crept in on his belly. "Old Snowy puts all his money into the business. There ain't nothin' left for the family." For the task at hand, Steve wore a complete uniform of open-front linsey-woolsy shirt, blue kerchief, dark blue cavalry trousers with a yellow stripe, tall leather boots, and a gun belt with a holstered Remy on the left, butt-forward for the cross-draw. On his right hip his Comanche war axe waited to enter the coming fray, its blood-thirsty flint head polished to a sharp, gleaming edge.

Lin could almost imagine the thirsty tomahawk crying out for blood.

"You see what I see?"

Several yards from the open barn, a livery corral door hung open and two men crouched down at the threshold, eating beans from a single, shared plate. Standing at the side of the building was Robin Alexander's horse.

"Those two men were with Alexander when they brought us in to Gruber's," Steve said.

One of the men let go of the shared platter to pick up a tin cup and wash down his beans. They were dressed in dark clothes and bareheaded with rat's nest hair, like they had just rolled out their cots.

Lin felt the sweat trickle down the back of his neck to soak into his shirt collar. The morning sun was still behind the far horizon, but the air was sticky and thick in his lungs. A hawk sailed in across the range and skirted a line of elm trees and cedar oaks behind the house and to the right before breaking the silence with a loud screech.

The cup man looked up from his sipping and pointed out the bird to his pal.

The quiet morning was about to get a lot noisier. Houston had wrangled more than 30 hard men armed to the teeth and fighting mad. Dispersed in small, tight-knit doubles and triplets around Dalton Farm, the warriors should soon have Dalton Farm surrounded.

Lin licked his lips in anticipation of the siege, giving eye to the winding lane in front of the livery station. Houston's plan was to come in with a dozen men on horseback behind a lead wagon free of horses.

The wagon, horseless and loaded with Klein's matches, would be on fire.

Steve's job was to tear down the iron fence and make an open path to the house for the rolling inferno.

Lin figured on raising one hell of a ruckus all by himself.

He wanted Robin Alexander.

Houston could have the Daltons, and the Brushy Creek boys could avenge their communities. Lin was on the lookout for the slender, cock of the walk Comanchero. Houston expected him to be here, wrangling over a price for the captured governor, awaiting his arrival by Hellbenders' Concord.

"Well, old Sam Houston's gonna show up all right," Lin said, under his breath. "But not in the way Alexander thinks."

"They shoulda been here by now."

The first wave of the attack was supposed to come up from the draw behind the house.

"What if they don't show up?"

Lin pulled his Colt-Walker and checked it a final time. "Might have to go anyway."

Steve had his tomahawk in hand.

Lin risked raising up on his heels to get a better picture of the landscape. Dalton Farm smelled of hay and horse apples. It carried the light conversational murmurs of the men with their breakfast. The bubble of morning coffee percolating over a stove in the livery.

The hawk flew past, and Steve followed its soaring path until it disappeared.

"Let's have it," Lin said. "You likely got an old Indian saying about the bird?"

"The bird says go."

"Go?"

"Go!" Steve jumped from the brush at the exact same instant Mal Billingsley and three Brushy Creek men clomped over the back yard to appear on the far side of a hemp clothesline. Mal yelled out, "For Quincy," and the boys "Yee-hawed" along with him. Lin was up and moving behind Steve, legs churning, his finger wrapped around the steel trigger of the Colt.

One of the Comancheros at the entrance to the livery was more alert than the other. First to see Steve running toward the fence, he ducked inside the doorway and came out with a long gun. Throwing the carbine to his shoulder, he barely had time to lower his cheek to the wood stock before Lin shattered the side of his rib cage with a booming ball of lead.

The rifleman toppled over sideways, rolling free of the gun so his buddy could snatch it up.

Smooth, flawless in his movements, the second man already had a bead on Steve when Lin cut him down with two blasts from the Colt.

Impressive. The Comancheros showed a cool sense

of professionalism under fire Lin hadn't expected. Clearly Robin Alexander had been accompanied by his top men, leaving less accomplished imbeciles to guard Gruber's Station. A tactical blunder.

Lin intended to show Alexander the error of his ways. Personally.

A volley of gunfire rained down on Mal Billingsley from one of the second story windows and his three vig companions returned fire. Together they pulled in behind two outhouse buildings, slid from their mounts and slapped the horses away into a direction away from the fight.

Spinning at the sound of a door cracking open at the porch, Lin fired at a run, slamming a pair of warning slugs into the painted wood siding. The door jerked shut at the assault but popped back open long enough for a furious shot of return fire.

At the iron fence, Steve had used his tomahawk to lop apart the spindly hinges before tossing the gate aside. With the open way as a starting point, he'd put his weight behind the steel pickets, ripping three posts free of the soil, opening the maw wide. Lin ducked into the yard behind him and ran perpendicular to the walkway of paver rocks leading to the porch.

The heavy front door swung open, and Lin popped off a lead ball. This time he hit somebody as a scream erupted inside. Glimpsing a scrawny dog of a man exit the egress with gun in hand, Lin careened into the turf as a final bullet cooked the air above him.

He reeled up out of his crouch onto his boot heels as his opponent plummeted to the porch floor, arms outstretched, smoking gun still in hand. The man kicked off a dying gasp, and Lin holstered his first Colt, its cylinder empty, then covered the doorway with his backup gun, expecting a follow up assault.

He wasn't disappointed when a rifle barrel reared through the gap with a belch of fire.

The Dalton boys were definitely home, and Lin figured at least two or three Comancheros were inside too. Nothing to do but draw them out.

"Jarret," came Steve's cry from the front yard and Lin saw the space was now wide enough for Houston's flaming wagon. Steve reached across for his Remington and Lin peeled off a shot toward the door. When he did, the barrel jerked toward him, and Steve leveled his gun.

Whether or not the Mountain Man hit anybody, Lin didn't know because a dozen men with booming, smoking percussion suddenly poured around the sides of the house from a rear exit.

Steve pounded leather in a sudden, backwards run to the livery barn while Lin slid and made a dive for the busted hay wagon.

Trapped behind the twin outhouse buildings, the Brushy Creek boys engaged some of the men, but the Dalton-Comanchero army was overwhelming.

Where the hell was Houston with his wagon and the other men?

A pair of dedicated Dalton boys, brawny and strong with leather braces holding up their trousers over pink long underwear worked together at the side of the porch to shower the outhouse site with lead. While one fellow pulled the trigger, the other fellow reloaded with his powder horn and percussion. Efficient and well-practiced, they kept up an almost continuous barrage.

Driven to an explosive fury, Mal and his vigs weren't so professional. They unleashed all their powder at once, then took time in between to reload.

During one of their down times, the boys from the porch made a mad dash forward.

Lin tried to pick one of them off, but missed and by the next time he tried, the combatants were engaged. Mal's boys had bayonet knives iron-strapped to the barrels of their guns and alternated between slicing air and clashing with the Daltons' defense.

Mal crossed barrels with the biggest of his foes, then cranked a boot straight into the fatty's guts. When the boy lurched back, Mal ran him through with a bloody rending of flesh.

The other boy didn't see his comrade's demise. He was too busy frantically battling Mal's lieutenants. Two to one, they made short work of the attacker, sending him to hell with ruthless efficiency.

"Lucky sons-a-bitches," Lin said, and as another blizzard of lead ripped down from the manor's upper floor, he wasn't sure which men were the more fortunate.

Better to die quick than catch a ball fragment in the guts and lay dying for the next four days.

Now Houston's shock troopers came out of hiding to meet the Daltons, two here from the line of trees, three there up from the draw behind the Brushy Creek vigs, men tossing lead from the trees behind the house, pocking all sides of the manner with lead.

The battle was fierce, but equal.

Lin was glad they didn't have any fewer men.

If only Houston would show up.

Lin slunk deeper into the barn alongside the wagon, wondering if he had time to reload his empty Colt.

The outside air was momentarily quiet, and the space between him and the mansion shrouded with percussion clouds.

The inside of the hay bar was a place of shadows cut by stripes of sun leaking through the tall vertical gaps between the weathered siding boards. Dust motes swirled up from the hay, and whirls of powder smoke assaulted Lin's nose. He couldn't help but sneeze.

When he opened his eyes, he was staring into the muzzle of Robin Alexander's gun.

3 2

BESIDE THE BROKEN WAGON, its dusty load spilling out on all sides, Lin stood behind an ankle-high pile of hay facing six loads of blazing death.

There was no time to talk, only time for action. With less than a second until the Comanchero leader pulled his trigger, Lin kicked up with the toe of his boot, sending a dry comet of chaff rocketing into his opponent's face.

Alexander choked, fell back, and Lin shoved forward, bringing the iron hard side of his hand down in a savage chopping motion. He slammed into Alexander's wrist, breaking the man's grip on his gun, forcing him to lose it in the thick, roiling dirt floor.

Lin slashed out with his boot, knocking the shooting iron away, clipping Alexander's ankle putting him back on the defense.

But the Comanchero was no amateur. He recovered quicker than most, threw up his arms and pressed back in when Lin figured he wouldn't. A sharp-knuckled jab came out of nowhere, slicing open the skin over Lin's cheekbone, giving Alexander the taste of first blood. His toothy smile sent Lin into a rage.

"C'mon, amigo," the Mexican taunted. "You want to kill me, here I am. I see it in your eyes, the blood fury. The madness. Come ahead then."

Struggling to keep his control, Lin checked his temper, blinked away beads of sweat as blood ran down the side of his face. He took a measured step to the side, then came around with a hard, short right, hoping to score a blow to Alexander's ribs.

Instead, he was met with the swift arc of a shining steel blade and the sickening pull of sliced flesh under his arm. A warm wash of blood trickled down his side, soaking into his shirt cloth and a nausea gripped his guts.

"This knife, she is not unlike the one owned by your hero Jim Bowie," Alexander said, his dark eyebrows crashing down with concentration as he moved in for the kill. "You be sure to greet him on the other side, one dead man to another."

Alexander lunged forward and Lin pulled aside at the last second, whirling backwards outside the barn. The sole of his boot found another slippery pile of loose hay, dumping him headfirst to the ground where his skull bounced like a melon on the hardpan.

With bells ringing inside his head, Lin saw Alexander come at him fast. Moving anything was like pushing through molasses.

This was it, he thought. If only he could draw his Colt…but he couldn't push through the fog filling his head.

Alexandro kicked him in the side and Lin's breath whooshed out. Winded, he worked his way backwards in the dirt, fighting to grab his gun, to breathe.

The slashing knife blade came down at Lin in an awful swipe aimed at his throat.

Just in time, Steve Gardner's big tomahawk came between them, catching Alexander's knife on its poll with a vicious upswing. Propelled backwards, Alexander righted himself quickly enough and twirled the long knife between his fingers.

Showing off.

Steve wasn't impressed, dancing in with a whirl of motion, swinging the tomahawk through a spiral of dizzy parries, easily matching the smaller weapon's thrusts. But Alexander wasn't one to surrender.

He feigned an attack at Steve's mid-section, stepped in to follow up with a heel to his shin, then threw a rapid attack straight past the tomahawk defense, slashing at Steve's eyes. With a heavy thud the tomahawk's neck blunted the knife's edge, pushing it sideways.

Alexander came around with another kick, but this time Steve stepped aside and returned the attack with a jab of the duck head heel of the hasp.

Both combatants backed off and circled one another, but it was Alexander who charged ahead. Young, impetuous, he wasn't about to give up. *"Eras un anciano,"* he said.

You're an old man.

"¿Tú crees?" Steve grinned and, brushing past Alexander's meager defense, clopped him across the shoulder with the flat of his blade.

What could have been a killing blow was a rugged, painful counting coup. Alexander cried out and reached for his damaged arm.

As Lin watched, Alexander began to understand his deadly predicament. The Mountain Man was at least six inches taller than the Comanchero, and Steve had the heavier weapon.

The outcome was practically preordained.

His dark hair like a wild devil's halo spreading out around his head, Steve cut loose with a demonic war cry peeling the flesh from Lin's spine, forcing Alexander into a defensive crouch. With a smooth, clean chopping motion, he brought the tomahawk around laterally and flung it off to the side where—surprise! It caught the last of Alexander's Comanchero riders in the guts.

Distracted by the sneak attack, Steve had left himself open to Alexander's blade.

But by now Lin had his Colt free, he had simply been waiting for the right time to use it. "For Jim Bowie," he said, and plugged Alexander straight through the heart.

The Comanchero collapsed less than a foot from his lieutenant.

Steve dashed to Lin's side. "Are you okay?"

His arm had stopped bleeding, and his head began to clear. "Gimme a hand," he said, and Steve set him on his feet with one arm.

At the manor, the Brushy Creek boys were holding their own, but reinforcements kept pouring from the house.

"Just how many men do they have in there?" Lin said. "Where the hell are they coming from?"

"Doesn't matter now," Steve said. "Help is on the way."

Lin spun around, then he and Steve fell back as a roaring blazing horror on wheels came down the approach to Dalton Farm. Hurling down the yard, the buckboard churned up the final incline to collide with the porch. A blossom of white-hot sparks enveloped the front door, and clumps of flame set the siding ablaze.

Almost immediately the battery of Dalton men scattered.

But Sam Houston wasn't giving them time to regroup. Riding bareback on a black mare beside Reece's roan gelding, the governor unleashed a dozen more yowling men equipped with guns, clubs, and knives into the fray.

Having yet to see battle, these boys weren't at all tired.

————

As is always the case, the cleanup took longer than the battle.

By mid-afternoon the fire had been quenched with topsoil and water from the nearby well. Mal Billingsley and his boys had voted to watch it burn and roast supper over the ashes, but Houston wanted to save the telegraph.

While most of the posse worked to secure the house and line up the dead, Lin and Reece secured the remaining Dalton men and women inside the livery barn. Stripped of their weapons, the two dozen newly minted indigents gathered together behind the wagon in a three-sided grain storage area.

In front of them, Steve Gardner and three men from Pellum nailed long horizontal planks to both sides of the barn's support pillars. With the help of a couple ladders, they made ten rows of planks, ceiling to floor, leaving space between for a flow of air, penning the family in.

"We'll die in here, you bastards," said one of the fighting men.

Steve said, "You've got a tank of water and enough shelled corn to last a day or so. By then, I imagine you'll be able to work a few of these boards loose and get out of here."

"What then? You've torn the place apart, killed half of us, wounded the rest."

"Think about it next time you want to start a war." Lin turned to Reece. "What about Houston's plan for you to stay here and organize a relief effort."

"I'm delegating the effort to the folks of Pellum."

"They might not be too charitable."

"Last I heard, they were torching the cotton fields behind the house."

"My point exactly."

"They're more charitable than I would be." Reece reviewed the population of the makeshift jail cell. "I don't see any of Robin Alexander's Comancheros."

"I don't think any survived," Lin said.

"Just as well."

"You have no idea the enemy you've made today," a woman in a formal dress said from behind the planks. "We know your names, and we'll remember this affront in the weeks to come."

A younger woman who might've been the older one's daughter, agreed. "Nobody hands a whuppin' to the Daltons without them learnin' to regret it."

"So much bravado," Reece said. "It's always the same, no matter where you go. The men and women who start the wars won't be responsible when they lose." She turned to the snotty woman and let her voice carry. "I had hoped you'd learn something here, today. But you won't. You good-for-nothings have dogged the governor, made plans to kill him, and set half of north Texas on fire. Now you'll blame us for hitting back."

255

"I don't know what you're talkin' about," said the girl.

"The sad truth is you probably don't." Reece said, "It's another thing sets my teeth on edge when it comes to the adults who make war. None of you care a whit for the innocents who get hurt, or even worse," and here she directed her barbs directly at the mother, "the innocence you corrupt."

Lin's comments to the women were less philosophical.

"Just so you know. I voted with Billingsley to raze your damn house to the ground."

Both women turned up their noses and moved to the rear of the pen.

Outside and close to the iron fence, Mal Billingsley and two Brushy Creek boys stood over a third member of their cadre who lay dead on the grass. Lin kept one hand on his Colt as he approached them.

Mal spoke first, and his tone was far from affable. "I suppose you're happy to see another one of us Quincy fellows cut down. Well, I'm going to tell you something, Jarret. You might have flummoxed old General Houston, but you're still a Hellbender, and you're still no better than calf scours in our book."

"Ain't no peace to be had with emancipators," his friend said.

Mal said, "I still ain't so sure you didn't have something to do with all of this anyway. You were carrying matches."

Reece rolled her eyes. "Like I explained to our female captives. The same idiots everywhere we go."

Ignoring the barbs, Lin changed the subject. "I hoped you would take Sheriff Aggie's horse back to him."

"The horse you stole."

"The horse I commandeered."

"Aggie could hang you for it."

"Not by a long shot. It was taken for Texan Ranger business. A life and death issue involving Governor Houston. I think I've got the upper hand on this one, Billingsley."

The big man's face flushed red, the veins at his temple throbbed, but he held still long enough for his friend to pat him on the back.

"Leave it alone, Mal. The Ranger's got you over a barrel."

"My uncle is Jesse Billingsley. Him and me were at San Jacinto. We been taking guff from your good general for almost more years than you've been alive. I don't have to—"

"Just take the damn horse," Lin said.

"One day you and me might meet again, Jarret. One day you might not have Sam Houston in your back pocket to pull out and wave at me."

"When the day comes, he won't have to," Reece said. "Because I'll be happy to shoot you myself."

"Just tell us where Houston is."

"Kiss my ass."

Reece put a hand on Lin's shoulder. "He's there," she said. "In the house." She pointed at the manor and Lin saw the governor through the gauzy drapes of an open window.

Together, Lin and Reece crossed the lawn to where they could converse without shouting.

Houston put both hands on the windowsill and poked his head outside. "How's the truce going?"

"As well as can be expected. Did you find the telegraph in good condition, sir?"

"We did, indeed."

"You've sent a message to Rimrock?"

"I've sent a message."

But not to Rimrock.

Lin didn't push it.

He rubbed the back of his scalp and the muscles in his shoulders popped. Lord, he hadn't realized how much the last few weeks had taken out of him.

"I also found a slew of papers incriminating the entire Dalton Company of activities treasonous to the state of Texas and the Union as well." Then he held up a single piece of parchment covered in black hand-writing. "Written correspondence between Snowy Dalton and Rimrock concerning my demise."

"Foolish thing to leave laying around," Reece said.

"Oh, it wasn't laying around. We broke into the safe."

"I hope you weren't planning another military campaign before the Red River," Lin said.

"Based on what I'm seeing here, it might be a good idea."

"There's more than one bad apple there, I agree. But I think Brother Lambert's a good man."

"Haven't you learned yet, Ranger? There are no good men. We're all sinners in the sight of the Lord. Some of us just hide it better than others."

"We're gonna need fresh horses to make the journey."

The governor smiled. "I'd wager the Dalton family won't mind if we borrow a few good steeds in the name of making their Cotton Growers Meeting a success."

Lin liked the idea. "We can turn them in directly to Snowy Dalton when we see him."

"I'm counting on it," Houston said.

33

DALE HEMLOCK COULDN'T REMEMBER the last time he felt so weak, so tired.

Dressed in cotton pajamas, sprawled across the top of his guest-bed sheets, he prayed for even the most anemic slip of nighttime air to pass through his open window. But Rimrock Station was an unmoving tomb at midnight, and Dale Hemlock was burning up.

He flung boney fingers over the edge of the bed, hoping to find the glass of water he'd poured earlier, only to tip the tumbler over onto the ornate French rug. The crash of shattering glass grated on his aching ears, and he felt the bed spin.

He'd never been a sick man, what his mother called a Weepy Pete, even during his youth. Growing up on a Virginia tobacco farm, Dale was no stranger to daily toil. In fact, until the age of 30 he spent most of three seasons each year in a row crop field of one kind or other. During the next decade he managed three separate farms, covering the miles between on a saddle horse and sleeping under the stars.

Still, his health hardly suffered.

Intimate with tobacco, corn, sunflowers, and cotton, Dale secured a position at the San Antonio Farmers and Merchants bank during his fortieth year.

Awarded a leather chair behind a broad desk with open windows on a third-story floor designed to create a crossflow breeze, he began to wear a vest and string tie as opposed to burlap trousers and a straw hat.

If he was more susceptible to a cold than when he was younger, he attributed it simply to old age. A sneeze or three, a thickening of his tonsils, perhaps a headache or drippy nose. Such was the extent of his illness.

The coach ride to the meeting at Rimrock Station had been bumpy and hot, the last stretch—interminable.

But he'd felt hardy enough stepping down from Lin Jarret's Concord. After the first good meal of ham steak, sweet potatoes, bread, vegetables and coffee in Lambert's guest cottage, he'd felt good as new.

Waking up weeks later to a daily dizzying stupor didn't make any sense.

Somebody knocked on the mahogany door.

Then a sweet voice queried from the hallway. Sally Ann Powell, matron of the house. "Mr. Hemlock? I was passing by with some linens and heard a crash. Are you alright?"

Damnation, of course he wasn't all right.

"I'm...I'm fine, Miss Powell. Do carry on."

"You're sure?"

No, you dingle-berry little airhead, I'm dying.

"I'm fit as a fiddle," he said, forcing the second word.

If only he could sleep.

His mouth was pasty and tasted like wax and the

iron ball rolling around inside his head seemed to be gaining speed and heat from friction. He closed his eyes to the swirling pain only to open them—when? Minutes later? Hours?—as a determined rapping came from the hall.

The room's coal oil lamp still burned dimly, and it took Dale a moment to orient himself.

The loud knock came a second time, and when Dale answered, he felt a bit stronger.

"Thank you, Miss Powell, as I told you, I'm fine."

Apparently, Miss Powell didn't want to take his word for it. The crack of the door jamb as the lock broke through splintering wood was a six-gun's percussion, and before Dale understood the lovely Miss Powell wasn't behind the invasion, two men planted themselves at the foot of his bed.

"Get up," said the man on the left. "Get dressed."

"You're coming with us," said the other man.

"I hardly think—"

"Get him up," said Lefty.

"I should think not," said Dale. "State your business or get away from me."

The two bullies were little more than animals. Gorillas with heavy Germanic accents dressed in black sweaters, dungarees and heavy work boots, they worked together to hoist Dale out of bed and into his house shoes. "H-help," he said. "Somebody, please."

Lefty slapped him across the mouth with an open palm. "Shut up, you."

A rag doll in their hands, Dale still felt compelled to issue a warning. "I don't know what this is about, but you'll rue the day you undertook such an endeavor as to try and force me—" Another sharp rap in the face and Dale watched with sleepy interest as most of the room grayed out of existence.

Each of the men pulled an arm over their shoulders, balancing Dale between them.

"Get him into the carriage," said Lefty from a long way away.

"What about the spinster lady? What if she sees us?"

"Just tell her old Hemlock's been drinking and we're going outside for some air."

But of course, they didn't run into Miss Powell.

Once outside, the crisp whinny of a horse and the crunch of gravel under steel-rimmed wheels conspired to revive Dale. He wafted down into the land of the living where he discovered his body jostling across an open paving of inlaid brick.

He willed his blurry eyes to focus and made out the tall outline of a single-story frame structure with a tall false front. A sign across the front entrance said something about Boots, and a row of shoes and a cobbler's bench floated past in silver and black hues as if they were part of a tintype picture.

Dale knew he was being led down a hallway.

"Drop him there, at door number three."

His head clunked, as he hit the floor, and everything turned to black.

The next thing Dale knew, he was seated in front of a tall burning candle and the room smelled of old leather and sandalwood.

Somebody pressed a cold, wet, washcloth to his head, and he opened his eyes.

Dale sat at a round table. A man in a hood sat on the opposite side. Beside the Hood was a fellow Dale recognized: Daniel Ray, the constable of Lambert's police force.

"I d-demand to know what this is about," Dale said, proud of his ability to form a coherent sentence. "You have no right to bring me here."

The Hood's response was a scoffing sigh, and he carried his hands from his lap and interlaced his fingers on the table. "You're here to receive instruction, Hemlock."

"We talk, you listen," Ray said.

"See here."

Lefty came out of the dark behind Dale and slapped the side of his head. For a few seconds, everything was turned upside down.

When Dale reoriented himself, Ray was talking to the Hood in hushed tones.

"...more time. Clay might still turn up."

"We'll carry on without him," the Hood said. "Clay was always only a backup plan if Hemlock fails. We may be better off without him. The man was too independent. Too unpredictable."

"Still, if Hemlock should lose his nerve?"

The Hood turned his attention to Dale and spoke up. "I don't think Mr. Hemlock will lose his nerve. Do you think so, Mr. Hemlock?"

"N-nerve?" Dale said. "What are you talking about?"

The world went decidedly gray, and when Dale regained his senses, the Hood was still talking to him.

"...do everything in your power tomorrow to educate your colleagues to the folly of National Union. The meeting is the last full gathering of the association before Friday's closing address from Governor Sam Houston. Your oration will prime the pump for the governor's dramatic...departure."

The garbled words overlapped and echoed like bats in a cave, and Dale worked hard to focus his hearing and his replies.

"My s-speech is on textile price trends in European winter markets. It's not germane to American politics."

"Everything is germane to American politics," the Hood said. "You'll do as we tell you, or I will kill you right now and be done with it."

Ray stepped up to the table and put down a small Henry Derringer percussion pistol. The polished wood grip and engraved silver hardware gleamed in the candlelight.

"What's this?" Dale said.

"Next week, as President of the Cotton Growers Association, you will introduce Governor Houston to your constituent members in the town square. Just outside this building. Inside your suit coat pocket, you'll carry this gun loaded with a single .41 caliber lead ball."

Ray's words didn't make sense. Why would he want Dale to carry a firearm? The Cotton Growers were the most civil men in all of Texas. Surely there was no need for protective measures considering it's such a congenial crowd?

Ray continued. "When Sam Houston takes the stand to deliver his speech, you will step back, put the gun to the back of the governor's head, and fire."

Dale gasped in surprise. "Y-you can't be serious. Why…the very suggestion…"

"It's not a suggestion. You will perform this service for us," Ray said.

"Or you will die," the Hood added.

"I d-don't understand. Why me?"

"Consider it your duty. An obligation you owe the Order of the Ivory Compass for your station in life."

"O-order of the…?" Dale was confused. "I don't owe anybody for my station in life other than myself. I'm a self-made man who got where he is through hard work. Perseverance."

"Oh, hell, Dale." The man across from him removed

his hood and tossed it down to the table. "I'm too hot under the damn-blasted thing anyway."

Immediately recognizing the regal mane of white hair, beard, and icy blue eyes, Dale struggled to breathe. "Mr. Dalton," he said.

Snowy Dalton, patriarch of a family of ten sons and thirty-five grandsons, ten thousand acres of cotton and heir to the Revolutionary War chest of Sir Gerold Dalton, cut to the chase. "My family put you where you are. We propped you up and made you a rich man. I'm calling in the marker, now. Today. We stand to lose too much if Houston's call for union succeeds. We need him out of the way. You're the man who will do it."

"What if I don't?"

"You'll die a slow, agonizing death from the poison in your system."

"P-poison?" Dale's mind reeled. The fever. The dizziness. The water's chalky taste.

"We made sure you received your daily dose each day during the deliberations," Dalton said quietly. "Within the month you'll simply wither away...unless..."

Panic gripped Dale's heart and he jumped at the chance for survival. "Unless what?"

"Do this favor for me, and your debt to us will be repaid. The moment Sam Houston is pronounced dead, Mr. Ray here will hand you a small vial containing an antidote to the poison you've ingested."

"I'll live?"

Dalton closed his eyes and nodded with sincerity. "You will, indeed."

"But they'll arrest me immediately. I'll hang."

Dalton wagged his head. "We have it all planned out. During the confusion, Mr. Ray will whisk you away to a waiting carriage. We'll keep you safe and sound."

Dale bowed to the hideout gun on the table in front of him. After less than thirty seconds, he scooped up the pistol and jammed it into the pocket of his pajamas.

"All right, damn you. I'll do it."

Dale couldn't believe what he'd agreed to. But if it meant his life over Houston's? If it meant going home and seeing his wife? Eating well? Enjoying a few golden years? Was Sam Houston any more deserving than Dale Hemlock?

Well, then there really was no choice, was there?

"You'll be remembered forever as a hero in the coming Order," Dalton said.

"Just be sure you have the antidote."

"Have I ever let you down, old friend?"

Dale thought back across the years, trying to remember if Snowy Dalton had ever even offered him more than two or three words of greeting. "I guess you've always been a friend, Mr. Dalton."

"And friends don't let friends down, Dale," said Daniel Martin Ray.

"I suppose not."

But something about Ray's demeanor was off—a tremor in his voice or a nervous tapping with his fingers. The man was less sure of himself than Dalton.

And Dale Hemlock had just put his life into Ray's hands.

The weight of the Derringer pistol in Dale's pocket wasn't the only thing dragging him down.

34

AT THE FRONT of the train, Lin drove the buckboard wagon full of supplies, Reece on the seat beside him with the 10-bore shotgun, Houston arranged comfortably in a nest of bedrolls and quilts in the box.

They stopped at whatever freshwater springs they came across. Visited whatever homestead looked inviting.

At night they made cold camps on the open range and were entertained by the governor's endless archive of stories.

Steve Gardner followed the wagon on Romeo and was flanked by two brothers from Pellum who lost all they owned in the fire. Energized by the battle at Dalton Farm, Ned and Hans Wegner were eager to make sure the governor arrived safe in Rimrock.

And even more eager to visit Snowy Dalton.

Behind them, a string of a dozen men who felt the same way followed along.

"I was just thinking about Snowy Dalton," Reece said on their third day out as the noon sun tipped toward the west. "He's busy with Dale Hemlock running the show at Rimrock. I doubt he has any idea his homeplace has been destroyed. Imagine being the lord of all you survey, never suspecting your fellow countrymen are about to cut you down."

Houston's voice came from behind. "I've got some experience there, Miss Sinclair."

"I was talking about Dalton."

"I think the first time I was truly surprised by the treachery of my fellow man was when I fought the Creek at the Battle of Horseshoe Bend. Good land, I was barely out of short pants and would never share the gruesome story were I in polite company. I was tracking this band of Creek Indians when all of a sudden, I was beset by a blizzard of arrows. I received a most grievous injury below the belt in the area of my—"

Reece stopped him. "As I said, I was talking about Dalton."

"It's an interesting story, nonetheless. The barbs of those arrows were embedded so deep—"

"Enough."

After a few minutes of miffed silence, Houston said, "You'll learn, Miss Sinclair. You might have more in common with Snowy Dalton than you understand. As more and more people turn on you, you'll begin to comprehend the truth."

"I'm nothing like Snowy Dalton. And I know all too well about people who turn on you, people you thought you could trust. One day I'll tell you the story how Lin and I met up. How his uncle betrayed us, and I almost lost my ranch."

"What I meant, dear heart, is you and Dalton both share extreme convictions."

"But on opposite sides."

Lin spoke up. "I don't think emancipation is an extreme conviction, Governor."

"The extreme choice between Union and Disunion is a powder keg. Emancipation is a lit fuse. I would rather negotiate from a standpoint of state's rights. Let emancipation wait until cooler heads prevail. It's what my speech to the Cotton Growers will point out."

"If we make it to Rimrock. I've been concerned about crossing the river on Lambert's ferry."

"We've already had one near-death experience on the boat."

"I concur. Lambert's isn't a good option for us, which is why you'll want to make a left turn sometime in the next few miles and head straight north to Polk."

"No. No, no. Not Polk," Lin said.

"You want to talk about grievous injury," Reece said, "We'll be lucky if we make it to the river. We'd have to get through Polk alive."

"I have a friend there."

Lin couldn't imagine what kind of friend Houston had in the roughest town in Texas. Home to any vice imaginable, the settlement was home to any number of shadowy distilleries, sleepy opium dens, and scurvy brothels.

"It's why Lambert's became so incredibly popular. No man with a lick of sense would travel through Polk."

"My friend is a woman," Houston said.

"Now I'm really worried."

"Jillian Douglas. Jim's wife."

"I didn't know Jim was married."

"Now you do."

"But...," Lin swallowed before he finished the sentence, "does she know about Jim being killed?"

"If she doesn't, you'll have to tell her."

269

"Let's have Steve tell her."

"If I know the Mountain Man, he'll be a tad preoccupied."

"FIVE HUNDRED DOLLARS," Steve waved the paper money in Lin's face and bellowed with glee. "Half of a thousand. Enough to buy another round."

The inhabitants of the Thirsty Turtle cheered, and the barkeep tossed a bottle of amber liquid across the bar. Steve caught it with one hand and worked his way around the room, sloshing whiskey into everybody's cup.

When he got to Houston's table, the governor put his hand over the lip. "I'm having cider."

"You're crazy. Did you see what her roulette wheel paid off? I've got the luck tonight, old man."

Sitting at the counter's inlaid black and red wheel, a voluptuous woman of forty-odd years, stuffed into a lacy, sleeveless dress two sizes too small, called out, "Wanna spin again, Mountain Man?"

"Mrs. Douglas, you're singin' my tune."

Steve slammed the bottle down between Houston and Lin and strode back across the room to the amusement of all present. He waved a hundred-dollar bill in the air. "Let's go with Red 27."

Jim Douglas' wife gave the wheel a spin.

"You haven't told her about Jim yet," Houston said.

Lin shifted uncomfortably in his chair. Sipping his whiskey, he said, "I'm getting there."

"And then we need to move on," Reece said. "I'm not overly keen on staying overnight."

"Ah, like anything else, the bad qualities of the place are exaggerated. Jill runs a good place. Should we need to stay, we'd find a lot worse down the street a ways."

"Should we need to stay? I assumed we were stopping for supper and moving on. You've been awfully tight lipped about this stop-over," Reece said. "What are you hiding from us?"

"Hiding? Me?"

"Black 12!"

Lin watched as Jillian bellowed out the number and Steve hung his head, crestfallen.

But not defeated. "Spin 'er again," he called.

Jill stood on tiptoe and kissed Steve on the cheek, then moved back down the counter by herself as the barkeep took over the game.

"Now might be a good time to break the news to Mrs. Douglas," Reece said.

Lin agreed, steeling himself to the task at hand. The worst he'd get would be a wet shirt when, overcome with grief, she fell into his arms.

He removed his hat, approached her with morose. Put a hand on her bare shoulder.

Gave her the bad news.

"Praise God," she said with a throaty rasp and picked up a fresh bottle from the back wall shelf. "You're sure he's dead?"

"I was there, Jill."

"Drinks are on me, boys," she yelled, and for the fifth time, maybe more, the inside of Jillian's Palace erupted with glee.

It wasn't the reaction Lin expected. "You don't seem too busted up about it?"

Jill poured a full measure of rye into her gullet. "Tell me something, Ranger Jarret. What were my beloved husband's last words? Did he say my name? Did he cry out for the love of his life?"

Steve carried his drink over and stood beside Lin as the Ranger fingered the brim of his hat. "He, ah...said..."

"Spit it out, boy. What were his final utterances on this mortal plane?"

"Mountain Man."

Jill brayed like a mule and the backwash from her glass splashed up and over the rim. "I knew it. I knew the corn-shucking bastard like I know that trick wheel back there."

Steve raised an eyebrow. "Trick wheel?"

"Jim was still your husband, ma'am."

"Jim was never here. If he wasn't off with this one," she pointed at Steve, "or Sam Houston, he was running booze to the nations across the Polk ferry."

Lin let the words sink home.

"He lived in Polk with you? I mean, when he wasn't out with Steve and Sam."

"Yeah, sure. In the back room here."

"If the wheel is rigged, how did I win?" Steve said.

"Clear this up for me, Jill. If Jim ran booze to Indian Country across the Red River here, why would he risk running it across at Lambert's ferry?"

"Lambert's?" Jill said. "As far as I know he never went to Lambert's."

"But the constable there, a man named Daniel Martin Ray, said he did."

Jill poured herself another drink. "Ray's a liar. He used to run booze here all the time. Direct competition for me and Jim."

"Ray sells liquor in the nations?"

"Sure. He lived here for nearly a year before moving on. I had no idea he was over at Rimrock now. And constable no less?" Jill let loose with a loud cackle. "Mr. Ray sure is moving up in the world."

A wandering cowboy walked up and slung his arm over Jill's shoulder. "How about a refill, pretty lady?"

"How about it, Clem?"

Lin went back to his table, his mind a whirl.

"What'd you find out?" Reece asked.

Lin was just about to tell her when the batwings doors of the saloon opened. Ten men dived for the floor while ten more drew their sidearms and cocked the hammers.

The gang of men who walked across the threshold carried themselves with an attitude of assurance and authority. Dressed in long-sleeved shirts of worn cotton with tall hats and tough expressions, they fanned out inside the establishment without a word.

All of them were armed with six-shooter pistols. None of them made a move for the guns.

The leader balanced a matchstick on his lower lip, using his tongue to play with it as he assessed the inhabitants of the saloon.

Lin said, "Aw, dammit."

Sam Houston stood up and spread his arms wide.

"My friends, we are delivered."

"As I live and breathe," Jillian said. "It's the Texas Rangers."

Oscar Bruhn plucked the stick of wood from his mouth. "Set 'em up, Jill."

Lin pounded his fist into the table and stood up to face his uncle.

IN THE GUEST HOUSE GARDEN, Brother Lambert most likely saved Dale Hemlock's life, catching him as he tripped on the presentation stage. It was a long way down from atop the high wooden platform to the checkerboard rock patio below.

"Steady, my good man," Lambert said. "Are you quite alright?"

Hemlock rested on Lambert's firm shoulder and ran skeleton fingers through his thinning hair. "Y-yes," he whispered. "Just lost my balance for a moment." His breathing came in rapid, shallow gusts—like a bellows with a substantial rip at the seams.

He pulled a handkerchief from his suit coat pocket, stepped away, and dabbed at his lips. "I'm fine, fine, Lambert. Please don't…don't bother with me."

Lambert stepped backwards toward the quartet of wood folding chairs beside the speaker's podium, ready to pounce forward if Hemlock took a second tumble. "Why not sit down for a spell? Rest yourself a bit. Lord knows it's hot enough to bake a gopher in his hole."

The sky above agreed with the sentiment but did nothing to help. The clear blue ceiling didn't have a single cloud to offer the bench rows of garden seating. Lambert decided if it were this hot tomorrow, he'd need to rig up awnings of some sort in the grass beyond the patio for the reception and for lunch.

The lavender petunias and rows of zinnias may soak up the sunshine, but he doubted the guests would appreciate the midday sun bearing down on them.

Hemlock pulled his coat tails straight and adjusted his string tie. "As I indicated, I'm fine, Mr. Lambert. Though, perhaps a sip of coffee…"

"I carried a pitcher of water out with me. Let me pour you a drink."

Hemlock flinched at the idea. "No…no water." He shuffled forward and, squeezing his eyes tight, gripped the back of one of the chairs as if in sudden pain.

Lambert ran his index finger across his chin and studied the old man. Hemlock was clearly ill, but never had a malady been so fickle with such strange symptoms. One minute the man was on death's doorstep, the next he was hale and hardy, then sick again before the snap of a finger.

"Tomorrow will be a busy day what with Governor Houston's presentation. Perhaps you should retire to your room for the rest of the day."

"Nonsense."

Lambert couldn't deny Hemlock's loyalty. He clearly cared deeply for his organization and had dedicated his life to the continued success of the Cotton Growers in Texas.

Hemlock said, "You mentioned Houston. I'd like to go over the plans for his arrival while I have you here."

"Oh, certainly."

Hemlock was an integral part of the ceremony

275

welcoming the esteemed governor to Rimrock. Not only was Houston's presence an honor for the Regional Cotton Growers, but the visit was a coup for Lambert. Never had he been so proud of his station, and he was satisfied to see it looking perfectly manicured.

He took his watch from its vest pocket and checked the time. "Hmm. Yes, we're scheduled to begin in less than 24 hours."

"As I understand it, Houston will cross the ferry at some point this evening?"

Lambert clicked shut the watch lid. "Yes, indeed, though I don't expect his entourage to arrive from Austin until after dark."

"And you've received confirmation they're on the road."

"Oh, yes—just yesterday as a matter of fact."

"Please update me on the itinerary for tomorrow?"

"We gather at nine o'clock, with a coffee reception inside the guest house. Then we'll adjourn out here to the garden for Houston's address to your membership. Afterwards, lunch will be served at the long tables in the back."

Hemlock dragged his hand along the side of his face. "You might want to consider setting up some awnings for shade."

"I had just thought so myself."

"Will Houston be staying on in the afternoon?"

"I don't believe so, no. His address is the final item on your agenda, isn't it?"

"The final item."

"I'm confident his people will want to move on. The governor is a busy man."

"Of course."

"It's certainly going to be quiet tomorrow night," Lambert said. "Once your members have dispersed and the Dalton Company packed up and gone, I won't know what to do with myself."

"One never can tell," Hemlock said. His voice was weak. Distracted.

"I understand you'll be traveling on to Arkansas as a guest of Snowy Dalton."

"Hmm? What're you saying now?"

"Snowy Dalton. How long have you known him?"

"Oh...uh...not long." Hemlock closed his eyes and appeared to sway like a willow in the breeze.

"Damnation, man, take a seat." Lambert guided him across the stage to the second folding chair beside the speaker's podium. He quickly reached for the pitcher on the nearby table and poured water into a glass.

He pressed the drink into Hemlock's hands, but Hemlock wouldn't drink.

"It's no good to dry out in this heat, sir," Lambert said.

Hemlock nodded but sat quietly. After a while, he said, "This is where I'll be sitting tomorrow?"

"Yes. The governor will be here next to you on the podium side. You'll introduce him, then sit down. I'll be seated on your right. Then our constable, Mr. Ray, next to me."

Hemlock still wouldn't take any water, though he seemed a bit stronger. "It's good Mr. Ray will be here."

"Just as a precaution, you understand."

"Of course," Hemlock said.

"We're living in turbulent times."

"More than we know, I think," Hemlock said.

————

HE HAD TO HOLD ON.

Less than 24 hours and the deed would be done.

On the way back to his room from the garden, Dale avoided the meeting hall and the voices of his colleagues. He dragged himself back to the shade of his room and tore at the strictures of his collar and tie.

Falling onto the bed, his eyes were level with the top drawer of his dressing bureau.

Inside was the single shot Derringer pistol—in all ways the answer to his problems.

For a few minutes of speculation, Dale wondered about taking the gun out and using it now. It would be a simple way to end his physical pain and quell his mental suffering.

Dale imagined the cool wooden grip of the hideaway gun in his trembling fingers. He fantasized about its smooth curves, its seductive ornamentation. He could taste the metallic tang of the barrel inside his mouth, feel his tongue probing the muzzle, his finger caressing the fine, crescent trigger.

One twitch, and the powder would erupt with a furious charge, sending the ball through the back of his skull, closing out one life while simultaneously saving another.

Dale's worries would be over, and Sam Houston would carry on.

He snapped open his eyes to cold reality.

Had he truly spent all those years tending crops, managing property and men, educating himself on the science of agriculture to end his own life simply because he felt weak? Hadn't he already come this far? His speech on textile price trends in European winter markets had gone over well with the organization. He'd managed to slip in some obligatory critiques of the Union—just as Snowy Dalton had asked. His finale included a resounding appeal to secession.

Should he quit now, when he was so close to the goal?

Hemlock felt a surge of inner strength. Hoisting himself up off the bed, he moved to the bureau mirror and combed his hair. The man who gazed back at him seemed capable enough to finish what was already started.

Tomorrow, he would greet Sam Houston with an enthusiastic welcome. He would make all the proper introductions to the association. He would announce the governor's address. Then, as the governor rose, Hemlock would make an impassioned cry for the Order of the Ivory Compass.

Instead of retaking his seat, Dale would assassinate one of the men standing in the organization's way.

It wasn't an organization he had ever expected to support. He had never been in favor of disunion.

Funny how circumstances could change a man's perspective.

After the daring deed, Constable Daniel Ray would be at the ready to slip Dale away to the ferry in a fast carriage.

Hemlock would swallow the antidote to the poison coursing through his body.

Then, after arriving in Texas and a brief period of biding his time, probably at Dalton's plantation home, Hemlock would be brought into the Order as one of its top officers.

Not only would Dale Hemlock be remembered as one of the founders of the new order, he would be a hero.

Looking forward to such a bright, glittering future,

he realized what a fool he'd been to resist the idea of disunion for so long. He straightened his shoulders and put the comb down gently on the bureau top.

It would all be so glorious.

He desperately needed a drink of water.

ON A PAIR OF FAST HORSES, Lin and Reece flanked Oscar Bruhn, the three of them leading Sam Houston and the Texas Rangers along the northern shores of the Red River. They would make the outskirts of Rimrock by Thursday night, but Houston had already opted to wait until the morning of his scheduled address to make his first appearance before the assembled Cotton Growers.

Always keep 'em off-balance, he had told Lin after riding the Polk ferry across the Red.

With his traitorous kin at his left hand, Lin Jarret knew what feeling off-balance was like.

When they slowed their gallop to a walk through a hilly region of shrubbery, he tried to right himself while Reece hung back a few lengths.

"By what right is a scum-sucking spider like you pardoned by the governor?" Lin said.

Oscar didn't try to hide his smirk. Casually scratching at his bushy red mustache, he answered. "One hand scratches the other in politics. Houston got me made a captain."

"I see. You're not gonna tell me."

"One day you'll understand."

"Houston won't tell me either."

"You're just sore because of what happened at the Sinclair rancho."

"You say it like it's a trivial thing. Tom Sinclair was your friend. You betrayed him to the Cortinistas. You and your damned Ivory Compass."

Oscar was quiet for a long time as they steered the horses down a steep incline between scores of cedar elm branches. Clopping through a narrow, muddy bottom, hiking up a rutted dirt incline, they reached the crest of the hill and saw an open pasture filled with sheep.

"I could tell you I'm sorry, Lin, and it wouldn't help either one of us lose the load we're carrying. I won't even ask you to believe me when I say I'm a changed man."

"Good, because I wouldn't believe it."

"I spent my time in prison talking to the chaplain there. Whether you or your girl accept it or not, God has forgiven me."

"So naturally we should be expected to forget the murders you helped instigate."

Oscar tipped back his hat and scratched his neck. His face beamed with shameless dignity, his eyes clear and bright. "I don't expect anything, Lin. Other than your loyalty to the man riding behind us."

"Me and Reece, and Steve Gardner—we've brought Sam through a lot. We didn't need you and your troops to finish the job."

"The governor thought otherwise, which is why he wired us from Pellum. He told us to meet you at Jillian Douglas's place in Polk. By the way, if I ain't already said so, I'm awful sorry to learn about Jim's passing."

"Go to hell," Lin said.

Oscar nodded. "I deserve whatever scorn you've got." He chuckled to himself. "And then some. For a whole bunch of things you aren't privy to, but it's just the way the world works sometimes."

"How do we trust when we get to Rimrock you won't pull your hog iron and shoot the governor yourself?"

"Son, I go back with the general a lot farther than you do. Remember, I was at San Jacinto. When Billingsley and Burleson called him coward for retreating almost all the way to the Louisiana line, Tom Sinclair and I backed Houston."

"I don't ever want to hear you mention Tom Sinclair's name. By God, Oscar, if you say his name around Reece, I swear she's liable to put you in the ground right then and there."

"She hates me worse than you do," said Oscar.

"Damn straight."

"All I can do is work the rest of my life to make amends."

"You might think about disowning the Ivory Compass."

"I disowned them and all blackguards like them the instant I was baptized into the Lord."

Lin pushed back the gorge of skepticism rising in his throat. "Of course you did."

"None of it matters, now, Lin. Like I say, we need to watch out for Sam. He's what's most important."

Oscar's ability to cut through to the bare bones of a situation was one of the reasons he'd been Lin's favorite uncle growing up. Being trusted kin was the reason the dirty egg sucker's betrayal had been so hard to take.

Lin wanted to believe Oscar was a changed man, but he didn't think he ever would.

"You're right," Lin said. "For the next twenty-four hours, Sam Houston is our priority."

"Afterwards, maybe you wanna beat tar outta me, I'll sit there and let you."

"You can bet I want to beat tar outta you, and I might just take you up on the offer."

———

THE GOVERNOR'S party had a chance to make plans later in the night, camping under the stars a scant five miles northwest of Rimrock.

So as not to be seen, they made a cold camp in an unobtrusive little valley. Not quite a box canyon, but with sloping grades high enough to hide the troop of more than two dozen, the site lent itself to a sentry's watchful eye and straws were drawn to see who got the duty.

Nobody would sneak up on them in the dark.

After the animals were cared for and the men had enough to eat and drink, Houston called a meeting beside a boulder jutting out from the landscape. This would be his final council of war, he said, unless the world turned upside down during the next year.

A probability everybody expected but nobody dared voice.

The next day, at first light, everybody had their assignments.

Lin and Reece rode within walking distance of Lambert's mill where the trees and underbrush were overgrown, offering plenty of places to hide.

Making their way along the street in dusky morning shadow, Lin said, "When we were in Daniel

Martin Ray's office the first night when Jim was killed, I noticed a back door. The lock on it was broken, and I'd wager one good yank would jerk the thing open to the alleyway behind the shoe repair building."

Reece said she also remembered the door. "What if Ray's not home?"

"We wait."

"And what happens when he shows up? What happens if we're right about his role in the conspiracy?"

"I guess what happens will be up to him."

Reece pondered his words, then said, "This business gets awfully dirty, doesn't it?"

"I sleep pretty well most night."

"I guess I do too."

"Let's do that together sometime again real soon."

"Keep your mind on your work, Ranger."

As it turned out, the door at the back of the shoe store wasn't only unlocked. It was standing wide open.

Quiet as winter snow, and twice as cold, Lin crept up to the entrance, Walker-Colt cocked and ready to fire. Directly behind, Reece gripped the same model shooting iron.

Voices from inside the office drifted into the alley.

The constable's voice—but whining, complaining about something.

Then a second man: Lambert.

Lin mouthed the big Chickasaw's name to Reece, then held up his finger.

Wait.

Reece raised a questioning eyebrow. Lin cocked his head at the rising sun.

Within minutes, the bright yellow ball had broken over the horizon, piercing the office with morning light, a blinding background Lin took advantage of.

Stepping with casual ease inside the door, his gun hand unmoving at his hip, he took Ray completely by surprise.

"'Morning, constable," Lin said with a relaxed tone.

Ray didn't bother to converse. Instead, he went for his gun.

Lin shot him through the forehead with a boom.

"Good Lord," Lambert exclaimed through the powder smoke.

"Don't move a muscle, Brother," Reece said. She held her pistol less than an inch from the station master's head.

"I assure you, I will not," Lambert said. But then he warned them, "Half the town will have heard your shot. You'll be inundated with townspeople within seconds."

"I guess right about now your townspeople are preoccupied with the parade coming down the street."

"What parade?"

Lin waved his gun toward the front window, and Lambert stood up to look outside.

It was early morning, but crowds were gathering as a string of Rangers, two riders abreast of each other, marched down the street on their trusty steeds. Situated in the middle of the first four, Sam Houston waved at the onlookers.

Lin was right. Nobody seemed to have noticed the gunfire.

Lambert was dumbstruck at the sight of the governor and his contingency of Rangers. With a lot of effort, he said, "W-we wondered where you were. Or, where Sam Houston was. I never would have expected you two to show your faces here after what happened here before. Certainly not with the governor in tow." Lambert turned to Reece to see her gun still aimed at his heart. "Please, Miss Sinclair…please. I can assure you I'm not armed."

"Check him," Reece told Lin.

After the Ranger patted Lambert down and nodded, Reece put away her gun. Lin kept his Colt drawn and ready just-in-case as he perched on the corner of Ray's desk.

Daniel Martin Ray, sitting in his chair, dead, staring at the ceiling, didn't mind.

Lambert cleared his throat. "At any rate, the Indian police will arrive shortly. I can't believe Governor Houston will sanction you killing my constable."

Lin waved his gun in Ray's direction. "You're not telling me you still trusted him?"

Lambert chewed his bottom lip. "If I did or if I didn't is beside the point. You had no right to walk in here and kill a man."

"He drew on me, boss."

"Funny. Governor Houston got wind of a little plot. Seems Ray was in cahoots with the Dalton Company to assassinate the governor during his speech today," Reece said.

Lambert exhaled deeply and sat back in his chair. "I see."

Lin thought the expression on Lambert's face was genuine. Not surprise, so much as a confirmation of deeply held suspicions.

Lin was convinced Lambert wasn't involved with the plot.

"I'm sorry to be the one to tell you," Reece said.

Lambert said, "The Rangers are here as protection?"

"They are," Lin said. "In case Ray's police force decides to cause any trouble."

A ruckus at the door brought both men to their feet.

In a flash, Reece had her gun out even as Steve Gardner hustled Snowy Dalton into the office.

"Unhand me this instant," said Dalton, jerking away from Steve's grip, the fabric of his eggshell white suit fraying at the shoulder seems. He glared at Lambert like a cornered lion, his white mane flowing out in all directions. Then he took in Lin and Reece.

"What's this about? Who are these people?"

Lin motioned toward an empty chair and Steve put both hands on Snowy's shoulders, forcing him into an empty chair beside Lambert. "Mr. Dalton, you are hereby detained in the name of the good people of Texas."

"Are you insane? I'd like to know by whose authority?"

"The authority of the man outside," Lin said.

"Do you know who I am, sir?"

Lin smiled and gave the man a sympathetic pat on the shoulder. "I knew who you used to be."

"BROTHER LAMBERT, it's good to meet you," said Sam Houston on the bricks outside the constable's office. "Miss Sinclair has had nothing but glowing endorsements for your charm and hospitality."

Reece smiled with resignation as Houston gave her a pat.

Another excuse to touch her arm. The shameless old duffer.

Lambert, for his part, was at a loss for words. When he spoke, it was with the deepest reverence, and a hint of shame. "I only hope we might live up to such kind words." He lowered his eyes. "And your expectations."

The spectacle of the Texas governor arriving on horseback surrounded by the hard men of the Rangers, the revelation of Dalton's assassination plot, the execution of Ray behind his desk—it had all be a bit much to digest so early in the day.

"Would you like to...ah, freshen up?"

"I expect the day to go on completely as planned," Houston said. "I apologize for not arriving last night, but certain priorities warranted a change to our travel plans." He held Lambert's arm in a firm grip. "You understand, I'm sure."

"Oh, yes. Yes, I certainly do, sir."

"Good man."

"We have a room for you at the guest house. Our best, of course."

"I'd take your worst and appreciate it."

While the men traded the necessary pleasantries, Reece studied the chatty excited crowd surrounding them. The affect Houston's arrival had on the people of Rimrock was magical. Three dozen or more settlers and Indians alike milled around the Rangers' perimeter mesmerized by the legendary figure from across the river. Clair, the red-haired Irish broomstick was in the front line, as was her friend, and several other familiar faces from Reece's first visit to Lambert's station.

"…know he was so heavy-set."

"More hair than I imagined."

"Younger than expected."

"Seems a bit old to me."

"Can you imagine…?"

"Wait until I write back east…"

Snippets of conversation, whispers of delight, Reece wondered when the Cotton Growers would begin to emerge from the guest house.

Would they be so congenial? It was only by chance Steve Gardner had spied Snowy Dalton strolling along the sidewalk on an early morning walk. His apprehension, and Ray's death, weren't yet universally known.

As soon as those facts became public knowledge, the crowd's chatter might take on a darker tone. While Lin and Steve interrogated Dalton inside Ray's office,

Reece thought it was best to get Houston in off the street.

She had worked hard to avoid speaking with Oscar Bruhn during the entire trip from Polk.

She hated to start now, but...needs must.

"Don't you think it's time for the governor to retire to a more private venue?" Reece said.

From his place in the saddle above her, Oscar agreed. "You've got it right." His head was on a constant swivel, and his fingers played a staccato beat on his gun belt. "I'm not comfortable with the crowd, either." He deliberately made friendly eye contact—a peace offering.

Reece looked away. "Let's wrangle him inside," she said.

But before either one of them could make a move, the crowd parted for an emaciated old gentleman leaning on a cane.

"Mr. Hemlock?" Reece jumped forward. "Dale Hemlock?"

At the sound of her voice, his expression was vacant.

"It's Reece Sinclair, sir. Lin Jarret and I drove you here to Rimrock."

"Oh, yes, of course," Hemlock said.

The withering transformation was startling. Dale had lost at least twenty pounds, maybe more, and his posture was stooped and listing to port. Stature wasn't the only thing he'd lost. Since Reece carried Dale to Rimrock a majority of his hair had fallen out, and his skin was covered in liver spots. It was as if he'd aged thirty years overnight.

"Is this the governor?" he asked her. "Is this Sam Houston?"

"Why, yes, it is. We escorted him here to address your association."

A dark cloud passed over Dale's features, and he nodded. "I'm to introduce him on behalf of Mr. Dalton and the Cotton Growers."

"I'm afraid there's been some trouble, sir. Mr. Dalton's been arrested."

Dale staggered back with the news as if Reece had tossed him a ten-pound lead cannon ball.

"Arrested?"

"It's a complicated story," she told him. "He intended to harm the governor."

For more than a few heartbeats, Dale was silent. Reece wondered if he heard the news. Or maybe he didn't comprehend what she said?

But when he regained his senses, it was clear he understood. "You...you're part of all this?"

And by all this, he meant the Rangers' entourage.

"A small part."

"But you know him, then. Would you introduce me to the governor?"

Reece felt a wave of pity. Cranky and belligerent during the stagecoach ride up from Texas, Dale now seemed humble and self-deprecating. Obviously, some sort of sickness had gripped the poor devil. No doubt it had been a struggle to stay with the meeting, to persevere to this point.

"Of course, I'll introduce you."

Dale put his right hand in his suit coat pocket and offered Reece his left elbow.

Taking his arm, she indicated her intent to Oscar.

He gave her the go-ahead. "Afterwards, we get the governor in off the street."

Ahead of them, Houston still engaged Lambert in animated conversation.

"I don't believe I've ever seen such a beautiful day," said Dale. As they walked, his eyes searched the crowd eagerly.

"Are you looking for somebody, Mr. Hemlock?"

"Oh, no...er, that is, I expected to see Mr. Ray at the proceedings."

After witnessing Dale's reaction to the news of Dalton's capture, Reece thought it was best to withhold the grisly news about Ray. At least until after he'd met the governor.

"Have you seen Daniel Ray? He's the constable here at Rimrock?"

"I'm sure he's around somewhere," Reece said.

Dale's tongue touched his bottom lip and Reece felt a shiver run through his body as he took a deep, struggling breath.

"If you're not up for the introduction, you'll certainly have the opportunity to meet him before he speaks—"

Regaining his nerve, Dale said, "Now. It's got to be now."

Reece led him toward Houston, and they stopped only a few feet away.

"So then I said to her, Mrs. Stevenson, are you sure you want to put something so heavy in your bed?" Houston laughed at the punchline to his story, as did Lambert. The two men clearly were getting along well, and Reece hated to intrude.

"I'm sorry to interrupt, Governor, but Dale Hemlock, the President of the Regional Cotton Growers association would like to meet you."

"Ah, so?" Houston said.

Turning.

Lambert followed with his eyes.

Reece stepped behind Dale so he could shake

hands.

"Governor, this is Dale Hem—"

Houston shoved out his hand. Dale's fist came up from his side pocket on the side away from Reece.

His fingers wrapped around a gun.

"No!" Brother Lambert bulled ahead, shoving Houston out of the way even as Dale's shot hammered through the air, cloaking the scene in a shroud of smoke.

Lambert hit the ground, squealing with pain.

Reece gripped Dale's wrist, crushing his bones beneath paper skin. He dropped the gun onto the street, and Reece slammed a tight fist into the side of his face.

He landed on the street beside Lambert and was completely still.

Volleys of screams and expulsions rang through the Rimrock square, echoing off the building façades as mothers gathered their children, men reached for their wives. A trampling madness spread through the crowd and a wide circle of space formed around Houston, Lambert, Reece, and Dale.

Oscar and the rest of the Rangers entered the fray, forming a boundary of horses around the four, guns out, threatening to level anybody who didn't do exactly as they were told.

Inside the circle, Lambert gasped. "The governor...is...he?"

"He's fine," Reece said with a reassuring tone. "You saved the governor."

"Am I...am I...?"

Reece examined the big hole in Lambert's suit jacket and felt a twinge at her own shoulder. "The wound looks superficial," she said, "at least from what I can see. I had one like it myself recently."

Lambert grimaced and gave her a nod. "Long as... the governor..."

"I owe you my life, sir," Houston said, crouching down beside Reece. This time he ignored her hand for Lambert's big paw. "By God, who'd have suspected Dale Hemlock of such subterfuge?"

Reece picked up Dale's gun and passed it to Houston. "Single shot Derringer. He needed to be close."

Houston wrapped his arm around Reece's shoulder, and this time she didn't resist. "It's not your fault, dear," he said. "You couldn't have known."

When she opened her eyes, a doctor knelt in front of her, his medical bag on the ground beside Brother Lambert. The doctor stood up and asked Oscar, "Will some of your men please help me get him to my office?"

Oscar signaled and three men jumped down from their horses.

"What about Hemlock?" Houston said.

The doctor cocked his head over his shoulder. "He's dead."

"Dead? What happened to him?"

The doctor's expression was stoic, uninterested. "First glance, I'd say poison of some kind. He's clearly not been well for some time."

"He complained his water tasted chalky. I didn't think much of it at the time, but I bet the conspirators poisoned his drinking water. I'm sure of it," Lambert said, gritting his teeth as the doctor helped strip away his coat. "It's...the hold they had over him."

The doctor nodded agreement with Lambert's theory. "The deluded fool was probably holding out hope for an antidote. It's a common enough extortion scheme. The only thing is, with those types of poison, especially for a patient so far gone, there's no hope of reversing the injuries."

He clucked his tongue.

"I'm afraid Mr. Hemlock was dead from his first sip of poisoned water."

Lin and Reece sat at Brother Lambert's supper table with their host on one side and Sam Houston on the other. Lambert wore a clean shirt and vest modified for a bandage and sling.

Houston wore his best suit coat, Sunday shirt and cravat.

The morning hubbub was put to rest, the Gubernatorial address delivered, the Cotton Growers meeting officially closed.

The Dalton Company wagon train moved on to Arkansas without their patriarch, and Daniel Ray and Dale Hemlock spent their first night of eternity at the Rimrock Funeral Home.

"An excellent meal," Houston said, complimenting his host.

"I have a fine chef," Lambert said, complimenting the African woman who methodically removed their plates to the kitchen.

Houston turned his attention to Reece. "It's a shame you lost your Concord, sweetie. Though perhaps it's for the best."

"For the best? In what way?"

"Maybe now you can reconsider your passions. Rather than worry about emancipation, turn your energy toward preserving the Union. It's where our future is—if we're to have a future."

"I have a counter-proposal for you, Governor. You too, Brother Lambert."

Both men raised their eyebrows with apprehension.

"Free your slaves."

Houston chuckled, and Lambert relaxed into his chair. "I thought you were serious."

"I am serious. You know it's the moral thing to do, Governor."

Houston's blue eyes locked with Reece, and his expression was open and filled with admiration.

He tossed down his napkin and changed the subject. "As I said, a fine meal. And a fine wine, which my beloved Margaret would not want me to indulge in."

"Which none of us needs to indulge in this side of the river," Reece said.

"Let's make an exception," Lin said. "We've given up a great deal today. All of us."

They lifted their glasses in a somber toast.

Lambert grimaced in his sling. "It's going to take a while getting used to doing things with one arm."

"You'll heal, my friend. Believe me, you'll heal." Houston put down his glass. "Why, did I ever tell you about the time I engaged the Creek Indians at the Battle—"

Lin's eye caught sight of Oscar Bruhn standing outside the French doors leading to Lambert's back yard garden. The older man gave a tidy two-fingered salute beside his temple, and Lin put a napkin to his mouth.

Signaling to Reece, he said, "If you gentleman will excuse us, please."

Reece stood and followed Lin outside.

They joined Oscar on the patio, closing the door behind them.

"I wanted to speak with you both while I had the chance."

Lin said, "That makes one of us."

"Enough with the back and forth. I've got a question for you."

Oscar stroked his mustache and gazed past them into the dining room where Houston sat regaling Lambert with another tall tale.

"The governor's tasked me with creating a new office. Call it a security office."

"You mean within the Rangers?"

"No, it's separate and distinct from the Rangers. It's, ah...more clandestine. Less public."

"To what end?"

"To deal with the coming struggle."

Reece had heard enough and turned on Oscar. "I've already heard Sam's plea to work for the Union. You can tell him once and for all, I'm really not interested."

"This ain't about that. You wouldn't be working for the Union."

Lin said, "Hell, Oscar, we don't even have a coach anymore. As of now, the Jarret-Sinclair line is out of business."

"Ain't none of us who has a stout heart ever out of business. I'm living proof of it." Oscar took a wooden match from his pocket and bit down on it. "In fact, it's time to embrace our stout hearts. Time to buckle down and choose sides."

RICHARD PROSCH

Lin shook his head. "Who would you have us work for? If not the Union, who? The Southern fire-eaters? The goddamn Ivory Compass or Golden Circle?"

"Sam Houston wants you to work for Texas."

"Last I checked, Texas is still a slave state and pretty much nobody supports emancipation."

Oscar coaxed Lin. "Give up that part of it. Forget about abolition."

"Or not," Reece said.

"All right," said Oscar. "Or not. I guess I ain't asking you to give up something your soul's committed to—foolish as I personally think it is. But don't throw away the chance Houston is giving you."

"Texas Hellbenders?" Lin said. "And we'd work for you?"

"If anybody knows what it's like to have a new chance, it's me."

"I'm not giving you a new chance," Reece said, "and I wouldn't be working for you."

"No," Oscar said, "you'd be working for Sam."

"Damn you," Reece said.

"Ultimately, we're not talking about me. We're talking about you. Pick a side, Miss Sinclair. Everybody else is. If you don't, you're liable to get hurt."

Oscar took the match from his lips.

"What's it going to be?"

Reece took a long time answering.

Finally, she looked straight at Lin.

"Yes."

Oscar turned to Lin. "What about it, nephew?"

"Yes, and damn you to hell for making me say it."

"You look at what's coming over the horizon," Oscar said. "We're already there."

Lin took Reece by the hand and walked back in Lambert's dining room knowing his uncle was right.

ACKNOWLEDGMENTS

We sit in rooms and write alone, but none of us writes alone. For this one, a big ol' tip of the Stetson goes to Johnny D. Boggs and my fellow Western Fictioneers: Gordon Rottman, Troy Smith, Micki Milom, and Vicky Rose. Special thanks to Mark Hatmaker for the tomahawk and spirit guidance (Mabitsiar'u Haits'i, brother!), and to Paul Bishop for always being only one ping away.

TAKE A LOOK AT HOLT COUNTY: THE COMPLETE SERIES

BY RICHARD PROSCH

SPUR AWARD-WINNING AUTHOR RICHARD PROSCH BRINGS THE WEST TO LIFE IN A WAY FEW WRITERS CAN...

Holt County, Nebraska, 1882

Deputy sheriff Whit Branham lives on the edge of unorganized territory seeking revenge for the death of his best friend. With moneyed cattlemen and killer horse thieves, anything goes and everyone is suspect.

Branham is still the law, still the man called in to clean up after a killing. And he'll do it, too—with guts, grit, and guns.

Collected for the first time: Holt County Law, Holt County Iron, and Holt County Justice, plus the Whit Branham short stories "Branham's Due," "Buffalo Wolves," and "Leonard in Jail."

OUT NOW

ABOUT THE AUTHOR

Richard Prosch's western crime fiction captures the fleeting history and lonely frontier stories of his youth where characters aren't always what they seem, and the wind burned landscapes are filled with swift, deadly danger.

His work has appeared in *True West*, *Roundup*, and *Saddlebag Dispatches* magazines and online at Boys' Life. He won the Spur Award from Western Writers of America for short fiction, and his Jo Harper stories have received nominations for the Peacemaker award from Western Fictioneers.

Richard lives in Missouri with his wife and son, Gina, and Wyatt, assorted cats, and a Great Pyrenees named Moose.